SHADOWS ON THE BAYOU

BY

LISA LEPOVETSKY

PublishAmerica
Baltimore

ISBN: 1-4137-7697-3
PUBLISHED BY PUBLISHAMERICA, LLLP
www.publishamerica.com
Baltimore

Printed in the United States of America

This book is dedicated to
Howard, Shari and Rachel,
For their unflagging
Belief in me.

ACKNOWLEDGMENTS

I wish to acknowledge some people who were instrumental in getting this book published. Dr. Michael Hall, who took the time to give me medical information, and Edie Hanes and Virginia Martin, who took the time to critique this manuscript. Many thanks to all of you.

PROLOGUE

The man stood with his head bowed in the hot afternoon. The air hung very still beneath a grey sky, and dark thunder thudded softly to the west like distant gunfire. A dragonfly buzzed past the man's face, then disappeared into the honeysuckle.

His dark blue uniform was faded, and a cut on his knee showed through a new tear in the pantleg. His hands were tied behind his back with rough heavy cord, so tightly that the palms appeared a dark crimson edged in purple. He said nothing to the two grim men who grasped his upper arms. A bead of sweat trickled through his unruly dark hair to drip from the stubble on his chin.

A blond man approached from the barn behind, his boots brisk in the dust, but the prisoner never turned his head, never looked up. The blond man wore no jacket, and carried a black, silver-topped cane. He paced tensely behind the darker man. A tripod was set in front of them, and the photographer screwed his camera onto it with exaggerated care. He stood to one side when he'd finished, and dusted imaginary grit from the lens with a soft cloth. Finally, he turned to the blond man and cleared his throat.

"Are you sure this is what you want, sir?"

"I am. Is there a problem?"

The photographer coughed once. "It's just that it's a bit unusual. Perhaps —"

"Just do your job, Mr. Smith. There must be a record. My poor wife must have proof that the Yankee cur who defiled her is truly dead. I am paying you well, am I not?"

"Yes, sir."

"Then on with it."

The photographer opened the cloth bellows of the large camera and scurried around the tripod to duck beneath the dark shawl. Just before he snapped the shutter, the prisoner's head rose to face the camera squarely.

"Now you may go," said the blond man. The photographer hurried away without another word.

The little party of men skirted the maze of hedges and headed toward the front of the large house. In the center of the lawn stood a huge live oak tree, a noose dangling from its largest branch. A rough wooden stool stood beneath the noose. In the tree, a large flock of dark birds rustled and muttered uneasily.

While the blond man watched from the veranda, his cane clasped tightly in his pale hands, the other two men pulled the prisoner up until he was standing on the stool. One placed the loop of the noose around his neck.

One corner of the blond man's mouth twitched. "Would you like a blindfold?" he asked.

"No," growled the prisoner. "I want you to watch my face when I die, you bastard. And I want to watch yours."

The rope was adjusted so that it was tight around the prisoner's neck. He didn't move though his hands twitched behind his back. His dark eyes remained locked on the eyes of the blond man. The two executioners moved away from the stool and looked questioningly toward the porch.

The blond man descended the steps slowly and waved them aside. When they had moved out of hearing, he approached the prisoner and looked up, his mouth twisted into a vicious grin, his eyes unnaturally bright.

"I offered her her freedom," he said quietly. "I promised her that she could leave with you if she wanted, save your life. I wouldn't interfere. She chose to stay."

The prisoner's eyes narrowed and a tight muscle twitched in his jaw, but he said nothing. He looked up at the windows of the house as though searching for something.

"You're wasting your time," sneered the blond man. "She isn't there; she couldn't be bothered."

Without waiting for a response, he turned on his heel and went back to the porch. He gestured to the other two men, and they returned.

The prisoner's eyes fastened on an upstairs window as one of the men grasped the two front legs of the stool.

"Damn you," he muttered.

"May God have mercy on your soul," said the executioner, and the stool was jerked away. The black birds rose in a dark silent cloud from the branches of the tree.

CHAPTER ONE

"How long you plannin' on bein' here?" The old man peered at Kirsta over the tops of his glasses. Light from the buzzing mercury lamps overhead turned his white hair into a ghostly halo. "I mean, you be stayin' at Lost Oaks more 'n' a couple a days?"

Startled by the question for a moment, Kirsta decided the gas station attendant must be an example of the famous southern hospitality she'd heard so much about back in Pennsylvania. It seemed more like nosiness to her, but she'd try to write it off as neighborly interest.

"I'm not sure," she answered. "At least a couple of weeks, maybe a month. Why?"

The watery, unblinking eyes peered at her, as the old man shrugged and seemed to consider whether or not to answer her. Kirsta listened to the strange noises of the night creatures hidden by the dense foliage and darkness around her, and tried not to squirm as her discomfort grew. A bat fluttered low to catch the moths drawn to the lights overhead.

"I'm doing some research for a colleague of mine at Parthenon University, back in Philadelphia," she continued, finally. "But I've been driving for such a long time since I left the Baton Rouge Airport, I'm sure I must have missed it somewhere in the dark."

"Nah. You've not even got to it yet," he said. "If you're sure you want to stay at Lost Oaks, it's about five mile up this road, on your left. I won't say you can't miss it, because the drive's pretty overgrown. Them briars and honeysuckles have near covered that old sign, too. But if you're careful lookin' for it, you'll probably see it okay."

Kirsta thanked him, then studied the half-moon rising over the dilapidated gas station as he coughed into a red bandanna. He pulled the wire-rimmed glasses from his forehead onto his nose, and finished writing out the gas receipt.

"You spent much time in Louisiana?" he asked. He pronounced it "Lou-siana."

"No, I don't get much opportunity to travel. This is my first time south of Virginia." Kirsta tried to smile, but the expression didn't feel right on her face. The old man was getting on her already-frayed nerves. "But I'm looking forward to some new experiences while I do my research."

"Mmmmm. New experiences. Mmmm-hmmm."

He took a step back and seemed to contemplate what she'd said. After a moment, Kirsta figured the conversation must be finished, and put the car in gear. As she prepared to drive out of the gas station, he stepped up to her open window again. One gnarled hand grasped the door frame, and Kirsta jerked to a stop. She realized she was staring at the raised blue veins and swollen, arthritic knuckles, where the finger joints bent outward. She forced her eyes up. The old man had leaned down toward the window, and the trembling head was closer than she'd have liked.

"You might want to finish up that work of yours as soon as possible, missy," he said. "Lost Oaks is a strange place."

Kirsta raised her eyes to his face, looking for some sign of drunkenness, even insanity. But the pale eyes behind the wire-rimmed glasses, while a bit moist, were clear and steady. Maybe this is a joke, Kirsta thought. The standard scare-the-yankee-tourist haunted house story. But she couldn't quite make herself believe that. The old man's face was deadly serious; he was surely no prankster.

"What do you mean, 'strange'?" she asked, not sure she really wanted to know.

He looked up the road in the direction he'd recently pointed, and shrugged. "Strange, that's all. Probably just stories; you know how folks talk sometimes. But all the same, I'd not spend more time there than I had to, if I was you."

Kirsta forced another strained smile through clenched teeth. She was exhausted after the long flight, not to mention the two-hour drive in a rental car with a faulty air conditioner. Late April in Louisiana was much warmer and more humid than it was back in Pennsylvania. Kirsta had no desire for veiled warnings from some nutty old coot at a gas station, no matter how well-intentioned he was.

"I appreciate the warning," she said, as pleasantly as possible. "I'll certainly keep it in mind. Although I have to admit, Louisiana's such a beautiful state, I'd hate to have to rush through it. Especially plantation country."

"Louisiana's like a beautiful woman," mused the old man. He stared off into space, and seemed to be talking more to himself than to Kirsta. "She gets under your skin, but she's got too many contradictions: real old and real new, big city and bayou, livin' and dead folks, all side-by-side. Sometimes they get all mixed up with each other. She's a beauty, sure is, but she can be a little crazy, too, and a little dangerous."

Crickets chirred and a bird screamed somewhere in the darkness behind her. The old man waved a crooked hand vaguely in the direction Kirsta had come. "There's lots of other places to stay round here," he said. "No need to be sleepin' at Lost Oaks if you don't want to."

"Thanks again," she said, easing the car forward, "but I'm afraid it's getting a bit late to drop in anywhere else. I'll at least give Lost Oaks a chance. I'm expected there."

Before he could detain her further, she drove out of the gas station, waving at the diminishing figure of the old man as he stood watching her. What a nut, she thought, shaking her head as the warm evening wind whipped her hair around her face. Maybe he has some personal vendetta against Mrs. Woodring, the owner of Lost Oaks. From her phone call, Kirsta knew Daphne Woodring to be an older woman, probably in her sixties or early seventies. What could she have done to cause the man at the gas station to try to steer people away from her home?

As Kirsta pondered the question, she almost missed the carved wooden sign at the side of the road. The only visible word was "lost," but that was enough to let Kirsta know where to turn. She drove up the twisted lane to Lost Oaks, watching trees and flowering shrubs suddenly appear in the white circles of her headlights, then just as quickly disappear into the blackness.

The house she finally saw as she rounded the top of the elliptical drive was not the stereotypical "Gone With the Wind" plantation house with an imposing white facade and towering pillars. The line of soft lights nested in shrubs across the front presented a large grey home with cream-colored trim, its second story rising in neat peaks and dormers above the ground floor. Kirsta imagined the veranda sheltered the ceiling-high windows on the bottom floor from the wild weather she'd read about. The guidebooks warned about storms that rage angrily around the area in the spring and fall.

A friendly house in spite of its size, Kirsta thought, pulling the car around to the rear. A home. Though she'd never been this far south, she felt strangely as though she'd been here before, and sat in the car for a long moment after turning off the engine and headlights. Perhaps it was all the research she'd done on the Civil War already. Or maybe it was the hours she'd listened to David talk about his childhood near Memphis.

David. Fear caught like a bubble in Kirsta's throat. Though she'd never have admitted it to anyone, David Belsen was one of the reasons she'd jumped at this chance to leave Pennsylvania for a while. She'd convinced herself for most of the six months they lived together that his verbal abuse came from some flaw in herself, that she somehow deserved it — he was so loving most of the time. Then he'd almost hit her.

They'd been having one of their pointless arguments when David backed her into a corner and picked up the antique snow globe he'd bought her for her birthday, raising it over her head. He'd realized at the last second what he was doing. He was able to keep himself from hurting her, but the glass shattered against the wall behind her.

Kirsta had moved out of the apartment they shared the next day. Martin Radive, a colleague on sabbatical from Parthenon had said Kirsta could use his empty apartment, but only for three weeks until he returned from India.

That was three months ago, and Kirsta still couldn't believe she'd let herself be dominated like that. She swore it would never happen again, not with any man. After a few days, David began leaving messages on her answering machine. She never answered them. Then he wrote thick letters, which she returned unopened. She didn't have to read them to know they were filled with the same uncontrolled outpouring of guilt and obsession he'd tried to convey over the phone.

Kirsta had thrown herself into manic, meaningless activity at work for two weeks, not answering phone calls from friends or students, terrified David would somehow be on the other end. She canceled her classes after he started showing up on campus, following her around, pleading with her to listen to him, to come back to him. She found an inexpensive efficiency apartment near the university, and only left when it was absolutely necessary, constantly looking over her shoulder for David.

Then Harrison Kahn, the head of the history department, had sat down in her office cubicle one of the rare days she showed up. He'd told her she needed to get a handle on things, before she lost her chance at a full-time position. Kirsta thought he didn't know the half of it; she couldn't even afford to rent her own apartment when Martin returned from India.

Before she could think of how to respond, Harrison had offered her a research job in Louisiana at an excellent salary. He'd always told Kirsta she could make a living as a researcher, but David had convinced her she should be a teacher, and had helped her get started at Parthenon. Too late, she'd realized she was stuck in a job and a relationship he'd created for her, both of which made her unhappy. Kirsta agreed to Harrison's offer, almost without thinking. She'd allowed him to hire a teaching assistant to take over her classes. She needed the money desperately to help pay for a new apartment, but needed the distance from David even more.

Kirsta's reverie was broken by the sight of a figure in white floating down the back porch stairs toward her.She fought down a scream of fear as the back-lit specter wafted toward her car. The face was in shadow. One thin arm reached up slowly, pointing a long finger toward Kirsta, and a light breeze ruffled the gauzy fabric that trailed along the flagstone path.

"You must be Kirsta." The soft voice broke the spell, and Kirsta breathed again. "I was getting worried about you. I hope you didn't have any trouble finding Lost Oaks."

"Not a bit," Kirsta fibbed, as she opened her door. "You must be Mrs. Woodring."

"The very same." The open car door cast a dim light on Mrs. Woodring's face, and Kirsta liked what she saw. The woman had one of those ageless faces that could have been forty-five or sixty-five, with clear green eyes and a quick smile. Laugh lines creased the corners of her eyes and lips.

As Kirsta opened the trunk of her car, Mrs. Woodring said, "You'll be in the old cook's cabin over there by the pond. It's quiet and out of the way." She glanced down at herself. "I hope you'll excuse my nightie and robe, but I thought Sean — that's my nephew — would come down to greet you. Should have known better, I suppose. He's a bit ... shy sometimes."

"Don't worry about a thing," Kirsta smiled. "I do my best work in an old bathrobe."

As the women headed down the brick path toward the small white-washed building, Kirsta glanced back at the big house behind her. The figure of a tall, slender man was silhouetted against the light from an upstairs window; he seemed to be watching them. Kirsta felt a chill ripple through her.

Unaware that Kirsta had paused, Mrs. Woodring continued walking and speaking. "I put some juices and muffins in the refrigerator for you, and there's fruit in a bowl. I don't bake myself, but Etta Patton down the road does baking for most of the bed-and-breakfasts around here. She's housebound with some kind of arthritis in her legs, and the baking gives her something useful to do. Lives with her brother Henry. They're twins — Henry and Henrietta. His hands are crippled with arthritis, too, but he still runs his gas station alone."

Mrs. Woodring paused to open the door of the cabin. Kirsta said, "I think I met him when I stopped for directions. He seemed a bit …" she searched for the best word "… over-dramatic."

Mrs. Woodring laughed. "That's a nice word for it. Oh, Etta and Henry get a little caught up sometimes, but they're wonderful folks. They just spend too much time alone is all. Well, here you are."

Kirsta put her suitcase on the carved oak dresser and looked around the cabin as Mrs. Woodring hung her clothes bag on a wooden clothes tree in the corner. "As you can see," the older woman continued, "we've tried to keep things as much the way they were as possible. But we've added a few comforts that the slaves who originally lived here wouldn't have had. There's a little refrigerator and microwave over there in the corner by the sink, and of course, there's a bathroom beyond that door there. We found a big old claw-foot tub at an estate sale, and hung some rattan shelves by it to go with the loveseat on the porch."

"It's lovely," Kirsta said, smiling. She ran her finger around the wooden curlicues on the dresser. "The leaf pattern on this oak bed matches the dresser and armoir. They must be hand-carved."

Mrs. Woodring sat in the high-backed rocker next to the stone fireplace. "We found those pieces in the attic when my nephew decided to rent this place out. I think there was a mirror, too. I remember my mother—that would be Sean's grandmother — saying something about her grandfather carving a bedroom suite for his new bride. It must be this outfit. I don't know why they weren't being used in one of the rooms in the main house. There was some awful French provincial stuff in the master bedroom, but of course Sean wouldn't even discuss changing the furniture in there."

Kirsta thought Mrs. Woodring looked older in the overhead light, as if suddenly tired. She had stopped rocking, and stared into the cold grating of the fireplace. Her thoughts were obviously not on Kirsta and the cabin. Kirsta smoothed the patchwork quilt on the bed.

"Do your nephew Sean and his family live here at Lost Oaks, too?" she asked.

Mrs. Woodring glanced up quickly, as though surprised to see someone else in the room. "I'm all he has for family — now. When he's in town, he lives here. But his antique business keeps him on the road, so he's away more than he's here."

"And you run the bed-and-breakfast for him?"

Mrs. Woodring's smile returned. "I like people. I worked as a receptionist at a hotel in Baton Rouge for a while. Then, when I retired and Sean was …

alone again a couple of years ago, he suggested I live here and run the rental cabin. You're our first guest, you know. We plan to open up a couple other outbuildings to renters, but this is the first one we finished fixing up."

Kirsta wanted to know more about Sean, but had the feeling Mrs. Woodring didn't want to talk about it just then. "You've done a beautiful job," she said. "I feel right at home here, almost as though I've been here before."

"I'm glad you feel that way," Mrs. Woodring smiled. "Well, you must be ready for some sleep. I can give you the grand tour of the plantation tomorrow." She rose and opened the door. "Extra blankets and towels are in the chest there. It's been a cool April. Usually the temperatures are much warmer by now, but the evenings have gotten pretty chilly. If you want, I can start a fire before I go."

Kirsta patted the bed. "I'm fine. I'm used to cold nights, remember. This quilt will be more than enough for me, I'm sure."

Standing by the window, Kirsta peered through the lace curtains as Mrs. Woodring followed the narrow path through the trees and low shrubs toward the house. In the moonlight, the long nightie looked like pale wisps of a ghost, darting between the low branches of the ancient live oaks. Kirsta was reminded of her earlier shock at seeing her landlady drifting down the back stairs of the main house. She rubbed her upper arms and turned away to get ready for bed.

Within minutes, she was snuggled beneath the heavy quilt, easing into sleep, the soft cries of night birds drifting like a dark lullaby from outside.

When Kirsta woke, the sun was streaming brightly through the curtains, dappling the floor and furniture with lacy light. She didn't know where she was for a few long moments, still lost in her strange dreams of the night before. After orienting herself, she settled again into the down pillows and closed her eyes, trying to bring the dream back. As she forced herself to relax, it returned…

She was in a strange, yet oddly familiar room, gazing at herself in a mirror. The glass was framed in finely-carved oak that matched the bedroom furniture in Mrs. Woodring's cabin. The other pieces stood behind her, but the room was a large, elegant bedroom, not the cozy cabin in which Kirsta had gone to sleep. Moreover, the woman who looked out from the mirror didn't have Kirsta's feathered, medium-length hair and blue eyes. This woman had hair the bright gold of aspen leaves in autumn, piled on her head in complicated knots and waves. She couldn't have been more than five feet tall, a full four inches shorter than Kirsta, and her eyes were jade green. Those eyes bored into her own, as though trying desperately to impart some terrible knowledge through that gaze.

Oddly, Kirsta wasn't surprised by this distorted reflection, and reached one hand down to smooth the folds of a floor-length yellow gingham frock with wide lace edging the square collar and wide sleeves. She touched the amethyst brooch at her throat, and watched in the glass as her forefinger traced an ornate silver letter "I" embedded into the stone. The brooch felt warm, as though radiating heat from within. Round and round moved her finger, round and round the delicate silver filigree border and the faceted edges of the stone. Round and round, round and round.

Kirsta began to feel faint, and the room behind the woman in the mirror swam out of focus. She swayed for a moment, sure her knees would soon weaken and she'd crumple to the floor. Then she heard a man's voice outside the unfamiliar bedroom door. She instinctively knew this voice belonged to the husband of the woman in the mirror. He sounded angry, annoyed about something, and banged on the door, ordering her to unlock it. In the dream, the knock sounded unnaturally loud, echoing in her head.

She watched herself quickly pull the brooch from her dress and tuck it into a small leather pouch, which she then stuffed into a jewel case. She locked the case with a tiny gold key and put the key into a pocket hidden in the folds of the yellow dress. She hurried over to unlock the door.

A large pale man stepped into the room. He towered over Kirsta, growling at her about the locked door, his hand clenched tightly around a black, silver-topped cane. He smelled of liquor and old sweat. He paced the length of the room, without waiting for an answer, muttering and cursing, then stopped suddenly, staring at Kirsta's chest.

"What's that?" He pointed a finger at the top of her dress.

Kirsta went to the mirror and saw a small dot of red on the bright fabric. In her haste to remove the brooch, she must have pricked herself with the sharp pin.

She mumbled some excuse about a mosquito bite, but the man wasn't listening. He began talking about a lover she was hiding from him. Kirsta had no idea what he was talking about, but heard herself answer him.

"You know there's nobody else," she said, backing away. "I don't know what puts these crazy ideas into your head."

"Crazy am I?" He raised the cane to strike her and she saw her face distorted in the silver ball at its tip.

That was when Kirsta had awakened. She opened her eyes again, a sick feeling in the pit of her stomach. The dream had been so real. But of course it would be — she had combined this historic place with her recent experience with David. Kirsta wondered what blond woman she'd pulled from some long-forgotten memory to represent her in the dream.

She rose from the bed and padded across the bare wooden floor to the bathroom. She pulled the plastic curtain around its metal ring and hooked the spray hose onto the faucet of the old clawfoot tub. The hot water felt wonderful, and her spirits rose as she scrubbed with the fragrant soap Mrs. Woodring had left. This research project was just what she'd needed to pull her life back together, she was sure.

After rubbing her skin dry with the thick towels, Kirsta wiped a circle of condensation from the small mirror over the sink and glanced at her reflection. She gasped and blinked hard, clutching the towel to her chest.

For a moment, in the steam swirling around the little room, she'd thought she saw a small woman with golden hair looking out at her. The silent green eyes pleaded with Kirsta to understand something. Then it was gone, leaving Kirsta's image looking out at herself, trembling and wet, but very real and very normal. She started to smile at her momentary terror. Then something else caught her eye, something that turned the warm sunny morning cold and dark. On the pale skin between her breasts, a small scratch was beaded with tiny droplets of blood.

CHAPTER TWO

Kirsta was still trembling when Mrs. Woodring knocked gently on her door an hour later. Kirsta opened the door, and invited Mrs. Woodring in, glad of the unexpected distraction.

Mrs. Woodring gestured at Kirsta's outfit, a hunter green turtleneck and cream-colored jeans. "I knew you'd be too chilly," she said, shaking her head. "Why, your hands are even shaking. I should have turned on the furnace or at least laid a fire in the grate for you."

Kirsta smiled. "No, I'm not really cold," she admitted. "I just had some disturbing dreams, and can't seem to get rid of the feeling they left me with."

"What kind of dreams?"

"Just something silly. I suppose it was brought on by the history all around me and my job." Kirsta waved a hand dismissively. "I always have strange dreams in a new place. Nothing to worry about, but thanks for asking."

Mrs. Woodring stood. "Well, if you're still interested, I'd be happy to give you the grand tour. Unless you have something else planned for today. I wouldn't dream of interrupting your work schedule."

Kirsta led the way to the door. "I'd love it," she said. "I want to organize the background information on my laptop computer before heading out to the local archives, anyway. That'll take a day or so. Lead on, Mrs. Woodring."

As they stepped off the small wooden porch, Mrs. Woodring said, "By the way, you don't need to call me Mrs. Woodring; I'm just Daphne. We're pretty informal around here."

"Daphne it is then." Kirsta locked the door behind them.

"You probably don't have to do that, either," Daphne Woodring said. "There's nobody around but you and me — and Sean, of course, when he gets here."

"Force of habit," Kirsta said. "I probably wouldn't be able to leave without locking the door behind me. I've even been known to lock my car in my own garage."

In David's garage, she silently corrected herself, recalling how possessive he'd become near the end of their relationship — about the car, the apartment, about her. Kirsta shook her head angrily. She was determined not to let David ruin this trip, this chance at a new beginning. He'd ruined too many things in the past. Harrison Kahn had told her David had threatened him, trying to find out where she was living. Fortunately, Harrison was a good friend and wouldn't tell him. Kirsta forced the memories away, and concentrated on her hostess.

"Before we get started," the older woman said, "how about something to eat and a nice glass of home-made lemonade? We can even carry it with us, if you want."

"I've already had a muffin," Kirsta answered, "but lemonade sounds great."

They walked up the narrow flagstone path that led beneath the hanging branches of a large live oak tree, and entered the small kitchen in the back of the house. A tall slim man stood at the sink, running water into a glass of ice. His back was to them, but Kirsta could see the outline of muscles through the thin fabric of his knit shirt. His black hair curled softly along his collar.

He turned to face them, and Kirsta felt an immediate tension in the air, as though an electric wire carried current between them. This was the man she'd seen watching her from the upstairs window last night. His face was long and thin, with lines deeply etched around the dark, sensuous lips. Kirsta thought he looked tired — not from lack of sleep, but from some invisible weight he carried. Still there was something intriguing, compelling about the chiseled features that suggested incredible energy beneath. She felt as though she knew more things about this man she'd never met than about any man she'd ever known.

"Sean. You're finally home," said Daphne. "I was beginning to worry about you." She crossed the floor to kiss him lightly on the cheek, then pointed toward the doorway, where Kirsta still stood awkwardly. "This is our first guest — Kirsta Linden from Pennsylvania."

His blue eyes bored into Kirsta's for a long moment, as though he wanted to say something, then moved slowly the length of her body. He didn't smile, though she was sure she saw some strong emotion flicker across his face. Was ·it possible he felt the same strange attraction?

"Sean McLeod," he said, not moving from where he stood. "Nice to meet you."

Surprised by this cool response, especially after his aunt's ebullience, Kirsta forced herself to move to him, her hand outstretched. "You must be Daphne's nephew I've heard so much about."

He grasped her hand briefly, and her fingers tingled where he'd touched them. "You've heard so much about?" he asked, then turned a quizzical eye toward his aunt. Daphne shrugged and blushed, glancing at Kirsta guiltily.

"I told her you were away on a buying trip for your antique business," she mumbled. "How about some lemonade, Sean?"

"No thanks." Sean took a long swallow from his glass, and Kirsta watched the muscles of his throat ripple as he drank. Suddenly thirsty, she nodded to Daphne.

"Well, I'd love one," Kirsta said. She turned back to Sean. "How was your trip, Mr. McLeod?"

He hesitated a moment before answering, his eyes searching hers warily, as though looking for some hidden meaning in her innocent question.

"Not very productive, I'm afraid," he answered finally. "The furniture in the house I went to look at wasn't nearly as old as I'd been led to believe. But then, things are often less than we expect."

"Or more," Kirsta said, thinking of David Belsen. "And that can be just as bad, sometimes."

Sean's dark eyebrows knitted together and he peered at Kirsta for a long time. She felt her face flush, and her heart beat loudly in her ears. It was as though he somehow knew what was in her mind. Kirsta had the feeling they were both saying something other than what their words conveyed.

"Yes," he said slowly, "that's more true than you could ever imagine."

Ice cubes tinkled and snapped as Daphne poured lemonade into two glasses. They sounded like firecrackers in the silence, and Kirsta welcomed the excuse to glance away from Sean's eyes. She took the cold glass from Daphne and drank deeply, not at all sure she wanted to continue these double entendres with a virtual stranger. And yet, she had to admit, Sean McLeod seemed less of a stranger than she'd expect. There was something disturbingly familiar about him. She decided he must remind her of someone back in Pennsylvania, but Kirsta couldn't imagine who. She decided to forget about it, the name would come to her later.

Sean cleared his throat and glanced at his watch. "Well, you two enjoy your lemonade. I have a meeting with a buyer in Natchez in two hours, and I still have to shower and change. I'll be lucky to make it on time."

Daphne's face crinkled in annoyance. "Oh, Sean. I thought you'd be here for lunch. I haven't seen you in three weeks."

"I'll be back for dinner," he called over his shoulder, hurrying through the archway into the dining room. "We can catch up then. I've really got to get going now. Nice to meet you."

Before Kirsta or Daphne could say anything else, he was through the room and taking the stairs two at a time.

When he was gone, Kirsta realized she was a bit breathless and disappointed, as though she'd run to catch a train, but had missed it by seconds. She smiled weakly at Daphne, who continue to frown at the empty doorway, shaking her head.

"That boy," she muttered. "I don't know what gets into him sometimes." She turned to Kirsta. "I'm afraid I have to apologize for him, my dear, he just doesn't seem to care what anybody thinks or feels anymore. He's really charming when he wants to be."

"I'm sure he is." Kirsta wasn't at all sure she believed her own reassurances. Sean was certainly attractive, but she had yet to see his charm. She set her half-filled glass in the sink. "He's obviously in a rush to get to his meeting in Natchez. I can understand that. We'll have a chance to talk again, if he's home for a while. I'll be here for another few weeks, at least."

Daphne opened the dishwasher to put the three glasses in. She said, "Oh, I'm not worried about that. You'll see him at dinner tonight."

"Dinner?"

"Didn't I mention it?" Daphne turned. "I must be getting senile. I bought a standing rib roast from the butcher for dinner tonight, and the smallest he had was five pounds. That's much too big for Sean and me. I was hoping you'd help us out by joining us. We don't dress up or anything; just casual clothes. And I won't even charge extra; it would be fun. What do you say?"

Kirsta had to smile at the breathless speech and childlike hopeful expression on the older woman's face. "What could I possibly say," she laughed, "except what time do you want me here?"

"Then it's settled," Daphne wiped her hands on her denim skirt. "Now for that tour I promised. Let's start out back, by the path from your cabin."

They headed through the lawn, Kirsta trying to listen to what her new friend said. Her mind kept straying back to the kitchen, though, and the brief conversation with Sean, replaying it over and over, analyzing every word. She remembered the way the light was trapped in his eyes and felt too warm, even in the shadows of the live oak.

"Of course, the plantation was much larger when my ancestors built it in the seventeen hundreds," Daphne explained as they strolled past the little pond near Kirsta's guest house. The water was almost hidden by wild irises and rushes. "Almost half the acreage has gradually been sold to pay for the upkeep of the main house. These old places cost a fortune to keep up. That's why so many of the owners turn them into tourist homes. It keeps the integrity of the plantation intact while helping to pay for the upkeep."

Kirsta waved a wasp away. "It must be awkward sometimes," she said, "having strangers traipsing around in your home."

Daphne's face clouded, then she smiled. The moment was so brief, Kirsta wasn't even sure she'd seen it. "I enjoy taking care of guests," the older woman admitted, "but you're right — not everybody is as enthusiastic. Some folks really resent what they see as an intrusion, no matter how necessary that intrusion may be."

A small turtle scuttled into the water, and Daphne shooed a goose that hissed at them as they crossed the lawn toward the house. "Be careful," she said, "that old bird will bite, if you get too close to her. She just hatched a couple of goslings. She's had a lot of trouble with the foxes eating her babies the last couple of times her eggs have hatched. I think she's determined not to let anybody or anything get near them."

"That's sad," Kirsta said.

"It really is. And the truth is, she's getting too old for this. Hardly any of her eggs hatch anymore. But she still tries, poor old thing. She makes a great watchdog, though. The only one she lets anywhere near her now is Sean. In fact, she follows him around when he's outside. He's always been good with animals."

Kirsta decided this might be a good opening for her to learn more about Sean. "You mentioned last night that Sean travels a lot," she began. "Isn't there enough antique business in the area for him to stay around here more?"

Daphne Woodring hesitated on the path, then continued on, away from the house. "Sean doesn't want to stay around here," she said.

"But why not? From what I've seen so far, Louisiana is beautiful. I can't imagine wanting to be anyplace else." Kirsta realized she meant it. She'd only been in Louisiana for less than twenty-four hours, but she felt as though she'd lived there all her life.

Daphne looked at her, surprised. "Oh, Sean loves it, too," she said, stopping near the rose garden. "Or at least he used to. Before the tragedy."

Kirsta couldn't stop herself from asking. "What tragedy?"

When Daphne turned toward her, Kirsta noticed a tear trickling down her left cheek. But Daphne's voice was firm and gentle. "Sean's wife Edwina had taken their two-year-old son Andy to visit her parents in Memphis. On the way, their plane flew into a freak snow storm. The wings iced before the plane could get above it, and they crashed into the river, killing all on board."

"My God." Kirsta's voice was a whisper. "How long ago did it happen?"

"Two years ago this past February. Sean and Edwina had been married three years. He hates it here now. He doesn't have to say anything; I know it reminds him of the wife and child he loved so much and lost so cruelly to a quirk of nature."

"I'm sorry," Kirsta said a moment later, as they resumed walking past the house. "I didn't mean to remind you of the pain. I shouldn't have asked."

"No, that's all right." She stopped at the opening in some tall hedges. "I feel for Sean, of course, but I hardly knew Edwina. And I'd never met the child, though it's still very upsetting. Sean had lost touch with most of the family after he married. The newly-wed syndrome, I guess. It seemed as though he and Edwina just wanted to spend all their time together."

"They must have been very much in love."

"Apparently so. Sean even hired someone else to run the antique business, which he swore he'd never do. Love can make us do things we'd never expect."

"That's certainly true," Kirsta agreed grimly.

"Well, enough gloom and doom," Daphne stated, straightening her shoulders and facing the tall hedges. "I'm supposed to be cheering you up after your nightmare. Now I'll show you the topiary maze and the old magnolia tree."

They zig-zagged through the narrow passageways between the hedges, a strong musty scent rising around them. Kirsta felt oddly trapped by the bristling green walls closing around her, and felt an overpowering urge to burst through the tightly-woven branches, to escape this living prison. She considered asking Daphne to lead her back out. Then they turned a corner into the center of the maze, and the sun shone again, warm and golden on her shoulders. Her panic a moment ago seemed more like a bad dream.

As Kirsta felt her breathing return to normal, she tilted her head back to look up into the dark limbs of a towering magnolia tree. Its large emerald leaves blocked out most of the sky behind it, and several blossoms still drooped on the ends of its branches. Though their white petals were edged in brown, the sweet, heavy scent still hung in the warm air.

"That's the legendary Marryin' Magnolia of Lost Oaks," Daphne said.

"Marrying Magnolia?" Kirsta asked.

Daphne smiled and walked over to the tree. "They say that when a woman wants to marry a man, she gets him to chase her into the maze, then climbs into these branches. While he's standing beneath her, she imagines their wedding as vividly as she can. The tree is supposed to grant her wish, if her heart is pure."

It was Kirsta's turn to smile. "'If her heart is pure'?"

Daphne patted the massive trunk. "I suspect that's the catch. If your young man doesn't propose, it's because your heart isn't pure enough, not because the magic didn't work. I also suspect a few weddings were encouraged by outraged parents because a girl claimed her young man had been peeking up her skirts from below."

"Or because she let him catch her before she got to the tree," Kirsta suggested. They both began laughing, and Daphne led Kirsta back through the maze to the lawn outside. Kirsta listened to Daphne's chattering, trying to ignore her growing claustrophobia. As they stepped out from the tall hedges, a faint burring sound drifted toward them.

"Darn," Daphne sighed, "that's the phone. I'll have to get it. How about we continue the tour later in the afternoon or tomorrow?"

Without waiting for an answer, she trotted up the walk, leaving Kirsta still standing by the topiary maze. Kirsta smiled and headed back to her cabin. She liked Daphne Woodring already. This trip was turning out to be better than she'd imagined. Then she thought of the dark, intriguing man standing alone in the kitchen, looking through her. There was something a bit dangerous about Sean McLeod — Kirsta was sure of it. She'd have to watch out for him. A shiver raised the hair on the back of Kirsta's neck. A shiver of excitement or fear? She wasn't at all sure which.

The rest of the day passed slowly, as Kirsta alternately tried to imagine what dinner with Sean would be like and tried not to think about him. By the time she was deciding what to wear, she'd considered all the possibilities. If he's as reserved at dinner as he was in the kitchen, she thought, Daphne would have her work cut out for her, carrying the brunt of the conversation. But he'd lost an adored wife and son recently, and of course that grief could account for much of his reticence toward strangers, particularly women.

On the other hand, she was sure she'd sensed something smoldering beneath Sean's cool aloofness. Some raw emotion deep inside him struggled to escape. Kirsta's skin prickled as she considered this, wondering whether that emotion would be good for her or not.

"You have more important things to think about right now than Sean McLeod," she said out loud, and set her laptop computer on the coffee table.

Kirsta let the computer boot up while she pulled a stuffed manila envelope from the pocket of her briefcase. She smiled as she slid Harrison's notes and lists from the envelope. His enthusiasm for research had been contagious when she'd taken classes from him, and only increased when they'd become colleagues after she graduated from Parthenon. Kirsta loved delving into lives and stories from the past, putting the pieces of history together like the parts of a jigsaw puzzle until they made a complete picture of how people lived. She set the timer on her travel alarm clock and began to work.

It seemed only moments later when the buzzer sounded beside her, but Kirsta could see hours had passed. She stood and stretched, pleased and relaxed by the work she'd already gotten done. She pulled a dark green floral dress from the armoire and held it up before her in the mirror. She wondered whether Sean liked green. As she gazed at her reflection, she felt a chill. How could she have packed this dress? David had helped her choose it when they'd gone to Cleveland one weekend last winter, shortly before Christmas.

"You fool," she chided her reflection in the carved oak mirror. "Who do you think you're kidding? You're lucky to have gotten away from David just in time, and already you're half- interested in another man. Stay away, far away from him. Once burned ..."

Kirsta looked away from her face in the glass. She considered going up to the main house to tell Daphne that she didn't feel well, and skipping dinner. But such a last-minute change would be inconsiderate, and she would probably have a pleasant dinner with Daphne and Sean. Recognizing and confronting her emotions would only help her to overcome them. Straightening her shoulders, she grabbed a hand towel and went into the bathroom to freshen up.

At the sink, Kirsta suddenly remembered her experience that morning, and took a deep breath before glancing into the mirror. She told herself that she'd scratched herself when she grabbed the towel, but dreaded seeing blood on her breast again — or, worse yet, the face of a stranger in the mirror.

To her relief, all she saw was a familiar brunette woman frowning back at her, worry lines etched a little deeply around the corners of the mouth, dark circles barely showing below the deep blue eyes. She drew a brush through her hair several times, and pulled sides back loosely with tortoise-shell combs. Then she brushed on a touch of blush and a dash of coral lipstick.

Kirsta buttoned the soft skirt and shirt, and fastened the matching belt, nodding at herself in the mirror. Alright, she thought, I'll be as charming and pleasant as possible tonight, no matter how Sean McLeod acts. She locked the cabin door behind her and started up the narrow walk to the main house.

The scents of honeysuckle and roses and magnolia drifted in the warm evening breezes, and Kirsta paused by the garden to pick up a fallen rose blossom. The stem had been broken, probably by the old goose that had run after Kirsta and Daphne that morning. Now, bathed in the dark amber of the setting sun, the red flowers almost glowed with richer, more exotic colors. A few of the dark, delicate petals drifted to the ground as Kirsta straightened and lifted the flower to her nostrils. She glanced at the house, then frowned.

Lace curtains flicked closed in one of the upstairs rooms. Someone had been watching her, she was sure of it. Why would Sean or Mrs. Woodring step away from the window, rather than call out to greet her as she approached the house? Kirsta felt gooseflesh raise on her arms and prickle the back of her neck. Suddenly, the evening seemed a little too damp, the sweet flower smells a bit cloying. Something fluttered past her cheek, and Kirsta hurried up the walk toward the comfort of the waiting porch light, dropping the broken rose behind her.

Daphne quickly showed Kirsta through the spacious ground-floor rooms, pointing out interesting heirlooms and unusual antiques. Portraits of some of the McLeod ancestors hung on the walls among yellowing photos of proud Civil War soldiers in Confederate uniforms. Kirsta felt a chill, wondering how many of them were killed in battle shortly after these photographs were taken.

"Those two rooms were restored in eighteen-eighty-one, after a fire," Daphne sighed. "Some of the paintings were lost in it, and a few others have been sent to Baton Rouge for restoring. You may see copies or photos of them while you're doing your research. If you want, I could get hold of some for you."

Kirsta thanked her. "I'll be sure to let you know if I need them."

Daphne sniffed the air and led Kirsta back to the dining room. "Well, I'd better get back to the kitchen or dinner will be burned to a crisp. I have to take it out of the oven, but I'll keep it warm until Sean gets here." She glanced at her wristwatch. "I'm surprised he's not back yet."

"Is he working late?"

"In a way, yes. He's helping some of the members of the Allindea Historical Society restore the chapel near the old cemetery. It dates before the Civil War. It's in terrible shape, and we can't afford to have professionals do it — the stonework itself would cost a small fortune. So, Sean convinced some of the local residents that they could do it themselves with a little advice from the professionals."

Just then, a car drove up behind the house. Daphne Woodring hurried to peek out the dining room window and smiled. "It's Sean. He shouldn't take long to clean up; then we can eat."

Kirsta felt a wave of relief pass over her, and realized she'd been worried he wouldn't be there for dinner. She felt the muscles of her stomach tighten at the anticipation of seeing him again. She felt annoyed by this strong reaction to a man after what had happened back in Pennsylvania, not five months ago. Kirsta tried to slow her breathing, telling herself that the last thing in the world she needed now was another relationship.

Of course, the dinner was excellent. Mrs. Woodring had baked a Yorkshire pudding with the roast, and served a bright combination of chilled steamed vegetables in a light vinaigrette dressing. The coffee afterward was strong and dark, and the red wine full-bodied. Sean seemed a bit more relaxed than he had earlier, and had discussed the progress of the restoration and some of his more interesting clients during dinner.

Afterward, the three of them relaxed in the candlelit dining room. As Sean and Daphne talked quietly about things that needed taken care of around Lost Oaks, Kirsta often found her eyes straying to his face, angular and sensual across from her in the flickering shadows. He agreed the hedges had to be trimmed again soon, and a plumber should look at that leaky pipe in the laundry room. After a few minutes, their conversation died away, and in the silence Kirsta could feel her heartbeat.

"What kind of wine is this?" Kirsta finally asked, glad for the sound of her own voice. "It's delicious, but different from anything I'm familiar with. But then, I'm not much of a connoisseur, I'm afraid."

"You wouldn't be likely to have tasted this, even if you were," Sean answered. "It's called Fruit de Coeur — Fruit of the Heart — and it's made at a tiny vineyard south of here, between Baton Rouge and New Orleans."

"Fruit de Coeur," Kirsta mused. "What a lovely name, very romantic." She glanced at Sean. His eyes were in shadow, but she sensed he was looking at her, and felt his gaze on her as though it were a physical thing, touching her flesh.

"There's a story behind it," Daphne said, rising to collect the dirty dishes on a large lacquer tray. "Robert Granchet, the man who runs the vineyard is a fourth-generation vintner, and his family is from the south of France. He says Fruit de Coeur is the oldest of their wines, and they have only a few vines of the kind of grapes needed to make it. They only sell that particular wine every third year. Robert claims there's a secret ingredient or process or something that makes this wine act as a mild aphrodisiac."

"Aunt Daphne likes to perpetuate the local mythology." Sean handed his plates and silver to his aunt. "It seems to be a regional pastime down here, finding new ways to amuse the tourists."

Daphne put her hands on her hips and sniffed. "I don't tell any stories that I don't believe myself. There's nothing wrong with stimulating peoples' imaginations, young man." She hefted the tray of dishes and carried it into the kitchen.

Kirsta cleared her throat awkwardly. "I don't mind the stories, Sean. Actually, I enjoy hearing all the old tales and legends. They add flavor to the history of an area."

Sean's eyes darkened with emotion. "But they're lies, don't you see? They only bring more rich tourists down here, eager to feed off a dying culture. We need to revive the life of the South, not cannibalize its corpse."

Kirsta felt her face flush under that smoldering gaze, and looked down at her hands, trying to think of some way to defend herself. She didn't want Sean thinking she was just another tourist hungry for scandal and sensationalism. After all, she was an educated, interested scholar, searching for the truth, not just some half-formed legends. And if he thought she was rich, she could show him the red ink on her bank statements.

But Kirsta discovered she was unable to find the right words. She rarely drank alcohol, and had had two glasses of the dark, heavy wine during dinner. Her brain seemed to be swimming in a hazy vortex. She wanted nothing more at the moment than to go back to her cabin, pull the quilts over her head and drift off into the oblivion of sleep. But she felt she needed to explain herself first.

Kirsta vaguely realized Daphne had returned, and sat down again at the table. Perhaps the older woman would be more receptive to what she had to say, would help Sean understand. Kirsta looked up at Daphne and opened her mouth to speak.

But the words died on her tongue, as she realized Daphne wasn't looking at her face. She was staring intently at Kirsta's hands on the tablecloth. Kirsta glanced at Sean, confused, but his gaze too was fixed on Kirsta's hands. She lowered her eyes, and gasped.

With no conscious awareness of the action, she had dipped her forefinger into her wineglass and was drawing on the linen tablecloth. Her fingernail rested on a crimson curlicue at the edge of a strange, decorative letter "I", soaking into the white fabric as they all watched silently.

CHAPTER THREE

Cold rain slashed at the trees, and their branches bowed to the vicious gusts of wind, tiny leaf buds trembling. David Belsen stared through the window of his second-floor apartment, past the nearly-empty parking lot and city streets to the hills beyond, where he knew Parthenon University perched like a red-brick spider waiting for victims.

He'd been one of those victims until three months ago, when Kirsta had finally shown her real colors. She'd loved him, she said, even moved in with him. But she was only leading him on, like all the whores Mother had warned him about. He hadn't listened to Mother then, thinking she was only a bitter old woman, trying to cling to her only child. But Mother had been right — and now it was too late to tell her. He hadn't even gone to her funeral in February. Too far to Atlanta from Pennsylvania, he'd said, too cold and snowy to travel.

Winter was trying to hold on too long this year, keeping spring at arm's length. It seemed to David that winter would always be there, inside him, blowing snow through his days, chilling his soul with her white fingers. He felt the three rooms behind him begin to close, the walls pressing inward, the ceilings crawling relentlessly down. He told himself it was his imagination, but refused to turn around for fear that this time it would be real. His hands gripped the edge of the window sill to keep him from screaming.

David knew Kirsta was out there in those hills somewhere, in a little apartment or house near the university — probably shacked up with some other man. He'd easily found out that she'd moved into Martin Rajive's house, and had tried desperately to call her. He needed to explain, to apologize. He could make her understand, if she'd just give him the chance. He'd left hundreds of messages on the answering machine, but she never returned his calls.

Then he began writing letters — two and three a day, most of them eight or nine pages long. Surely this would work. But after a week or two, the letters came back, unopened. She hadn't even given him a chance. David had waited another week, to let her realize how much she missed him and get in touch.

But still nothing happened. Finally, he'd decided to take more assertive steps and try to see her in person. Surely enough time had elapsed for her to put the whole situation in perspective. Their love couldn't be destroyed by one little lovers' tiff on New Year's Eve. Her pride was simply getting in the way. He would go over to Rajive's house and talk her into moving back in with him.

But when David had gotten there, he'd found that Martin Rajive had recently returned from India and moved back into his own house. For one horrible moment, David had thought Rajive and Kirsta were lovers, but then he realized she'd moved out. Rajive didn't know where she'd gone — or wouldn't say — and David hadn't been able to find out from her colleagues.

He'd finally gone into the office of Harrison Kahn, the head of her department. Kahn had refused to give David her new address, even when David threatened him. That was when David realized Kahn and Kirsta were having an affair. It was disgusting to imagine, Kirsta with a balding, paunchy man old enough to be her father. In fact, Kahn had a son nearly Kirsta's age. But that didn't stop some people.

David closed his eyes and pictured Kirsta in Kahn's bedroom. The wife was downstairs cooking something for dinner, and the son was in the next room studying. Kirsta lay naked on the red satin sheets, her auburn hair spilling across the pillowcase, her eyes closed in ecstacy. Harrison Kahn was on top of her, naked and sweaty, panting like a Saint Bernard as she took him in her arms.

When he opened his eyes again, the light was different outside, the shadows deeper. David was confused — was the weather changing? No, the rain continued to abuse the tree branches, the wind still blew. He glanced at his watch — six-thirty. Two hours had escaped while he'd been standing at the window. Two hours had simply disappeared from his life.

Not again, he thought. How was that possible? He was losing more and more pieces of time these days. He'd even canceled his classes for the term because he couldn't keep track of his schedule. The dean had threatened to fire him, but David was too smart for him. He'd claimed emotional distress over his mother's death, and the dean had bought it.

David rubbed at his face and winced at the stiffness in his muscles. Emotional distress, that was a laugh. Everyone — even Kirsta — had thought his mother's death had upset him, but he knew he was stronger than that. And she wasn't really gone. As long as he took the time to remember her, to think about what she would have wanted him to do, then she'd never be gone completely.

He turned away from the window. Suddenly, he couldn't bear to watch the wind and rain racing through the streets outside. His chest felt tight, as though he were afraid of something. He laughed out loud, his voice unnaturally loud in the apartment, bouncing from wall to wall. David Belsen wasn't afraid of anything or anybody. He was invincible, Superman, the Avenging Angel.

"Avenging Angel," he said it out loud, and liked the way the words felt in his mouth. "I'm the Avenging Angel. There's nothing that can stop me from my holy quest."

Mother would have liked him as the Avenging Angel. She had always called him her 'little angel,' even when he'd grown up. It had always irritated him, but she wouldn't drop it. In fact, just before she died, David had gotten annoyed with her during a telephone conversation and asked her not to call him that.She'd cried and told him not to shout at her. But he hadn't been shouting. He never shouted. Why had Mother always said he was shouting, when she knew how angry it made him?

Then she'd had her stupid heart attack and died before he could call her back and apologize. She was always doing things like that to punish him. When he was a little boy, she'd simply refused to speak to him for a couple of days. When he got older and moved out, she'd left the phone off the hook for days after they'd had a fight, so he'd have to wait before saying he was sorry. So when she really died, he'd played her own game and refused to go to her funeral.

He paced back and forth in the living room, keeping an eye on the walls to make sure they stayed put. He caught sight of his reflection in the mirror across the room. His pale hair was uncombed and stood in spikes around his head. He moved closer to the glass. For a moment the bright light from the floor lamp was directly behind him, and his hair lit up like the corona around the sun. David looked like a god — or an angel. He remembered a picture Mother had given him when he was little. It showed a frowning guardian angel, glowing sword brandished high above his head. The angel's hair was exactly like this, wild and glowing gold. An omen, David thought. He must pay attention to omens.

He realized he was clenching and unclenching his fists. His hands felt so stiff, he needed to move his fingers, loosen them up. And his legs felt as though he'd been crouched all day. What was that called, restless leg syndrome? Good name, he thought, restless leg syndrome. He had restless legs all right, restless everything. He had to get out of that apartment, now.

David jerked open the door and slammed out, coatless, into the hallway, not bothering to lock the door behind him. He had no idea where he was headed, but he'd know when he got there. The hallway smelled like garlic and tomatoes — probably Mrs. Carpelli in 306 was cooking spaghetti sauce. It must be Thursday, he realized, because she always made spaghetti on Thursday.

The grey carpet muffled his footsteps, and David frowned at the silence. He wished he could make lots of noise on the floor, to show how big and important he was. He decided to take the stairway down the two flights. The elevator was carpeted, but the steps were bare, and he could make as much noise as he wanted. He opened the door into the stairwell, and pounded down the steps. The leather bottoms of his shoes slapped noisily on the stairs, and echoed up and down through all the floors. David felt power radiate through his muscles and bones as the sound clattered around him.

If only Kirsta could see him now. She'd give him another chance, if she'd take the time to see the real David Belsen. He knew she really loved him, deep down, if she'd let go of her stupid pride and allow those feelings to bloom. He'd planned a life for them, and she had ruined those plans. He had to find her and make her understand — they were meant to be together. She was his and nobody else's, no matter what Mother said. Mother wasn't here to control his life anymore.

David hit the push bar in the center of the metal door, and it slammed against the outside brick wall with a crash. He liked the sound, and when the door started back, he hit it again. A white-haired man opened a window several floors up, shouting at him, but the voice was lost in the wind. David laughed, and hit the door one more time.

"I'm the Avenging Angel," he shouted up, but the old man had already closed the window. David shrugged.

He moved away from the building, and the wind tore at his clothes. The rain had stopped, but icy drops flew from the eaves and branches to spatter against his face. David shivered, but knew it wasn't from the cold. His muscles were responding to the power growing inside him.

David hunched his shoulders against the wind and walked aimlessly down the wet streets. Rush-hour traffic whizzed past him, but very few other pedestrians were out fighting the weather. Street lights were flickering on, and he watched their reflections appear and disappear along the sidewalks like dreams or fantasies.

Or lives, David thought. And what was life but a dream, a fantasy? He slowed down and purposely moved in front of a lamp post. The reflection disappeared, blocked out in an instant by little more effort from David than a step or two sideways. Power. He sensed it surging through him again. Life was like that, he thought: anybody with power could snatch it away in the blink of an eye.

David resumed walking, turning down a side street he recognized. Kirsta's friend Ginny lived in one of these tidy little cottages, he recalled, but he wasn't sure which one. He'd been there once to a party. He remembered what the inside looked like — particularly a large painting over the fireplace. It showed a flock of black birds flying against an autumn sunset and had terrified him for some reason. He'd been nearly unable to keep his eyes off it the whole evening, and had become angry with Kirsta when she'd asked about his fascination. Why did she always have to be so analytical about everything, so intrusive? When she was back with him again, he would have to teach her to be the kind of woman he needed.

He began peering in the lower windows of the houses he passed, careful that nobody was around to see him. It wouldn't do for the Avenging Angel to have an audience; mere mortals could never understand how important it was for him to find Ginny's house. Ginny would know where Kirsta was. And David was sure he'd convince her to tell him — one way or the other.

After a while, he found the house he wanted, a little yellow cottage with white doors and shutters. He recognized it right away, and remembered commenting to Kirsta that it looked more like a lemon meringue pie than a house. He ran his fingers comb-like through his hair as he climbed the front steps, trying to tame its wildness. He rang the doorbell and peered in the narrow window beside the door while he waited. He could see into the living room, and shuddered as his eyes fell on the painting above the fireplace. Why, he wondered, did it disturb him so much?

His question went unanswered, because Ginny opened the door just then. She was dressed in a grey tweed skirt suit, the hemline a sedate two inches below her knees. She managed a computer store, and had met Kirsta when they both took a drawing class several years back. David knew Ginny had always been interested in him sexually, though her friendship with Kirsta had prevented her from approaching him.

"David." She was obviously surprised to see him.

David wondered how much Kirsta had told Ginny about their break-up. Had she mentioned his momentary loss of control, when he'd tossed the snow globe in her direction? He doubted it. Kirsta was very private about her personal affairs, even to her friends. He decided to assume she hadn't. He'd know soon enough, by Ginny's response to him.

"I know this sounds corny," he said, "but I was actually in the neighborhood. I saw your lights on, and on an impulse, I thought I'd see whether you were home."

Ginny smiled. "It's been a while."

So Kirsta hadn't told her. "Nearly four months," he said, then adopted what he hoped was an appropriately regretful expression. "Since Kirsta left me."

A vicious gust of wind nearly ripped the door from Ginny's grasp, and she blushed. "Oh my God, you must be freezing. Would you like to come in?"

"I thought you'd never ask." David smiled at her. "If it's not a bad time?"

"Not at all. I just got home a little while ago. Would you like a drink?"

"Thanks. Sounds great."

She poured them each a glass of red wine. David was pleased to note that she twice checked her makeup and dark hair in the small gilt mirror by the bar when she thought he wasn't looking. This was going to be easier than he'd expected.

Ginny sat on the end of the sofa, crossing one leg over the other, showing quite a bit of thigh. David remained standing, keeping his back to the fireplace so he didn't have to look at that awful painting. He could feel the eyes of all those birds fixed on his back like creatures from a Hitchcock film.

"So," Ginny said, "what brings you to this neighborhood on such a nasty night?"

David almost told her he was out taking a walk, then realized how strange that would seem, since he'd worn no coat. He'd have to think fast.

"Actually, I was driving by and had some car trouble a couple blocks away on Third Street."

"Do you need to call a garage?" she asked. "The phone's in my bedroom."

You little tramp, David thought, trying to find a way to get me into your bedroom. He must concentrate on Kirsta and his quest to find her; he mustn't be deterred by such temptations. He felt a shudder of revulsion at Ginny's blatant attempt at seduction, though he was careful to conceal it beneath a charming schoolboy smile.

"Thanks," he said, "but there was a garage just down the street. They're working on it now. I took the chance you'd be home, and that you'd let me hang out here until they're finished. I gave them your phone number. I hope that's all right."

She looked pleased. "No problem. I'm just marinating some chicken for dinner now, and I have plenty. Would you like to stay?"

He pretended to consider it, then said, "Sounds delicious, but I'll have to take a rain check. I have a lot of papers to grade tonight."

The smile flickered from her face for a moment. "I thought you'd been …" She stopped.

"Yes?"

"Nothing," she said, smiling again. "Never mind."

Damn, he thought. Had Kirsta told Ginny about Parthenon firing him? He couldn't be sure, but the smile didn't seem quite as bright now, and her eyes looked a little guarded. He decided he might as well get to the point before something else happened.

"You know," he said, looking around, "Kirsta and I had a wonderful time here at your party. You're one of her best friends."

Ginny said nothing, just sat and sipped her wine, waiting for him to continue. He sat next to her, letting his knee touch hers. She didn't move away.

"You know, I've always felt a certain closeness to you," he went on, his voice dropping a few decibels. "And I feel comfortable here now."

"I'm glad," she said, and he felt her knee press his, ever so slightly. The guarded look was gone from her eyes, if it had ever been there. "I feel comfortable with you, too, David."

"I've been thinking about starting to date again," he said. "I think it's time I got out."

"You're probably right." He thought he noticed a huskiness in her voice that hadn't been there before. "If you're sure Kirsta isn't coming back."

"Oh, I'm sure," he lied. "But there's one problem. I'd like to be able to go out without worrying whether or not I'll run into Kirsta somewhere. I'm over her, of course, but there's always that awkwardness when that kind of thing happens."

Ginny looked confused. "I don't understand. Why don't you just avoid her, then?"

"That's exactly the problem," he said. "I don't know how. She didn't tell me where she was moving. I suppose it was an oversight, but I thought you'd probably have her new address."

A frown flickered across Ginny's face, and she set her wine glass on the coffee table. She stood and moved to the fireplace.

"I don't know how to say this, David, but I'm afraid I can't give you her address."

The bitch. David drew a long, slow breath to calm himself, then tried his schoolboy smile again. "Sure you can. You do know where she is, don't you?"

Ginny looked at him oddly. He couldn't read her expression. "Yes I do," she said slowly, "but she asked me not to tell anybody — especially you, to be honest."

"She was upset," he said. "She didn't mean that literally. You know how Kirsta is — she blows up and then everything is over."

Ginny shook her head, her hair drifting around her face like dark feathers. "No, she's not like that at all," she said. "And it sounds to me as though you want to know where she lives more than you want to avoid her."

David felt his smile slip. He thought he heard the flapping of wings behind Ginny, but of course that was ridiculous. It was only a painting. He stood and moved toward the fireplace until he was only a few feet from her. Ginny didn't move, but he saw a shadow of fear deep in her eyes.

Good, he thought, be afraid. "Tell me where she is," he said very quietly.

Ginny moved a step backward. "I think you'd better leave."

He reached out suddenly and grabbed hold of her hair, pulling her head sharply sideways. He liked the way her eyes squinted in pain and then grew very wide.

"I'm not leaving until you tell me where Kirsta is," he whispered into her face, "and I've got all night."

CHAPTER FOUR

Kirsta lay awake for a long time that night. Daphne Woodring had pooh-poohed her apologies, insisting the wine would come out of the tablecloth without any hint of a stain. Sean had said very little, staring at the ornate letter until the lines were obscured completely by the spreading liquid, and the whole design was no more than a red blotch on the snowy background.

To Kirsta's dismay, Daphne had insisted Sean accompany her back to the small cabin. Kirsta had tried to tell them she could do it on her own, but Daphne was firm, worrying about hidden tree roots and broken flagstones. Sean didn't seem particularly concerned one way or the other, but shrugged distractedly at his aunt's suggestion, glancing one more time at the dining table.

Neither Kirsta nor Sean had spoken as they walked, and the chirping of the frogs and crickets seemed very loud in the misty darkness, the smell of honeysuckle too sweet. Kirsta felt Sean's presence strongly beside her, even when she wasn't looking at him. She smelled his musky cologne over the scents of flowers, and heard his footsteps on the walk, firm and sure on even the roughest places.

Once, he grabbed her arm when she stumbled over one of the exposed roots of a live oak, and she shuddered at his touch. His hand seemed to linger just a moment longer than needed before letting go.

"You have to be careful out here," he murmured, and Kirsta felt his breath tickle her cheek. "There are too many hidden things that could hurt you."

God, she thought, he was so close, she could hear his heart beat. Or was it her own? She tried to answer him, but her voice failed her. She nodded.

When they reached her porch, she pulled out her key. "Thanks, Sean," she said softly as she opened her door, anxious to be away from his disconcerting presence, and yet secretly praying he'd stay. "And thank your aunt again for the dinner."

"I will," he said.

Kirsta thought she heard something in his voice that suggested there was more, so she turned back. She hadn't realized how close they were until her face nearly touched his chin. His hair rippled slightly in a warm breeze. Kirsta backed up instinctively, her heart pounding. What was she afraid of, she wondered.

Kirsta waited, but Sean said nothing more, just stood looking at her. His back was to the light, so Kirsta couldn't see his expression, but she felt a tension in the set of his shoulders that convinced her he wanted to say or do something. His hand lifted to brush a wisp of hair from her face and his fingers trailed along her cheek like feathers.

Kirsta shuddered deliciously, and closed her eyes to savor the sensation. Her heartbeat thudded loudly in her ears as she waited for the kiss she knew was inevitable. She knew she shouldn't want him, but there seemed to be something more than simple physical attraction between them.

When nothing happened after a few seconds, she opened her eyes again and peered at him curiously. Sean's head was bent close to hers, as though studying her features. He seemed confused about something. Kirsta opened her mouth to ask what the matter was, but before she had a chance to speak, he put one finger to her lips. He shook his head and touched his lips to hers.

Kirsta wanted the moment to last forever, but it was over all too soon. They both backed away from one another. Kirsta's legs trembled a bit, and she noticed Sean's brow was furrowed as though he wasn't sure of what had happened. What had happened, she wondered. It seemed something had passed between them, something more than a simple good-night kiss.

Sean cleared his throat. "Goodnight, Kirsta," he said quietly. Then he turned and was gone into the shadows.

Kirsta could still feel his touch as she lay naked beneath the clean sheets, listening to the quiet noises of the night creatures around her. Did he feel it, too? Was he filled with the same longing, the same sense of emptiness? It was possible she reacted too strongly to his presence because of her emotional vulnerability. Their attraction might be purely physical. But no, she thought, there was something more…

She touched her breasts lightly, feeling the flesh rise, wishing her fingers were his. She sighed and snuggled deeper into the soft mattress. She'd better get a good night's sleep; tomorrow she would have to get to work, visiting the local libraries and archives.

She still couldn't fall asleep, and began counting the chirps of the crickets. Her father had once told her that you could measure the temperature by the number of times crickets chirped: the greater the number of chirps, the higher the temperature. "Counting the crickets," he'd called it. Kirsta could never remember how to calculate the ratio, but counting the crickets always relaxed her — like the counting of sheep relaxed some people, she supposed. One, two, three, she began rhythmically.

Around thirty-five, Kirsta began to feel drowsy. Suddenly she stopped counting. She was not alone in the cabin. Kirsta realized she'd been subconsciously aware of this for several moments. She didn't know how she knew it, but she did. Her eyes strained to peer into the darkness, but very little light sneaked in around the edges of the curtains. She heard nothing over the pounding of her heart. Someone — or something — had joined her in the room; she sensed a subtle shifting of molecules near her, a new, dark tension in the air.

Kirsta didn't move. She knew that if she put out her right hand, it would connect with something that hadn't been there when she turned out the light earlier. She had to do something; she couldn't just lie there paralyzed all night. She remembered her dream of the previous night, and the odd feeling she'd had this morning that someone was watching her from the mirror. Kirsta trembled violently; her very blood seemed to have grown colder in her veins.

Without a thought, Kirsta suddenly rolled to the far side of the bed, next to the wall. She fumbled with the hurricane-style lamp, her trembling fingers finally finding the switch. She thought she heard a scuttling noise, but when she turned the lamp on, the room was empty. She glanced at the door. The small iron bolt still lay firmly in its housing. The back door was also firmly shut and locked, its chain in place.

Kirsta pulled her robe on and grabbed a heavy brass candlestick from the mantle. She clutched the front of the robe closed, and headed toward the bathroom, the only other door in the small cabin. Jerking the door open, she felt a momentary panic at the sight of her own terrified face in the mirror, but the room was empty — as were the armoire and all the cabinets in the kitchenette. There was no sign that anyone else had been there. Kirsta collapsed back onto the quilt as her knees finally gave way.

Was it possible for someone to have sneaked out before she turned on the lights, or could her imagination have invented the intruder? She had never been prone to such flights of fancy, but then the atmosphere of Lost Oaks seemed to have worked on her nerves last night; why not tonight as well? Maybe it was the Fruit de Coeur. She rarely drank wine, and in combination with everything else, it probably over-stimulated her imagination. With a sigh, Kirsta lay back down and tried to go to sleep. But she kept the light on for the rest of the night, and the candlestick beside her in the bed.

The next morning, Kirsta rose early. She'd slept fitfully, and had finally given up as dawn thrust its pale fingers beneath the curtains. She pulled on a fuchsia sweatsuit and rubber sandals, and strolled down through the wet grass to watch the sun rise over the pond. Long beams of pink light reached through the branches of the trees to rest on the water before her, and three small ducks paddled back and forth, ignorant of their audience.

Kirsta found a stone bench at the far end of the pond, and sat enjoying the serenity around her. She closed her eyes and leaned her head back, enjoying the warmth of the morning sun on her face. Her terrors of the night before seemed worlds away, impossible in such bucolic surroundings. She felt herself drift, as though on the purple clouds that ran before the sun. The light cast bright patterns on the insides of her eyelids.

Then the patterns coalesced and she seemed to see herself in a large rustic room, moonlight pouring through one small window in the far wall. Long skirts hampered her movements, and she wanted to tear them off, free her legs from them. She looked around her. The walls of the room were rough boards, and straw crunched on the floor beneath the leather soles of her high shoes. She smelled the ripe, musty smells of hay and manure, heard the soft snort of a large animal to her left. She was in a barn or stable of some kind.

Footsteps sounded behind her, but Kirsta felt no fear, only a thrill of joy, a shudder of anticipation. Someone she loved had just put his hands on her shoulders. She reached up to touch the slender fingers, but a chill sliced through her heart — the hands were wrong, the fingers too thick, the palms too hot. Before she could turn, they crept toward her throat and then she couldn't breathe …

Suddenly a shadow blocked the light, chilling Kirsta's skin and forcing her eyes open as she gasped for air. Sean stood before her, the early light glittering like amethysts through the dark waves of his hair. Kirsta squinted up at him, tried to force her mind to concentrate. But she couldn't make out his expression. The rosy light behind him seemed to blur the edges of his face, changing the set of his jaw, the angle of his cheekbones. He looked like a different man, Sean McLeod and yet not Sean McLeod. Kirsta struggled to identify the changes in Sean, but felt the world around her fading away somehow, as though a warm fog had moved in around her.

With a great effort of will, she shook her head and wiped hard at her eyes with the heels of her hands. When she looked up again, the sun's angle had changed slightly — or Sean's position had. At any rate, he was the same Sean McLeod she'd met the day before, tall and slim, his black hair mussed and slightly damp. He was wearing jeans and a red shirt with the sleeves rolled above the elbows. The dark hair on his forearms looked damp, also, as though he'd been out in the early-morning mists for a long time. Kirsta noticed again how long and slender his fingers were.

After waiting for him to say something, she said, "Good morning, Sean." Her voice sounded unnaturally loud in the stillness, and the ducks squawked and flapped into the tall grasses on the other side of the pond.

Sean said nothing for a moment. He just stood, clenching and unclenching his hands. Kirsta watched him warily. She wondered whether he were even aware of her, though his eyes seemed locked on her face.

Then suddenly he looked away toward the house as though he heard something from that direction. Kirsta glanced that way too, expecting Daphne to be waving from the back porch. But she saw nothing except the play of shadows and light against the windows as a small breeze rippled the leaves. Sean sighed and rubbed his eyes. When he looked at her again, his eyes seemed more focused, less intense.

"What are you doing out this early?" he asked.

"I could ask you the same thing," Kirsta said, but he didn't respond. She continued: "I had trouble sleeping last night, and decided to give up when the sun came up."

"Nothing you ate, I hope. Aunt Daphne would be shattered to think her cooking gave anybody a problem."

Kirsta smiled. "No, nothing like that. I just thought I heard a noise in the cabin, and my nerves were on edge."

He waved his hand dismissively. "Probably just your imagination working overtime in a new environment. Or an animal. There's no foundation or basement beneath these old slave cabins. We put that one up on cement blocks and beams to get it off the dirt, but sometimes racoons or foxes get underneath. They can make quite a ruckus at night. I'll have one of Henry Patton's gas jockeys over to check it out, if you want."

"No, don't bother." Kirsta felt a bit embarrassed she'd brought the whole thing up. "Probably just the new environment, like you say. I'm sure I'll get used to it."

"I'm sure you will." Sean glanced at his watch. "It's only six-thirty. Aunt Daphne won't be up for another half-hour, at least. I'm not much of a cook, but I could manage some coffee and toast, if you're hungry."

"Thanks, but I'm not really hungry yet," Kirsta said, rising. "I'm still full from that big dinner last night. I could use a cup of coffee, though, if you're having one. Then I think I'll just wander around the grounds for a while until the library in Allindea opens."

As they walked to the back porch, Sean pointed toward the towering hedges. "Did Aunt Daphne show you the maze yet?" he asked.

"Yes, she did. And the 'Marrying Magnolia'."

Sean scowled. "The 'Marrying Magnolia.' I should have known. That's just the sort of tripe people want to hear. Well, you'll probably want to see the barn behind it, then. There are all kinds of family legends about it, too."

"What kinds of legends?" Kirsta asked.

Sean's lips raised in a knowing smile as he held the back door open for her. The smile didn't reach his eyes, however. "I knew you'd be interested. Well, I don't remember a lot of it, but there's something about my great-great grandfather locking his wife in there during the civil war or something. Apparently, he was punishing her for doing something awful or was keeping her from doing something. As I said, I'm pretty vague on most of that stuff."

While Sean filled the coffee maker, Kirsta opened a couple of cupboards, and found two mugs. She set them on the counter next to the coffeemaker. They moved quietly around the kitchen for a few minutes, and Kirsta realized how comfortable she felt with him just then, how domestic to be preparing morning coffee. It seemed … natural, somehow.

"Have you ever been married?"

Kirsta was startled out of her reverie by Sean's blunt question as he handed her the creamer and sugar bowl.

He flushed darkly, as though startled by his own question, and said in a gruff voice, "I hope you like chicory."

"N-No," she stammered.

"No you don't like chicory?"

"No I've never been married."

"I was."

Kirsta hadn't expected to have such a personal conversation so soon, and wanted to steer it away from herself. She didn't want to discuss David Belsen with Sean. Did he want to discuss the death of his wife? How would he react if he knew Daphne had already told Kirsta about the plane crash? Maybe he was looking for an opening to talk about it with her, to become closer. After all, he'd brought the subject up, even if he'd seemed to surprise himself.

Kirsta decided to brave the minefield of Sean's marriage, rather than talk — or think — about David. She cleared her throat. "Your Aunt Daphne told me about your wife and child — and the accident. She said you were ... well, devastated. I understand; it must be awful to lose someone you love so much."

Before Kirsta could continue, Sean pounded his fist on the counter top and snarled, "Damn it, that woman has no idea how to mind her own business. How could she — or you, for that matter — have the first inkling of how I felt?"

Kirsta took a step back. "I ... I'm sorry," she began. "I didn't —"

"Forget it," he said, turning away tensely. He fiddled with the handle of the glass coffeepot as the brown liquid hissed into it. "I shouldn't have snapped at you that way," he muttered. "But it's a subject I never talk about. And it infuriates me the way my aunt feels she has to constantly lay our lives out for every stranger who drives up the pike. Especially when she couldn't possibly understand how painful it was."

Kirsta moved beside him and poured coffee into the mugs. She didn't want to be just some "stranger who drives up the pike" to Sean and Daphne. Ridiculous as it seemed, she already felt as though she belonged at Lost Oaks, and wanted Sean to see that, too. But if she didn't understand her feelings, how could she possibly make him understand them?

Kirsta handed Sean one of the mugs and sat at the little breakfast table by the window. "I think your Aunt Daphne's one of the nicest people I know," she said carefully. "She's made me feel right at home already. And I have to admit I think she has a real intuition about people."

Sean still stood by the counter. A lock of dark hair hung loosely across one thick eyebrow as his eyes seemed to swallow Kirsta. "Do you really?" he said. "And just what did Aunt Daphne intuit about you?"

She tried not to blush, but felt her face heat up. "Well, not much, I guess," she admitted. "At least not that we've talked about. But then, we haven't had much time for conversation."

"So, what deep, dark secrets does Ms. Kirsta Linden have that she wouldn't talk about to strangers?"

Kirsta glanced at Sean's face, but his eyes were guarded. She couldn't tell whether he was serious or kidding. She decided to assume he was kidding.

"I don't really have many secrets — at least not deep, dark ones. I've never robbed a bank or murdered anybody. And as I said, I've never even been married. I teach history for Parthenon University, and am down here in Louisiana doing research on pre-Civil War plantation life."

"So you're writing a book? The 'publish or perish' academic syndrome?"

"Well, not exactly," she admitted, stirring sugar into her mug. "I'm actually doing the research for a colleague of mine. He had too many classes this term to do it himself."

Sean's eyes narrowed. "Let's see if my intuition is as good as my aunt's," he mused. "You left in the middle of a term to do research on a book that you're not even writing for yourself. I think you're running away from something — or someone. How am I doing so far?"

Kirsta didn't answer for a moment. All she could see was David's face that last night as he paced the kitchen, shouting at her. His pale hair flew wildly around his face, big hands rubbed together like hungry animals. She heard herself trying to calm him down in a voice that didn't sound like hers anymore, and watched again as he raised the snow globe. Kirsta forced the memory from her. What's past is past, she told herself.

"Actually, I much prefer research to teaching." This was true, but only covered the surface of Sean's question.

Blood pounded behind her temples, and Kirsta watched her hands tremble through a pink haze. She tried to drink her coffee, but it was too hot, and she burned her tongue. Tears sprang to her eyes. They were tears of pain, but Kirsta knew the pain went much deeper than the surface of her tongue.

Kirsta stood and tried to straighten her shoulders. "I think I'd better get to work," she said, glancing at her watch. She was amazed by how calm her voice was. "This may feel like a vacation, but it's not. I do have a deadline."

Sean watched her go wordlessly, a frown crossing his face.

"Then just take the coffee with you," he said quietly.

Kirsta nodded and backed out the screen door. "Thanks for the coffee, Sean." She turned and hurried down the walk to her cabin, forcing her legs not to run.

Kirsta showered for a long time. She'd reacted badly to Sean's teasing. He'd wanted to get a rise out of her, and had succeeded. She only hoped he hadn't noticed. The hot water sprayed her breasts, coursed between her thighs and spattered the tops of her feet as she tried to wash her embarrassment away. She vowed not to let herself show that kind of vulnerability to Sean. There was something a little dark, a little dangerous about him. She recalled the odd moment by the pond, when he merely stood frozen, not responding to her, and wondered what he'd been thinking.

After drying off, Kirsta dressed in a rose-colored sundress and tan canvas shoes. She let her hair dry in the warm breeze that wafted through the big screened windows as she charged the battery of her laptop computer and sorted through her research materials. She phoned the Allindea library and found out which of the larger plantations in the area contained local archives she could visit for information. She made a list, but decided to check out the library and historical society files first, to get an overview of the area before targeting specific plantations.

As Kirsta slowly maneuvered her rented car down the gravel drive toward the main road, a motion to the left caught her attention. Daphne waved and hurried down the path toward her. Kirsta smiled and rolled down her window, waving back. She cringed inwardly, remembering her embarrassment after helping Daphne pull up the stained tablecloth.

"I'm glad I caught you before you left," Daphne panted. "I wanted to let you know dinner will be a little earlier tomorrow night — about six, if that's no problem."

"Dinner?" Kirsta had assumed last night's experience would be the last, especially after her own strange behavior afterward. She had planned on finding some fast food in Allindea after her research.

Daphne nodded. "I invited Henry and Etta Patton over for roast chicken and pecan stuffing — it's Henry's favorite. He's never liked coming over to Lost Oaks for some reason, but he can't resist my pecan stuffing."

"Thanks, it sounds delicious," Kirsta said, "but I wouldn't dream of intruding on your dinner party. I'll just catch something in Allindea. I'm sure there are plenty of places to get a quick dinner."

Daphne's smile faded. "But I set this up for you. The Pattons are a wealth of information about local history — you can't shut them up when they get started. And I thought you'd enjoy talking with them about your research. They're very enthusiastic about it, and Etta even talked about bringing some old scrapbooks of her grandmother's."

Kirsta couldn't think of a reasonable objection. She didn't relish the idea of spending another meal worrying about what Sean was thinking of her, but she hated to disappoint Daphne. And the truth was, she'd definitely like to see the Pattons' scrapbook. And, Kirsta told herself, as long as she avoided the Fruit de Coeur, she should be all right.

"Six o'clock sounds fine," she smiled.

"Wonderful." Daphne stepped back. "Well, you get going," she said. "And good luck."

Driving down the winding drive, Kirsta glanced into the rearview mirror. The grey house gradually receded behind her, framed in the Spanish moss draping from the heavy branches of a gigantic live oak that stood alone in the center of the front lawn. Nearly hidden in a network of shadows against the trunk of the tree stood a tall, slender man, watching her. Though she couldn't make out his features, Kirsta knew it was Sean, and she shivered in the musty warmth of her car.

CHAPTER FIVE

As Kirsta drove along the wooded roads toward Allindea, she realized she'd have trouble working on her research. Her emotions were too confused by all that had happened at Lost Oaks. Something was strange at the old plantation, but she couldn't put her finger on exactly what was going on. Without thinking, Kirsta pulled the car onto a dirt patch at the side of the road and got out. She walked alongside a wide field for a mile or so, enjoying the sweet, sharp scents of the wildflowers.

The morning was warm and steamy, and dragonflies darted between the high weeds. A hawk hung lazily in the high clouds, and a squirrel chattered at her from the safety of an old stump. Kirsta noticed a narrow path leading into the field, and followed it, heading toward the stand of high loblolly pines at the far side. The cool darkness of the woods seemed to beckon her. Glad she'd worn the canvas shoes instead of sandals, she checked the pocket of her sundress for the notebook and pen she always kept there. She'd take some notes on flora and fauna while she explored the woods.

Kirsta tried to think about Sean, then she tried not to think about him. She couldn't understand her feelings for him. His complexities seemed immense, and yet there was a sensual simplicity to the way he moved, the sparkle of his eyes, the gentle set of his mouth, that made her heart ache. What was the problem with him?

Kirsta laughed out loud, once, without much humor. Maybe the problem lay with Kirsta herself. Maybe she had to sort her own life out, come to terms with her past and her relationship with David Belsen, before she could even begin to understand anyone else. Though she knew intellectually it was ridiculous, she still felt sometimes that she could have made a difference in what happened with David if she'd only tried harder. Maybe if she'd seen it coming sooner, she could have gotten him some help. Maybe if she'd given him more time. Maybe she should have —

Kirsta stopped at the end of the path and shook her head angrily. "Kirsta, you're tired and confused," she said aloud. "Don't start trying to heap blame on yourself. You're okay, and you did the right thing."

She pushed on through the dense undergrowth at the edge of the woods. That kind of guilty second-guessing was just the kind of response David would have wanted her to have. Kirsta had done everything she could to make him happy and to make their relationship work. She knew that. All the time in the world wouldn't have made a difference to David.

Kirsta wondered what time it was and frowned when she realized she'd left her wristwatch back at the cabin. She would have to get her mind back on what she was doing; she seemed to be getting more and more absentminded lately, since she'd come to Lost Oaks. Since she'd met Sean.

She passed the tall, soldierly trunks of the pines, their branches beginning high above her with their long needles stretching upward to catch every ray of sun and every drop of humidity. Fallen leaves and brown needles softened her footsteps as she padded deeper into the woods. The smooth sweet gum trunks were thicker, sloping gradually from knobby roots, and the leaves blocked much of the sunlight. Grey vines wrapped themselves around the trees and dangled between the branches. One particularly thick vine seemed to hang above her in mid-air, doubling back on itself to form a narrow loop, for all the world like a hangman's noose.

Kirsta froze, at once fascinated and repelled by the image. There was something strangely familiar about the way the vine hung, silhouetted against a long beam of golden sunlight in the greenish glow of the woods. As she squinted against the glare, she could almost see a human shape form itself in the empty air, a shaggy head bent sideways before the loop, the vine around the shadowed neck. Black eyes bored into hers from the dead face.

Kirsta gave a little gasp, and turned away from the disturbing mirage. Whatever could have brought on such a grisly fantasy? Scrambling through the leafy green plants growing along the forest floor, she found herself breathless at the top of a small ravine. Something burst from a shrub near her head, and before Kirsta's brain registered that it was only a small bird, she descended, half-running, half-sliding down the embankment.

She paused at the bottom of the ravine to get her bearings and looked up at the place where she'd stood a moment before. It would be too difficult to try to get back up the same way — the ground was sandy and steep. She dusted her hands off and glanced around. The ravine had a silty bottom, studded with large rounded rocks, and snaked between the banks. This was apparently a dry stream bed, so she decided to follow it until she found a more gradual rise. She'd climb to higher ground and hike back to the car. The idea of taking notes in the woods hadn't been such a good idea, after all.

Which way would take her back toward the road and her car? Kirsta tried to remember which direction she'd come, but the ravine twisted away in both directions, so she had no idea which way would be best. She turned to the left and began picking her way through the stones and small plants along the stream bed. The broad leaves of tulip poplars along the banks created a dense canopy high above her, so she caught only glimpses of the sun reflected from their shiny green surfaces.

Kirsta felt very small and very alone. She rubbed her wrist and wished she had her wristwatch. She felt as though she'd been walking for hours. Somehow, she thought knowing the time would be reassuring, give her a sense of connection to the rest of the world. Where was the rest of the world? Wandering through these towering trees made her feel as though Lost Oaks and Allindea and the whole state of Louisiana around her had simply disappeared, as though time had stopped. Nothing existed but this forest and no time had ever existed or would ever exist except now.

Kirsta's chest tightened beneath the elastic threads that shirred the top of her sundress, and she felt a trickle of sweat on her back. She walked faster, and stumbled over a rock nearly hidden by the sandy dirt. Her shoe came off and she stopped to pull it back on. As she leaned against a thin tree growing crooked from the bank, she thought she heard something moving through the woods above her. Kirsta held her breath and listened. She heard it again — the slow, heavy steps of some large animal walking through the trees toward her.

Did they have bears in Louisiana? Wild boar? She cursed herself for not doing more preliminary research before coming down here, but she'd been in such a hurry. Somehow, the steps didn't sound like a wild animal's; they sounded more regular, more controlled — like a man's.

She started to call out for help, but then realized how isolated and vulnerable she was. Everyone knew stories of women who'd been raped or murdered in lonely spots like this. Even Kirsta had been chased across a deserted mall parking lot one night by a drunken motorcyclist with a knife. She'd made it to her car with only a few yards to spare.

And now she had no idea what kind of man might be lurking just above her.

"Oh my God," Kirsta whispered to herself, trying not to panic. Had he heard her before? Did he know she was down here? He seemed to be heading in the same direction; maybe he was following her.

Kirsta began running along the dry creek bottom as quietly as she could. She had no idea where she was running; she might end up trapped somewhere, right where he wanted her. Maybe he was herding her where he wanted her to go. Her breathing and heartbeat were so loud in her ears that she couldn't tell whether he was still following her or not. She thought she heard an angry shout and glanced at the top of the bank behind her as she ran.

Her foot slammed into another half-buried stone and she fell headlong, sliding across the pale soft sand. She rolled over once and hit her head hard against the stump of a tree. Bright flashes played in her vision as she tried to get up, and she collapsed back into the grass and moss, hoping she hadn't made as much noise as she feared she had. She closed her eyes, willing them to clear. Then she heard heavy footsteps pounding toward her. She tried to rise, and the pain in her head brought tears to her eyes.

A male voice called out, and she recognized it. Sean. She leaned back against the weedy bank in relief.

"Kirsta?"

She knew Sean was standing over her, but she said nothing. She didn't even open her eyes. She used all her concentration willing herself not to cry. Then hands gripped her upper arms, and Sean pulled her gently to her feet. He wrapped his arms around her shoulders, and held her against him tightly. Kirsta felt as though she'd come home.

"It's all right, Kirsta. It's all right," he whispered over and over, until her breathing became easy again.

"I'm sorry I scared you," Sean said as Kirsta brushed the leaves and grass from her dress, feeling a bit foolish. "I saw your car along the road, and thought you might have had some trouble."

"How did you find me in here, though?" Kirsta asked. "Frankly, I don't even know where I am. I fell down the bank into this ravine somewhere back that way, and just started walking, hoping I'd find a way back to my car."

Sean picked a couple of twigs from Kirsta's hair. "Actually, you're not that far from the path through Witchman's Field. I assume that's how you got in here in the first place."

"Witchman's Field? Is that what it's called?"

Sean nodded. "These are Witchman's Woods, too. I'm not sure of the exact source, but apparently there was an old Cajun fellow who lived in a shack back in the woods around the turn of the century. He was some kind of herbalist or healer or something. Nobody knew much about him — even his name — so he's just remembered as the Witch Man."

"The Witch Man." Kirsta felt her researcher's curiosity blooming. "Do you know whether his cabin's still back there?"

Sean hesitated, then waved a hand in the general direction Kirsta had come. "As a matter of fact, it is," he said. "I know these woods like my own backyard. I used to wander around in here for hours and hours when I was a boy. I never told anybody I'd found the cabin. It was my secret hideout. It's actually a pretty interesting place."

He ran a hand through his hair, and glanced away. Then he asked quietly, "Would you like to see it? Or do you have to get to work?"

"I'd love to see it. Lead on."

Kirsta was moved by Sean's sudden shyness about showing her his secret place. He was like a little boy who wanted to share something special with a friend. But there was nothing childlike about the hand that took hers and gently led her back along the stream bed. Or about the way he looked at her when he glanced at her as they walked side-by-side through the shimmering woods.

They finally reached a place where heavy roots jutting from the bank formed natural steps. Sean drew Kirsta up with him by holding one arm firmly around her waist. She struggled to keep up with him, but he moved so surely and smoothly that she knew she'd have been left behind if he hadn't helped her. It was obvious he'd done this many times before.

When they crested the top, Sean paused to let Kirsta straighten out her sundress, which had become twisted and was bunched around the tops of her thighs. His eyes followed her movements appraisingly as she pulled it down. She felt herself blush.

"I certainly don't have my mountain-climbing clothes on today," she said. "I didn't plan to do any heavy-duty hiking today when I left."

"That's obvious," Sean said, his eyes slowly moving up her body until they rested on hers. "So why did you?"

She shrugged. "I don't know. I wasn't in the mood for being cooped up in the library, and just stopped here on impulse, I guess. The woods looked cool and inviting. Where were you headed?"

Sean began walking again, his hand resting lightly in the small of Kirsta's back. "I guess Aunt Daphne's told you about the restoration project for the chapel at the Allindea cemetery?" Kirsta nodded. "Well, I didn't have any appointments today, so I decided I'd go in and help out there for a while."

Kirsta stopped. "Are they expecting you? If you don't have time to do this now, we can —"

Sean held up his free hand. "No, it's fine. I'll just get there a little later. Nobody stands much on ceremony or worries about schedules. There are plenty of people to work 'till I get there."

He pulled a vine out of their way, and Kirsta shuddered, remembering her earlier vision and asked, "What kind of vine is that?"

"It's called blackjack or ratpan vine. It makes a kind of honey some people like. And those low green plants are paw-paws; they have fruit near the end of the summer, about the same time the muscadine grapes are ripe on those other vines over there."

"Sounds like there's a lot to eat out here, if somebody got lost."

Sean nodded. "Or if somebody didn't want to be found. Sometimes escaped convicts or fugitives hide out in these woods, and there's plenty to keep them alive. Plenty of small animals, too — chipmunks, squirrels, rabbits, even armadillos. Lots of bad guys have been found back in Witchman's Woods by the law."

Kirsta thought about how frightened she'd been when she'd heard Sean's footsteps, and felt a bit less foolish for running from him.

Then they were at the edge of a wide, grassy clearing. On the far side of the clearing, protected by the overhanging branches of a sweet-gum tree, stood a large wooden shack. The floor was raised about three feet off the ground by several widely-spaced pillars of cement blocks. An uneven stack of truck tires in front led to a metal gate held across the open doorway by a rusty chain. The chain was hooked to a bent nail.

"Witch Man's cabin." Sean's hand on her back moved Kirsta forward, and they crossed the large grassy lawn.

"I can't imagine anyone living so far out in the woods alone," Kirsta said. "It seems … dangerous."

"Lots of people thought the witchman was dangerous," Sean said. "They came for his herbal concoctions, but they thought he was magical, and didn't quite trust him."

"I suppose their fear was his best protection," Kirsta mused. "But I'm surprised the cabin is still here. It seems as though vandals would have wrecked it after he died."

"Fear again," Sean said. "People still say his ghost roams the woods. Nobody would come near here right after he died, for fear of his spirit coming after them. And then people just forgot about it. After I discovered it, I finally found out whose place it was from Henry Patton, who'd heard about it from his daddy."

"Why haven't the insects and weather destroyed it, then?"

Sean laughed. "Well, it's not for lack of trying. When we get there, you'll see dirt-diver nests on all the walls."

"Dirt-divers?"

"Kind of wasps. They make nests that look like Pan pipes. But they don't really hurt the building. And the shack itself is made of cedar, like most of the houses down here. Termites hate cedar."

They reached the tire steps, and Sean went up first, unhooking the chain from its nail. Kirsta watched the way his strong leg muscles rippled beneath the pale blue denim. The gate swung open with a rusty squeal. Kirsta hiked her skirt up again before climbing to the doorway. She felt Sean's eyes on her as he held out his hand and pulled her up to him. Her foot slipped off the rough edge of a floorboard, and she nearly lost her balance. Sean's arms wrapped around her, and he pulled her to him.

"Be careful," he said, moving her away from the edge. "You wouldn't want to get hurt way out here."

Kirsta tried to erase the worried frown on his face with a small joke. "Especially since the herbalist's remedies aren't around to make it all better."

"Actually, that's not quite true."

Sean led her into the darkness of the main room of the cabin. The cabin had no windows, and the heavy cedar boards were nailed snugly against one another. The only light came from the doorway through which they had just come, so Kirsta's eyes took a moment to adjust. When they did, she gasped in wonder.

Two of the walls contained rough wooden shelves from floor to ceiling. These shelves still sagged beneath the weight of more than a hundred jars, bottles and vials, each labeled and filled. Some contained powders of various colors and textures, some were filled with liquid, and some had objects inside. Kirsta wasn't sure she wanted to get close enough to find out exactly what those objects were.

"This is amazing," she whispered in awe. "It's all still here, after so many years. What are these things?"

Sean moved toward the wall straight ahead of them. "Well, this wall contains mostly medical herbs and healing potions and tonics," he said. He began pointing at bottles and reading their labels. "Valerian root. Chickweed. Sassafras bark. White nettle. And here are some jars labeled according to how they act: nerve soother, stomachache remedy, burn salve, and so on."

Kirsta pointed toward the other wall of shelves. "And what's in those?"

Sean said, "The contents of those seem to be a little less scientific. They're more like ingredients for magic spells and potions."

He picked up a small blue jar. "This one has something that looks like caviar in it. The label says: 'pirhanah roe.'"

"Fish eggs," said Kirsta, moving alongside him. "I guess it is like caviar. But I don't think I want to taste it."

"Me neither. How about this?" He pointed to a large jar near the top. "'Vulture's feet.'"

"Yuck. What do you suppose anybody would want with vulture's feet?"

Sean peered at the jar and shrugged. "I don't know," he mused. "Maybe for some kind of flying potion?"

"Oh, I'd like that," she smiled. "I've always wanted to be able to fly. I remember lying out in the grass in our backyard on summer days, watching the birds soar above me. I wanted more than anything else to be up there with them. I even planned to be a pilot, because that's the closest I could get to being a bird."

"Why didn't you?" Sean moved closer to her.

"I don't know. Other things got in the way, I guess." She laughed. "And when I found out how much a pilot depends on math, I realized it probably wasn't for me. History was always more appealing."

Kirsta realized Sean was standing directly behind her. Though he wasn't touching her, she could sense his presence as though some energy field extended beyond his body. She shivered a little.

She reached out and dusted off the label of a narrow-necked bottle nearby. "'Potion of desire,'" she read. "'Attracts the opposite sex.' I wonder what ingredients this contains."

When Sean didn't respond, she turned to see whether he'd heard her. He was standing very close, gazing into her face intently.

"I don't think you need that one," he whispered huskily. "At least, not for me."

He bent he head toward hers, and kissed her. Kirsta felt as though the floor had suddenly dropped from beneath her feet, as though she and Sean floated somewhere in a vortex of light and color.

She closed her eyes and drew him closer, her arms slipping around his neck, her hands beneath the collar of his shirt. She opened her lips slightly and tasted him. He was all firmness and muscle against her, and his pelvis ground against hers. She felt the heat of his hands on her buttocks, searing her flesh even through the layered fabric of her dress and underwear. She felt imprisoned in her clothes.

Then his hands moved. Keeping his mouth locked on hers, he backed up enough to run his hands upward across her aching breasts, and still further up to her neck. Then his fingers slid slowly across the naked flesh of her throat and shoulders until she thought she'd melt. He pulled his lips from hers, biting her lower lip gently at the last moment, then moved his mouth along her shoulders, kissing her gently every few inches.

Kirsta's legs trembled beneath her. She felt feverish. These sensations were new and electric with Sean; her whole body seemed to pulse with an excitement she'd never known before. And yet, at the same time, she felt as though she'd always known Sean would be there for her someday, as though she'd waited her whole life for him.

Kirsta closed her eyes and let her head drop backward. Sean cradled the back of her neck gently in his left hand and kissed her throat. Through the shirred fabric, he stroked her left breast with his other hand. Her nipple hardened at his touch, and she moaned softly as he lowered his head to kiss her breast through the dress. Kirsta moved against him, her hands still clutching the back of his neck.

"You're so beautiful," he murmured, his breath tickling the flesh between her breasts. "Oh Kirsta, you're just so damned beautiful."

Something clattered loudly against the metal roof of the cabin, and Kirsta jumped back, her heart hammering loudly. "Wh—who was that," she stammered, trying to catch her breath.

Sean stepped to the door and chuckled. "Not a 'who,' but a 'what,'" he said. "Unless you consider a displaced squirrel a 'who.' Apparently we're trespassing."

He came back in and gently pulled her back to him, touching her lips once more with his. He ran his fingers through her hair.

"Or maybe it was the ghost of the Witch Man," said Kirsta. "Maybe he doesn't like people fooling around in his house."

"Impossible," Sean said, stroking her hair. "He couldn't have any objections to people being happy here. There are too many potions on these walls that prove that."

He glanced at his watch. "But we'd better be going. I really do have to get to the cemetery chapel pretty soon, and it's a bit of a hike back through the woods."

Sean showed Kirsta a shortcut back to Witchman's Field from the cabin, and they reached her car before too long. Sean's sports car was parked right behind it.

"So, you're going to the library now?" he asked, as she unlocked her car. "Will you be working for the rest of the day?"

Kirsta looked around and shook her head. "I suppose I should. But after such a pleasant morning out in the woods, being closed up in a little room seems like the last thing I want to do. I may just wander around town for a while, soak up some atmosphere."

"Well, if you're interested in old buildings, why don't you stop by the cemetery and see what's being done to the chapel. It's really got a lot of personality — and atmosphere."

Kirsta agreed to meet him in the cemetery parking lot after lunch, and watched him drive away. As she started her engine, she could still feel his hands on her skin, his mouth on hers. Oh God, she thought, she didn't need another man in her life right now. What was she going to do about Sean McLeod?

CHAPTER SIX

As she drove toward Allindea, Kirsta could still feel Sean's fingertips gliding along her shoulders. She heard his whisper in her ear again: You're so beautiful. He'd seemed so loving, so sincere.

She sighed, wishing she could trust him. She was undeniably attracted to Sean, both physically and emotionally. She wanted to believe in him, and in herself. But she had trusted David Belsen's words of love and passion not so long ago, and he too had seemed sincere and tender. But that dream of love had become a nightmare of violence and terror. Kirsta hit the steering wheel with the heel of her hand angrily. She must not allow herself to make that mistake again. Her eyes would be wide open this time.

The clock on the dashboard showed her that it was nearly eleven-thirty. Kirsta decided to wander down the main street of Allindea for a little while, getting a feel for the place. When she found somewhere that looked interesting for lunch, she'd just stop. She found a parking spot in front of the historical society, and went in there first, to see what kind of information they might have to help her research.

The Allindea Historical Society was housed in an unused church, with whitewashed plaster walls and dark wood trim. The sign on the front double doors proclaimed the museum "open." A tall, buxom redhead with large red lips opened the door as Kirsta climbed the front steps. She greeted Kirsta with a large smile.

"Come on in," she said, backing into the musty room to let Kirsta pass. "I'm Celeste Wallace, president of the Allindea Historical Society. Nice to see you."

"Thank you." Gingerly, Kirsta stepped inside, a bit overwhelmed by Celeste's enthusiastic greeting. "I'm —"

"Oh, I know who you are," Celeste laughed, her loud, deep voice dripping with a heavy southern accent. "You're the woman staying out at Lost Oaks with Daphne and Sean. You're here to do some kind of research for a book or something, right?"

Kirsta was taken even more off-guard by this remark. "Yes, that's right — Kirsta Linden. I'm sorry, do I —"

Again the large woman laughed and cut in. "There's no reason you should know anything about me," she said. "But Allindea's a pretty small place, and Daphne Woodring isn't the most stand-offish woman in town, if you know what I mean. Most of us have known you're coming for a couple weeks now. Not too many unfamiliar faces walk into the historical society on a weekday. I just took a chance it was you."

Kirsta relaxed and held out her hand. "Well, it's nice to meet you, Celeste," she said, "even if you knew me first."

Since the building was deserted at the moment, Celeste offered to show Kirsta around the ground floor. The Allindea museum consisted of two large front rooms filled with local antiques and artifacts displayed on shelves and in glass cases. Each room had two windows that reached from about waist-high nearly to the ten-foot ceiling. These windows should have made the rooms quite bright on such a sunny day, but the layer of dust coating them dimmed the sunlight and seemed to leach something from the place. Colors were muted, unreal.

Kirsta felt the whole place had a sense of timelessness. The thick walls not only kept the occasional noise of a car passing or a dog barking outside from reaching them, but deadened the sounds inside as well. Even Celeste's loud voice had a strange, muted quality as she described some of the more interesting objects in the large cases.

"Now, here we have some Indian artifacts from the area, both the Houmas and Tunica tribes." Celeste unlocked a small padlock and lifted one of the heavy glass lids. "Mostly, these are things local people have dug up on their property and donated to the society."

Kirsta gently touched the smooth edge of a pottery shard. "Are there any pieces from Lost Oaks?" she asked.

"Oh no," Celeste said, stepping back and looking at her curiously. "Neither of those Indian tribes ever went near that whole area. It was supposed to be bad medicine or something. In fact, that's how the plantation got its name. Didn't Daphne tell you about that?"

Kirsta shook her head; it ached dully from the stale air and she was beginning to regret coming in.

"Well, when Sean's great-great-great-granddaddy came to West Feliciana Parish, looking to build a plantation, he found all this land completely untouched a few miles from Allindea. Nobody knew who owned it. Everybody had just avoided it for years — all the rumors of strange things happening back there and all, you understand. But the old man was practical, if nothing else, and figured it was a good way to set up cheap. So he claimed the land as his, and built himself a house.

"But when they started clearing the land for building and planting, they found a whole grove of live oaks in the center of the woods. Live oaks aren't native to Louisiana — they were imported in the eighteenth century — so somebody must have gone back in there and planted them. But no one knows who would have done that. So they named the plantation Lost Oaks."

The room seemed very warm and Kirsta's mouth was dry. She glanced around the room for a water fountain, but there was none. "And they never had any problem later with supernatural things?"

"Oh sure," Celeste said, closing the glass lid. "At least, there are legends and rumors. Stories about curses and ghosts — the usual. But you know the historical value of local legends. One of those and a quarter won't buy you a cup of coffee."

She moved to a different case, beckoning for Kirsta to follow her. "If you're interested in Lost Oaks history," she said, "we don't have much here. The family still has most of the important papers. You can talk to the Pattons, though — I'm sure they'll be happy to help you with your research."

"Yes," Kirsta said, moving into the back of the building after Celeste. "I think I'm meeting the Pattons tomorrow night."

"You'll love them," Celeste said, "everybody's uncle and aunt, if you know what I mean."

Kirsta thought Celeste's voice seemed a bit fainter, but perhaps her ears were at fault. She felt a bit lost and lightheaded in the haziness of the big room. She had to ask Celeste to repeat her next comment.

"I just thought you might like to see the few things we do have from the Lost Oaks area," she said, reaching into the case. "Sean donated some old letters from Andrew Johnson and Teddy Roosevelt to ancestors of his, and a couple of business documents. But I think the most interesting thing is this. It belonged to his great-great grandmother."

Celeste took Kirsta's hand and placed something in it. Kirsta felt as though she'd gotten an electrical shock, and dropped the object on the wooden floor.

"I'm sorry," she mumbled as Celeste bent to retrieve what had dropped.

"No problem." Celeste held out a silver-topped comb for Kirsta to examine. Feathery engravings circled the deeply-etched, intricate letter "I" in

59

the center of the crossbar. Kirsta frowned. Though the engraving pattern was different, it was the same letter Kirsta had drawn on Daphne's tablecloth.

Celeste's voice pounded in Kirsta's eardrums. "This was David McLeod's wedding gift to his wife." Kirsta tried not to wince. She wondered how to make a graceful exit.

The pain in her head increased, but Kirsta tried to ignore it. "Why would Sean give something that personal to the museum," she asked, "and keep so many other things?"

"Good question," Celeste said. "I asked him the same thing. But he just said he didn't want it around. Said it makes him uncomfortable or something. Shouldn't surprise me, I guess. Sean's all right, but a bit odd at times, if you ask me. Don't you think so?"

Suddenly Kirsta felt as though she were unable to breathe. The musty room seemed to be closing in on her. She stammered an apology and thanks to Celeste, and hurried out onto the front porch. As soon as the doors closed behind her, she felt the headache recede. She leaned against one of the wooden pillars and drew several deep breaths, inhaling the scents of roses and honeysuckle from the garden next door.

The clock on the tower of the Allindea Inn struck noon, and Kirsta realized her hunger had combined with her strenuous walk in the woods that morning to create the lightheadedness she'd felt a moment before. She decided to treat herself to a nice lunch at the inn, and maybe absorb some of its gracious southern atmosphere while she was there.

Ten minutes later, Kirsta sat at a table in the corner of the veranda, behind a wicker folding screen. Spider plants and ivy draped from brass planters suspended above her, and a Scott Joplin rag tinkled from the speakers.

Kirsta sipped a minted lime drink in the small breeze created by a slowly-rotating ceiling fan. She released the tiny jitters that still hovered like gnats at the edges of her mind. She ordered lemon-chicken soup and a fruit salad, and leaned her head against the padded chair back. It had been a very unusual morning, she thought, and closed her eyes.

She remembered the strange shock at the touch of the silver comb. Perhaps static electricity had built up, or the edge of the silver had a spur which pricked her palm. She pondered the odd coincidence of seeing the letter "I" on the comb after what had happened at dinner. She wondered again why Sean donated such a personal item to the museum.

At the memory of dinner, Sean's face suddenly appeared in the violet darkness behind her eyelids, and she felt her stomach clench and her heart beat faster. His lips parted and he bent his head toward hers again, the way he had in Witchman's cabin. She shuddered, and opened her eyes, glancing around quickly to see whether anyone had noticed. Hers was the only table occupied on this side of the screen.

The waiter brought her soup and salad, and Kirsta settled down to enjoy her lunch. The drink had already improved her disposition, and the fruit was sweet and delicious. Kirsta caught herself listening to conversations at the tables adjacent to hers.

Just the other side of the wicker partition, two middle-aged matrons sipped glasses of chablis while they waited for their companion to arrive. The heavier woman was dark-skinned and wore gold bangles and a bright red turban wrapped around her head. She looked like an aging gypsy. The other one had on a pastel blue pantsuit that nearly matched her hair. They didn't notice Kirsta at the next table, and she moved her chair slightly, to further conceal herself behind the tall plants as she nibbled the juicy cantaloupe.

The women discussed local politics for a few minutes, the gypsy dismissing the local mayor and his assistants as "a bunch of dunderheads." Blue-hair laughed, and said, "I have to agree with you, cousin or no cousin. Granddaddy would have put him over his knee and paddled him for that paving decision."

Kirsta smiled, and wondered whether any residents of Allindea weren't related to someone else there. She doubted it. Then she heard something that caused her to pause in her lunch and listen more carefully.

Someone else had joined the table, and the gypsy sighed, "Finally we can order. I'm starving."

A loud female voice said, "Pricilla, you're always starving. What's the special today?"

As they discussed what to order, Kirsta realized the newcomer was none other than Celeste Wallace. Kirsta debated whether or not to announce her presence, but Celeste stopped her with her next comment.

"Sorry I'm late girls, but the strangest thing just happened at the museum. That woman from Pennsylvania came in this morning."

"The one staying at Lost Oaks?" asked Blue-hair. "What's she like?"

"Her name's Kirsta something," supplied Celeste. "And she's a funny one."

Kirsta felt her face burn as the others asked for an explanation. She recalled her discomfort in the old building and her hasty exit and wished she'd been more controlled. She looked for an exit behind her, but the only way from the veranda led directly past Celeste's table. She'd have to stay until they finished eating.

"She didn't even ask to see the town records," Celeste continued. "Hardly spoke at all, actually."

"Unfriendly." The gypsy sounded disgusted. "Typical northern tourist."

"No, not unfriendly," Celeste corrected. "Just really quiet, kind of … distracted, or uncomfortable or something. Especially when I mentioned Sean McLeod."

"What does she think of Sean?" asked Blue-hair conspiratorially, almost whispering.

"I don't really know," admitted Celeste, "though I tried to find out. I said I think he's a little strange, but she didn't take the bait."

"Well, he is strange. Ever since he brought that woman to Lost Oaks."

The gypsy said, "Poor thing. He got even worse after that terrible accident. I mean, it's been two years now — he should start living again. My oldest, Lydia, was interested in him last summer, but he pretty much ignored her. I'll be honest, I wasn't all that disappointed, considering his moodiness these days."

Celeste said, "I think he's a little scary sometimes. There's something about his eyes …" She left the sentence to hang unfinished in the air.

"Grief."

Kirsta wasn't sure who'd said it, but all three murmured agreement. There was silence for a moment, then the waiter asked for their lunch choices.

While they ordered, Kirsta thought about what she'd just heard. She was more intrigued than ever by the dark, intense man living at Lost Oaks. But she thanked Heaven for the squirrel who had interrupted them at the Witchman's cabin. Obviously, Sean still wasn't over the tragedy that took his beloved wife from him. He may have been looking for comfort, but Kirsta certainly didn't want to be a stand-in for the ghost of the woman he lost.

Her chance to leave discretely came a few minutes later, when the Gypsy saw someone they all knew in the main dining room. They bustled in to chat while they waited for lunch to arrive. Kirsta waited until they were inside, then left the payment and tip on her table and hurried down the sidewalk toward her car. She slid behind the wheel and breathed deeply in relief.

Kirsta started the engine and turned the corner to head back to Lost Oaks. At the stoplight she noticed the steeple of the old brick church by the Allindea cemetery. She swore softly to herself, remembering her promise to meet Sean and see the renovations. The last person she wanted to see right now was

Sean. After hearing what Celeste and her friends had said about him, Kirsta felt she needed to sort things out in her mind.

She decided to postpone her visit to the church, but when the light turned green, something made her drive into the church parking lot and pull the car in next to Sean's. She sighed and got out, feeling that even her car wouldn't let her avoid him.

The little brick church sat like a squat red sentinel against the high wrought-iron fence surrounding the Allindea cemetery. Branches of willows and oak trees hung protectively over it, shading it from the afternoon sun. Kirsta could hear hammering and the occasional whine of an electric saw from inside. A sign hung next to the open door, warning visitors to be careful during the construction. She entered the dark doorway, feeling oddly uncomfortable and anxious. She really wasn't ready to face Sean just yet — at the same time, she couldn't wait to see him again.

Nobody was in the large main room downstairs. The sounds of construction seemed to come from above her. All the pews had been removed, and the wall sconces were draped with rags, making them appear like ghostly arms raised in silent benediction over the missing parishioners. Kirsta headed toward the small door next to the altar, hoping it led upstairs. The gutted, deserted church made her uneasy, as though she were walking into a hospital — or a funeral home.

"Kirsta, you must leave."

The voice startled her. It sounded as though someone had whispered in her ear. She leaped forward a few steps, whirling to see who'd been right behind her. Nobody was there. The room was still as empty and deserted as it had been a moment ago. Kirsta glanced up, looking for a small balcony where someone could stand. Perhaps the acoustics of the room caused strange auditory hallucinations. There was nothing, no place for anyone to hide — although, why would they? Hardly anybody around here knew Kirsta, and even if they did, there was no reason to play such a joke on her.

Kirsta felt the hairs rise on the back of her neck, and rubbed goosebumps from her arms, though the air in the building was warm and stuffy. Had she imagined it, manufactured the voice from echoes of the saws and drills upstairs? It was the only explanation, but Kirsta hurried across the gritty floor, anxious to get away from the empty room.

She opened the door into a small hallway and saw a doorway leading outside ahead of her and a narrower door to the right. Stairs headed up to the left. The hallway was dark and windowless, and the air seemed dense, filled with more than the powder from crumbling old plaster and sawdust. Kirsta knew Sean must be upstairs with the construction crew, but something drew her to the closed door. She watched her fingers wrap around the antique brass knob and turn. The door opened.

At first, Kirsta could see nothing in the darkness of the room. She took a step or two into the doorway, thinking she'd try to find a light switch on the wall. It must be the rector's study, she decided. But before her hand got past the wood molding, she heard voices from within. At first, they were too faint to distinguish, and Kirsta thought she must be interrupting some clandestine meeting or rendezvous.

"Excuse me," she muttered, "I didn't mean —" Then she stopped. The speakers seemed not to have noticed her; they just continued talking. She listened. Now she could understand more of what was being said.

And she began to see. Perhaps her eyes were adjusting to the darkness, or maybe it was a trick of the sunlight through the door into the empty sanctuary behind her, but she could make out the figures of people before her. Apparently it was some kind of rehearsal for a play, because the two women were dressed in costumes, long dark dresses with hoop skirts and bonnets that might have been worn in the last century. The room shimmered around them, as though lit by dim candlelight.

One woman was taller than the other, and Kirsta saw pale wisps of blond hair fluttering from the edges of her dark hat. She wept into a lace hanky as she spoke in halting tones. The other woman patted her on the shoulder as she wept. They stood over the form of a man's still body, stretched out on a crude wooden table. Behind them stood a roll-top desk, cluttered with papers. An upholstered armchair sat in each corner and portraits of grim patriarchs hung on the walls.

"I was never permitted the chance to say good-bye," sobbed the blond woman. "And, by God, he'd have my neck if he knew I was here now."

"It's no matter," murmured the other, still patting the delicate shoulder. "Even now, he's signing the papers in Allindea. He won't be back for hours. Nobody else knows you're here; I took great care. You've nothing to worry about."

Kirsta realized the 'he' they referred to was not the man on the table. Her heart went out to the grieving woman. She felt like a voyeur, intruding on such a scene, but still stood, transfixed by the emotion before her.

The blond woman reached out one thin hand and stroked the cheek of the man on the table. Her back was to Kirsta as she bent to whisper in his ear. But Kirsta heard her words as clearly as though they'd been spoken in her ear.

"You blame me, I know, my love," the woman said. "You believe I betrayed you; it was part of his plan. And that's the worst tragedy of all, the worst." She dissolved into sobs.

Kirsta realized she was holding her breath, and backed out of the doorway, needing more air than seemed to be in the little room. A wave of dizziness swept over her, and she reached up to grasp the door frame for support. She leaned her head on her arm for a long moment and closed her eyes. When she opened them, the door had swung shut, and she could no longer hear the voices.

Kirsta turned away, trying to make sense of the tableau she'd just witnessed. Had she imagined it? No, that seemed impossible — everything was too real, too specific. Perhaps it was a rehearsal, as she'd first thought, for a play to be performed on the re-opening of the church after renovations. A surprise. That still made the most sense. And of course, they'd never noticed her, with the door swinging open and shut so silently. That had to be it.

Kirsta went up the old wooden stairs, anxious to be away from the unsettling scene she'd just witnessed. Her legs felt weak beneath her as she climbed toward the landing. Again, she heard voices from above, but these voices were somehow more concrete, more immediate.

"If we don't get the money we asked for," said a deep raspy voice, "there's no point in breaking through that wall. The balcony will just have to wait."

The other voice laughed. "After Sean talks to Robbison, we'll get it, no worry about that."

Kirsta hurried up the last few steps into a large open room with windows on each wall. Sawhorses and large tools were scattered about, and a layer of sawdust covered everything.

Several men were working at different places around the room, but two men stood to one side, studying a blueprint. One of them, a short red-headed man, was pointing at a corner of the paper.

The tall, pale man next to him was shaking his head.

Kirsta cleared her throat, and all heads turned to look at her. The red-haired man frowned at the interruption. He dusted off his hands and took a couple of steps in her direction.

"Can I help you, m'am?" His was the raspy voice she'd heard first.

"I'm looking for Sean McLeod. I was supposed to meet him here." The two men who'd been speaking glanced at each other, then back at Kirsta.

The pale man said, "Well, he's at the bank right now, but he'll be back any minute, if you want to wait downstairs." She nodded thanks, and turned to go back down.

The pale man turned his blue eyes on his companion. "And he'll have the money."

"I wish I had your confidence, Jerry," said the other, frowning again. "I don't know how you can be so sure."

The other men turned back to their work while the two spoke. They all seemed to have already forgotten Kirsta. As she descended, something the pale man said stopped her.

"I know Sean. And I know what he did for Robbison's daughter after her bike accident."

"They must be pretty close friends, then." said the other.

"No, they hardly knew each other up till then. Sean just has a special spot for kids who've been hurt. Probably something to do with his own kid's death. Anyway, I know Robbison would never say no to Sean."

Kirsta quietly descended the rest of the stairs and left by the back door. As she rounded the corner of the building, a blue station wagon pulled up. Sean exited the passenger side, and a thin, dark woman remained behind the wheel. Kirsta was surprised at the small pang of jealousy she felt seeing him with an attractive woman.

"Thanks," he said to the woman, then saw Kirsta. She hoped she wasn't flattering herself by thinking he looked very pleased to see her. He hurried over to her as the car drove away. She watched the way the sun seemed to glow in his dark hair, and how the damp edges of his hair curled at his temples.

"Have you been waiting long?" he asked.

"No, I just got here, and one of the fellows upstairs said to meet you down here."

He looked disappointed. "So you've already seen the inside? I guess I don't get to give you the grand tour."

"I'd love it. I just wandered through on my own. I'm sure you can point out things I missed."

Sean took her arm in his and led her around the back. "I'll leave the main sanctuary for later," he said. "First, I'll show you what we're doing upstairs."

As they entered the little back hallway, Kirsta pointed to the door opposite the stairs. It had been closed again.

"What's that room?" she asked. "The rector's office?"

"Probably was," Sean said. "But there's nothing in there anymore. No point in even looking at it. Right now we're storing all our extra equipment and supplies in there. It's a mess."

Kirsta was confused. "But I looked in there earlier. I'm sure it had furniture then."

"Not today it didn't," Sean laughed.

Kirsta felt herself bristle with annoyance at his disbelief. Why did he insist she was wrong when she knew what she'd seen, not fifteen minutes ago? "Well, open the door and look in," she said. "You'll see I'm right."

"That's what I mean," Sean said, still smiling. "You couldn't have opened the door. It's always kept locked during the day, so children can't wander in and hurt themselves with something. The only people with keys are Jerry, upstairs, and me, and we haven't been in there for several days. Try it, see for yourself."

Kirsta walked to the door slowly, telling herself that he must be mistaken, must be joking with her. But deep inside, she knew it was true, that when she turned the heavy old brass knob, the door wouldn't open. And it didn't. She tried again and again, rattling the knob angrily, almost frantically, but the door never budged.

"Would you unlock it, please." Kirsta's voice cracked with tension.

Sean inserted his skeleton key into the lock and turned it. The tumblers thudded into place. He twisted the knob and opened the door, reaching inside to turn on the light.

A naked bulb overhead showed Kirsta the contents of the room. Just stepladders, cans of paint and various electric drills and saws — no table or chair or roll-top desk. There was no way anybody could have changed the room so drastically in only a few minutes. Kirsta decided not to mention the grieving women she'd seen standing together. Somehow she knew they hadn't been there any more than the antique furniture — except for her.

Kirsta realized Sean was busy explaining her earlier experience in the chapel. She heard him as if he were speaking to her from a distance. He said something about paint and lacquer fumes causing strange hallucinations, and she agreed vaguely. But she knew in her heart that something else had occurred there in that tiny locked room, something beyond her realm of experience.

Kirsta didn't really believe in ghosts, yet she didn't disbelieve them either. She'd simply never seen one herself. She wanted to ask Sean whether the chapel was reputed to be haunted. Maybe there was something strange here that others had experienced as well. Maybe Sean would have some insight.

She opened her mouth to ask him, then stopped; she wasn't sure how he'd react to the suggestion of some paranormal occurrence. He might think her ridiculous, even asking such a question, or see her as some silly schoolgirl, looking for ghosts. She remembered his previous disgusted comments about tourists. She decided to let the subject rest. If she had seen something supernatural, it was over now.

They went upstairs and Sean introduced her to the workmen. The red-headed man she'd spoken to earlier was Leon Erikson, an art teacher at the local schools who helped with the design of the renovations. Pale, thin Jerry Harris proved to be an intelligent, soft-spoken carpenter who headed up the construction crew. He explained that all the workers were volunteers from the area, and many were specialists in some aspect of construction or design. Sean had spent nearly a year finding the right people and convincing them to work on the chapel.

"Mr. McLeod here can be a mighty persuasive guy," Jerry grinned as he handed a wad of envelopes to Sean. Without glancing at them, Sean tucked them into the hip pocket of his jeans.

"Those are the most recent bills," Jerry said to Sean. "I trust you had some success with Mr. Robbison down there at the bank."

Sean grinned back, but just said, "Some."

Jerry winked at Leon and raised his thumb in a signal of victory. Leon waved back, and continued measuring the wall that led into the sanctuary.

"I guess we can go ahead with the balcony, then," Jerry said. "We're almost finished with the rough work in here."

"We'll have plenty of money for the balcony," Sean said, "and probably part of what we need to repair the wrought iron fencing out front, if we're careful."

As Sean took Kirsta back down the narrow stairs, she was all too aware of their closeness and the feel of his arm draped loosely across her shoulders. He led her through the empty chapel, pointing out where the old part ended and the renovations began. Kirsta admired the flawless blending of the old and new, and he explained in detail the process for matching textures.

"You certainly know a lot about construction and architecture," she marveled.

"Most of it I've learned on this project," he said, opening the front door for her. "But I'm hooked; I'd like to do more. In fact, if you don't have anything else to do tonight, I'll take you to dinner at another place I'm interested in. I'm meeting the owner there later, and I think you'd get a kick out of seeing it."

Kirsta nodded. "Sounds great," she said. "I'll have to change, though. Can I meet you someplace? Back at Lost Oaks?"

She thought she saw a dark look ripple across his face, but decided it must be a shadow from the trees above them. "No," he said, "I have other clothes with me and have more work to do here. Why don't you come back to the church and leave your car? We can both take mine. About six-thirty?"

Kirsta agreed, though something in the back of her mind told her that a date with Sean might be the most dangerous thing she could do — emotionally, if not physically.

CHAPTER SEVEN

David Belsen wiped his hand along the thigh of his jeans as he drove across town. He wasn't really nervous — it was more an excitement, anticipation making his pulse quicken. His right hand patted the pocket of his leather jacket for the tenth time in the last five minutes, and felt the reassuring firmness of the long steel blade. The hunting knife was one of the few worthwhile things his father had left him before steaming to oblivion on a merchant marine freighter twenty-five years ago. The hunting knife, a volume of Sherlock Holmes stories and leather bomber jacket.

David had read straight through the thick mystery book in a week, enthralled by Holmes' insight. He was annoyed, however, that Watson never bothered to record all the details Holmes saw. David felt sure that if he'd been given the same advantage, he too could have solved the cases. He'd thrown the book in the garbage as soon as he'd finished reading it.

The bomber jacket had been too big for him, though he wore it everywhere, even in warm weather, until Mother threw it out. She never admitted discarding it, but he'd known she hated it. After she died, he'd bought another jacket exactly like it.

David had hidden the hunting knife under his mattress until he moved away from home, to keep her from taking that, too. Every month or so, David would jam a chair back beneath the knob of his bedroom door (his mother never allowed locks on interior doors), and slide the knife from its hiding place. He'd often stroked its cold surface with his index finger, admiring how it held his reflection. Once he intentionally ran his thumb along the razor-sharp edge, watching the beads of blood bubble to the surface and drip into his palm as he did so.

If he'd had the knife with him last night, he thought, he could have convinced Ginny to talk much sooner. But it was probably better that he used his hands on her. He hadn't wanted to really hurt her unless it was absolutely necessary — didn't even leave any bruises. She'd have called the police, making everything that much more complicated for him. No, the way he'd worked it, she couldn't prove he'd ever been a threat to her. Hell, she'd even invited him in and offered him a glass of wine. What policeman would take her seriously after that?

David chuckled softly, remembering her face as he held her head over the sink. The water had turned her feathery hairdo into a sodden mess, and the makeup streaking down her cheeks made her look like a refugee from a sixties rock concert. It really hadn't taken all that long to convince Ginny to give him Kirsta's address. She'd even told him that Kirsta was on sabbatical in Louisiana, staying at some plantation a little north of Baton Rouge. Ginny had actually been very helpful, once she got started. He'd almost hated leaving her there on the bathroom floor, sobbing and gasping.

David had slept the dreamless, deep sleep of the righteous, and had awakened around four in the morning more rested than he'd been in months — nearly four months, to be exact. Throughout the morning and afternoon, he had packed all his belongings into boxes and suitcases and canceled the apartment. He had to pay extra for breaking his lease, but Mother had left him enough money to live comfortably for a while. When he got to Louisiana, he and Kirsta would start again someplace new — maybe Baton Rouge or New Orleans, who knew? He'd loaded everything of importance — surprisingly little, when he thought about it — into his hatchback.

Now there was one more thing he had to take care of before leaving town. He pulled his car into the faculty/staff parking lot of Parthenon University, and hung his parking tag on his rearview mirror. He hadn't thrown it out when they'd fired him, knowing it would come in handy. He walked across the lot to a sprawling brick building. Most of the windows were closed against the brisk wind, but one was open slightly on the third floor. Probably just the window he was looking for, he thought. Some people thrived in harsh weather and hard times.

He glanced around before entering the side door of the building. There were never many people on campus just before the dinner hour, and those he saw showed little or no interest in him. He slipped inside, and started up the wide metal staircase to his left. After two flights, he opened the door onto the third floor, and walked as quietly as possible down the uncarpeted hallway. David had worn sneakers this time, so his footsteps were nearly silent as he approached the closed door halfway down the hall. He'd rather have heard his steps echoing like gunshots throughout the building, but he had to be practical. He slowed as he drew near the door. Black letters and numbers seemed to swarm like insects on the opaque glass. He blinked hard and they stopped moving.

He stopped outside the door and listened. A male voice murmured inside, and David's heart leaped. Did he have someone in there with him? After all this, would David be denied the first step of his quest? He cursed softly to himself. Then he realized he heard only one voice. Of course, the telephone. He waited until he heard the receiver being replaced.

The door opened silently. Well-oiled, David thought. Good, surprise was on his side. He entered a small dark anteroom, and closed the door softly behind him. Ahead of him, the inner doorway in the office was open, and he could see a middle-aged man seated at a large desk, his head bent over a stack of papers. David's lip turned up at the glimpse of thinning dark hair combed pathetically across the shiny scalp. The man removed his glasses and rubbed the bridge of his nose wearily. David stepped into the doorway and the man glanced at him curiously.

"Professor Radive?" David asked, though he knew very well who the man was.

"Yes. Can I help you?" The man smiled tentatively. His voice was soft and musical, with a slight accent. A woman's voice, thought David with scorn. He moved a few more steps into the room, until he was across the desk from Radive.

"You have a colleague in the history department," David said, keeping his voice steady, "a Miss Linden, I believe, do you not?"

David emphasized the formality of his speech, sounding like a judge at the bench. He felt the now-familiar power flood his veins, and he imagined himself pronouncing sentence on the condemned man.

"Yes," said Radive, "Kirsta Linden. Why?"

"And tell me, Professor Radive," said David, pacing to the side of the desk, "just where is this Miss Kirsta Linden right now?" He put his right hand into his pocket.

"She's on sabbatical, I believe. Is there something I can do for you?"

"Kirsta Linden has run away, hasn't she?" David asked, his voice louder. "She's living off your filthy money in Louisiana. Is that true or not?"

"My money? I don't understand." Radive frowned and stood. "Frankly, I don't think any of this is your business. Who are you?"

David raised his face and took another step toward the older man. He let his eyes bore into those of Martin Radive.

"I think you know who I am," he whispered.

Radive's eyes grew round and white. Yes, it was obvious he suddenly knew who David was — the Avenging Angel.

Radive cleared his throat, but his voice shook when he spoke. "You'd better leave."

"I don't think so," said David. "Not until our conversation is finished."

Radive glanced at the telephone in the center of his desk. David laughed, and reached out with his free hand and pulled it away. He jerked it hard enough to pull the jack out of the wall.

"We don't want to be interrupted, do we?"

Radive was trembling and sweating heavily. "I don't know what you want," he croaked.

"Maybe not," David said, "but I know what you want, don't I? I know exactly what you want."

Radive just shook his head. David slowly drew the knife from his pocket and pointed it toward Radive's throat.

"You want my woman," David said. "I know what you two were up to while I was suffering, trying to cope these last few months after that bitch left, trying to get my life back together."

"Please, Mr. Belsen," Radive whined, his back against the wall, one hand outstretched. "Let's just —"

"Shutup!" David placed the thick, razor-sharp blade against the pale flesh beneath Martin Radive's chin. "Don't you ever use my name. It's too holy for your disgusting lips. Understand?"

Radive nodded, but said nothing. His eyes no longer flitted around the room, but remained on David's face.

"I don't want any more of your lies," David snarled. "I know you seduced her, maybe even raped her. Kirsta would never be unfaithful to me, not on purpose. She loves me. Me."

"I'd never —" Radive began, but David's right hand twitched. The point of the blade seemed to move of its own accord, skimming lightly along the trembling wattles beneath the older man's chin. A tiny red line instantly appeared, and two drops emerged, trickling to disappear beneath Radive's white shirt collar.

David watched the drops fall, mesmerized. They seemed to grow until they swallowed him, enveloping him in a red world. The room was red, the day was red, his life was red and wet and warm around him. A crimson roar filled his head as he tried to concentrate, and he saw nothing and heard nothing but the blood surging through his body. He seemed to be swimming, floating in a river of blood.

Some time later, David realized the red was no longer inside him. He was sitting in the front seat of his car. Though the scarlet light still filled his vision, he could clearly see the objects around him — the dashboard, the steering column, the knife in his hand. He raised his head slowly, as though drugged, and looked outside, through the glass.

His car was still parked in the Parthenon University lot, and now the red light came from the top edge of the setting sun, which still hung over the low hills circling the far edge of town. David sighed and leaned his head back against the car seat. He felt more relaxed than he had in months. He flexed his fingers. Something sticky adhered to them, and he held his hands up before his eyes.

His right hand still gripped the hunting knife, and both hands were splotched with a dark substance. Blood, he thought without surprise. The blood of the guilty. He leaned over and reached into the glove compartment, tearing a packet of moistened towelettes along a perforated line.

Kirsta had always chided him about his frequent need to wash the filth of the world from his hands. Sometimes his sense of contamination was so great, he would have to pull over to the side of the road and wipe his hands clean. What would she think about him wiping her lover's blood away? Would she see the practicality of it now, or would she still say he was obsessive? David grinned, considering leaving the dark stains on his hands so he could explain to her what they were. He savored the image of her shocked expression when he held his palms to her face. Then he shrugged the notion away and tore the packet open. It took three towelettes to remove all the blood from his hands and clothes and the blade of the knife.

Now it was time to find Kirsta. David consulted his map. Several routes led toward Louisiana. He considered heading straight south, then cutting across Georgia, Alabama and Mississippi until he made his way to southern Louisiana. This way he'd find warmer weather more quickly. But the way he chose led southwest, through Ohio to Cincinnati. Then he'd follow the fastest roads south and west to Memphis, where Mother was buried.

David itched to get to Kirsta. He had to find her, to bring her back to him where he could watch her and keep her safe. He'd drive all night, catching cat-naps along the way when he needed them. Nothing could divert him from his goal — except Mother. He must stop and find her grave, explain his plans to her. He'd make her proud of him, tell her about the Avenging Angel. His heart thudded heavily inside his chest as he thought about her.

He put the car in gear, and drove out of the parking lot. As he pulled onto the main street, he saw a police car and ambulance approaching from the opposite direction, lights flashing. In his rearview mirror, he watched them turn into the shaded drive that led to Parthenon University. The sun dropped behind the hills, extinguishing the red glow. David flicked his headlights on as he drove through town.

He saw all the stores and restaurants and gas stations as though he'd never seen them before. He realized he'd probably never return to this town — maybe not to this state or even this part of the country. What a dreary little burg, David thought, with such dreary little people in it. He belonged someplace more important, perhaps exotic. Someplace that lived up to his personality and lifestyle, or at least the lifestyle he planned on assuming as soon as he and Kirsta were together.

As he headed out of town, he passed a little shop with a sign out front that read, "Teresa's Treasures: antiques and collectibles." That was where he'd bought Kirsta the antique snow globe he'd given her for her last birthday. He smiled, remembering the glow of excitement and love he'd seen in her eyes when she'd opened the box. He'd had to borrow the money from Mother, telling her it was for airplane tickets to Memphis.

David suddenly pulled the car into a driveway and turned around. New Year's Eve, Kirsta had goaded him into breaking the snow globe, throwing it against the apartment wall where it had shattered into a million shards. She'd run out that night, leaving him alone. He'd bled from hundreds of tiny cuts as he'd gathered up the pieces in his bare hands, crying and swearing never to frighten her again. But of course, Kirsta wasn't there to hear his apologies. She'd even sent a friend over to collect her things the next day.

Well, to prove to Kirsta how much he'd changed, he'd give her another chance, show her that he forgave her. He'd find another present for her, one even better than the snow globe. A gift she could treasure forever.

He pulled into the drive at the side of the little wooden building, and walked up the steps. As he opened the door, a bell tinkled softly above his head. The grey-haired woman behind the counter glanced up from the paperback novel she was reading. Teresa McCale, the owner of the store, he remembered. She smiled when she saw him.

"Hello. Mr. Belsen, isn't it?" she asked.

"That's right, Mrs. McCale," he answered. "I'm surprised you remember."

"Oh, I couldn't forget you. You bought that beautiful snow scene for your girlfriend's birthday. I enjoyed talking with you so much. How did she like the gift?"

"She loved it," he said, heading toward her. "Now I'm looking for something even more impressive."

Mrs. McCale rose slowly and placed her novel on top of the huge brass cash register beside her. She walked around the edge of the counter.

"Is this a gift for your girlfriend, too?" she asked.

David grinned until he thought his face would break. "Yes, it is," he said. "In fact, she's my fiancee now. I want to find a special wedding present for her."

"Oh, that's so romantic." Mrs. McCale glanced around her. "Well, let's see what we have. How about some sexy lingerie?"

David felt his stomach churn as he pictured Kirsta in bed with Harrison Kahn again. But this time, Kahn was covered in blood as he lay on top of her.

"No, I don't think that's what I'm looking for," he said. "Maybe something a bit more unusual."

"All right," she mused, moving toward the back of the store, "perhaps another antique would do the trick."

She reached above her head, and took something down from the shelf. "How about one of these?"

But David wasn't watching her, and didn't even hear her speak. His gaze was riveted to a pair of silver combs in a glass case. The light from the small lamp that sat on the case caught in the ornate carving, and the combs seemed to glow with a light of their own. David felt dizzy, and leaned against a mahogany hutch beside him until the feeling passed.

"I want those," he said, pointing at the combs. His voice was hoarse.

Mrs. McCale moved toward him and followed his gaze. "Excellent choice," she said. "Aren't they exquisite? I just got them in yesterday."

She unlocked the padlock on the glass lid, and lifted it. She took the combs out and held them out toward David, but he didn't move to take them. He just stared at them. His head felt as though it might explode.

She waited, then said, "I'm afraid they're a bit expensive. They're very old, you see, and —"

"It doesn't matter," David croaked, interrupting her. "I'll take them."

"Fine." Mrs. McCale straightened slightly, then relocked the case. She moved to the counter. "Cash or charge?"

"I'll pay cash."

"Would you like them gift wrapped?" she asked, punching keys on the electronic cash register that sat beside the large brass one.

"Yes," David said through clenched teeth. The vertigo, or whatever it was, seemed to be passing. "Wedding paper, please."

"I have some lovely paper," Mrs. McCale said as he paid her.

CHAPTER EIGHT

As she drove back to Lost Oaks, Kirsta's head spun, mulling over what she'd heard about Sean and the weird things that had happened, both in Witchman's Woods and at the chapel. Not to mention that intense moment at the Witchman's cabin. She shifted in the bucket seat as she remembered how good, how natural Sean's arms had felt around her.

"Get a grip, Kirsta," she told herself aloud as she pulled into the Lost Oaks drive. "Keep your wits about you this time. No more rose-colored glasses."

She showered and typed some notes into her laptop while her hair dried. She dressed in a long, gauzy Indian-print skirt and magenta silk shell with matching sandals.

As Kirsta climbed into her car at six-thirty, Daphne waved from the garden. Kirsta waited by the car until the older woman could scurry over.

"I'm glad I caught you," Daphne panted. "There was a message on the answering machine for you this morning. Some woman from Pennsylvania called. Now what was her name?"

Kirsta fought to keep from glancing at her watch while she waited for Daphne to remember.

"Jane?" Daphne was talking to herself now. "No, that's not it. "Jenny? That's closer…"

"Was it Ginny?" Kirsta asked.

"That's it, Ginny." Daphne looked pleased, as though they'd won a contest. "The message was from Ginny. She wanted you to call her when you got a chance."

"Is that all? Did it sound urgent that I get hold of her?"

"I couldn't tell you," Daphne said. "That's all she said, I'm afraid. If you'd like to use the phone …"

Kirsta finally looked at her watch. "No, I'll try her later. I have to get going."

"All right, dear." Daphne backed away as Kirsta got into the car, then waved again as she started to drive away. "Don't forget about dinner with the Pattons tomorrow night," she called.

Kirsta called back that she wouldn't, and drove off toward Allindea. She wondered whether Daphne knew that Kirsta and Sean were having a dinner date. Date. The word seemed so strange. She and David hadn't gone out much after she'd moved in with him, back in Pennsylvania, and Kirsta hadn't been interested in another relationship since that one ended. She had to admit, it felt good to be dressing up to spend time with an attractive, interesting man, even if there was little or no chance of anything romantic coming of it.

The sun was low on the horizon when she pulled into the chapel parking lot, and Sean's car was the only one left in the deepening shadows by the front door. Kirsta got out and stood by the front door a long moment, hoping Sean would come out. She remembered her uneasiness earlier and hesitated to enter the deserted building now that the rooms would be nearly dark.

She heard footfalls echo across the wooden floor of the sanctuary toward her, and nearly bolted for her car. Just then, however, the front door opened, and Sean stepped out. He seemed transformed. He'd changed from the jeans and work shirt he'd worn earlier to a light grey pin-striped three-piece suit with a pale peach-colored shirt. His dark hair was carefully brushed back from the temples, and he smelled of lime and musk.

His eyes caressed her body slowly, and he grinned. "You look great, ma'am."

She smiled back. "You're not so shabby yourself. What a change."

"From the back fields to the board room, eh?" He laughed. "I like to look like money when I'm going to be talking about it. You hungry?"

"Starved."

"Then let's get going." He opened the passenger door for her, and they slid into his car. Sean pressed a button on the dashboard, and the plaintive nasal tones of a jazzy saxophone solo surrounded them. Kirsta closed her eyes and sighed comfortably.

"You're going to love this place," Sean said after a few minutes, "a real hidden jewel. Old southern charm and some of the best food in plantation country. They even have live music tonight: two men and a woman who dress in Civil War costumes and perform nineteenth-century pieces — old ballads, waltzes, reels, things like that."

"What's the name of the place?"

"Mistmere. It's one of the outbuildings on the Mistmere plantation, just a few miles from town. It sits across the gardens from the main plantation house. The house is falling into disrepair, though, and the new owner wants to restore it and turn it into an inn. He doesn't know anything about old architecture, though, and asked me too look at it and make recommendations."

"Sounds interesting," Kirsta said. "From what I've seen of the cemetery chapel, you'd do a wonderful job, too."

Sean looked at her and beamed. "Thanks, ma'am," he drawled in an exaggeration of his usual slight accent, "that's mighty kind of you to say."

He reached his hand over and covered her fingers with his. Kirsta smiled at him and squeezed his fingers lightly. She felt so comfortable, sitting in the car with him, listening to the smooth sounds of the saxophone, watching the lush woods glow in the red light from the setting sun. It seemed as though she'd known Sean and Louisiana her whole life.

The car rounded a curve, and Sean pulled onto a narrow macadam road to the left. They twisted along this drive through the dense woods for almost a mile, then suddenly the trees parted and ahead of them the drive looped around a large formal garden filled with all manner of exotic flowers, looking like pools of bright color beneath the low gas lamps. In the center of the garden, a large wooden sign read simply "Mistmere" in elegant carved letters.

To their right was the huge old manor house, looking like every plantation house in every movie about the old south Kirsta had ever seen. Four white columns led from the veranda to the top of the second story, past a second-floor sitting porch. Huge ancient oaks flanked the house, and tall windows opened wide to let in as much air as possible.

Sean turned the car to the left, however, toward a much smaller building, nestled among some flowering shrubs. A screened porch ran the length of the building, and inside Kirsta could see flickering lamps hanging over the tables between vine-filled planters. Sean pulled into the grassy parking area, and she got out of the car, the mingled scents of a multitude of flowers wafting around her. A whippoorwill sang softly in the branches overhead as they entered through the screen door.

"Something smells good," Kirsta said when they got inside. "Fresh bread?"

A woman's voice answered from beyond the archway before them. "That's right. We bake a variety of our own breads and rolls fresh every day. You're probably smelling the onion-herb biscuits; they're one of the chef's specialties."

An attractive white-haired woman in a long gingham dress entered the foyer, smiling at them. She said, "Hello, Mr. McLeod, it's nice to see you again. Gene will be down a bit later. I'll show you to your table — we kept one on the veranda for you."

As they headed out toward the screened room, Sean introduced the woman as Edythe Elliot, the wife of the new owner. "They're practically foreigners," he said with exaggerated disapproval, "imported from Lafayette."

"Which is all the way down in the southwest corner of Louisiana," Edythe pointed out with a smile. "Cajun country. Same state, but almost like being in a different country."

The inside dining room and veranda appeared nearly full, but Sean and Kirsta were seated at a small table set off by itself in the back corner of the screened porch. Golden shadows created by the flame from a small hurricane lamp danced on the lacy white tablecloth. Fresh daisies and violets peeked between the greens in a pink antique vase.

Sean ordered a bottle of wine and asked about the musicians. "They will be here tonight, won't they?"

"Oh, yes," Mrs. Elliot said, glancing at her watch. "They usually start playing by about eight. That's when Gene's coming down to talk. That way, Kirsta will have something to listen to besides your shop-talk."

They ordered oysters and mussels for appetizers, and Kirsta decided on the crawfish etouffe for dinner. Mrs. Elliot waited on them personally, and seemed pleased by her choice.

"If you've never had etouffe," she said, "ours will spoil you. It's the best in Louisiana."

Sean ordered steak Diane, and their hostess left to begin their salads. During dinner, Sean talked about the various plantations in the area, and the kind of consulting work he'd like to get into. Kirsta had recently developed an interest in antiques, particularly from the eighteenth and nineteenth centuries, and they compared notes on unusual pieces they'd found and unexpected shops they'd run into in out-of-the-way places.

Parthenon University and her problems back in Pennsylvania seemed not to exist in this lush, relaxed world, and Kirsta gave herself over to the warmth she felt as she sat in the flickering shadows of Mistmere. Sean's eyes glowed with the candle's light, and Kirsta watched his lips move as he spoke to her, remembering the taste of him in the dusty heat of the Witchman's cabin.

Suddenly, a man's voice boomed from behind Kirsta, causing her to jump slightly in her chair. She'd been so fixated on Sean, she hadn't realized anyone else was near. From the look on Sean's face, neither had he.

"Sean McLeod, you son-of-a-gun. I never saw you come in here." The man held out his hand, and Sean smiled warmly as he shook it. He introduced the heavy, iron-haired stranger as Phil Robbison, president of the First Allindea Bank and Trust. Kirsta wondered for a moment where she'd heard the name.

"Pleased to meet you, ma'am," the man boomed, and pointed to Sean. "This here's my favorite neighbor in West Feliciana Parish. You know what he did for me?"

"No," Kirsta said, suddenly recalling the comments of Jerry Harris about something Sean had done for Robbison's daughter.

"That's ancient history, Phil," Sean said uncomfortably. "Kirsta isn't interested —"

"'Course she is," bellowed Phil Robbison. He turned his attention on Kirsta. She tried not to lean back in her chair, so overwhelmed was she by his huge presence.

"This man here," continued Robbison, clapping one meaty hand on Sean's shoulder, "did everything he could to make my little girl comfortable when she was in the hospital over Baton Rouge way. She and my wife and I had got all broken up in a car accident — hit and run, never did catch the fella. We were all laid up for close on a month down there.

"Anyway, Sean drove two hours down to that hospital every day to see her and bring her stuff. I didn't know who it was then, but the nurse said some nice man from up this way brought her a stereo and a VCR and even a video game set-up. I couldn't even leave my room for more than two weeks, but I rested easy, knowing there was this guardian angel coming to see my baby every day, reading her favorite books and getting her whatever she wanted. I figured I'd pay whatever he asked."

"That's a wonderful thing to do," Kirsta said. She could see how embarrassed Sean was by this conversation, but wanted to hear more. She was enthralled by these new revelations about him. Phil Robbison was more than willing to oblige.

"Turned out, he didn't want a penny. Like I said, he tried like the devil to keep his identity a secret, but I have ways of finding things out — bankers' connections, you know."

He chortled at his little joke, and patted Sean's shoulder. "When I found out it was Sean, I tried to at least make good on the stuff he'd bought. But he wouldn't have that at all, not for a minute."

The florid face grew serious for a moment. "I understand what drives him to help out kids in trouble," he said quietly, "but I'd do anything for you, Sean. You know that."

"I know, Phil," Sean muttered. Then he cleared his throat. "By the way, thank your wife for taking me back to the church earlier today. I enjoy the walk, but she saved me some time."

Robbison assured Sean he would, and returned to his table.

So the attractive woman in the car was Phil Robbison's wife. Kirsta tried to think of something to say. She was impressed by Phil Robbison's story, by the kind, gentle side of Sean he'd revealed to her. She wanted to reach across the table and tell Sean how proud of him she felt. But she was afraid she'd make him uncomfortable if she mentioned it. She tried to think of something to change the subject, but couldn't focus on anything except the image of that little girl in the hospital and Sean by her bedside.

She was spared any awkwardness, because Mrs. Elliot approached just then with a gaunt, man dressed in a white tuxedo with emerald green tie and cumerbund. The man limped slightly, though he carried himself straight and tall, as if he'd been in the military for a long time. Sean stood and introduced him to Kirsta as Gene Elliot.

Elliot bowed deeply from the waist as he took Kirsta's hand. She suddenly thought how much more appropriate she'd feel wearing a hoop skirt and white gloves.

"It's always a pleasure to meet such a lovely young woman," he said in a voice dripping with southern elegance, "and a crime to leave you sitting alone. I'll bring Mr. McLeod back as soon as humanly possible — no more than half an hour. But then, I'm sure he'd have it no other way."

"I hope you don't mind," Sean said as they turned to go, and Kirsta shook her head. "We'll order dessert when I get back."

The men excused themselves and headed across the garden toward the plantation house. Through the tiny mesh of the screening, Kirsta watched them go and wished it were she walking through the fragrant flowers with Sean. She sighed and fingered the edges of a daisy, drooping from the side of the vase before her.

"He loves me, he loves me not." She caught herself counting petals, and stopped. Love was not what she wanted from Sean, she told herself firmly — just a pleasant evening out with an attractive man. Nothing more.

Just as Edythe Elliot had promised, the music began a few minutes later, soft strains of an old folk ballad. Kirsta moved her chair to see into the dining room, where the trio had set up. The two men wore grey Confederate soldier uniforms, and both sported shaggy whiskers. One played a twelve-string guitar and the other played a violin. Between them stood a dark-haired woman in a long gingham dress and bonnet, who alternately played a glass flute and sang. Her voice was a soft clear soprano that crested the background music like white foam on a wave. The songs she sang were full of love and promise and the longing for a time long past.

"Dearest love, do you remember,
when we last did meet,
how you told me that you loved me,
kneeling at my feet?"

Kirsta closed her eyes and let the music flow over her. She could hear the soft chirping of birds and insects just outside the screen, a perfect accompaniment to the lilting, lovely music.

"Ah, how proud you stood before me
in your suit of blue,
when you vowed to me and country
ever to be true."

Kirsta cast her mind back through more than a hundred years, to the time when Mistmere Plantation was in its glory and life was gentle and slow among the magnolias and willows. She imagined she sat on the upper veranda of the plantation house in her hoop skirts and pantaloons, fanning herself and sipping a mint julep. She pictured Sean next to her, talking about his day quietly as the evening settled around them.

It seemed she sat there forever, basking in her fantasy, the music changing again and again from marches to dance numbers to lullabies and back again. In her mind's eye, Sean moved closer to her and reached over to stroke her hair. He placed a red rose between her breasts, leaned down and whispered in her ear.

"May I have this dance?"

Kirsta nodded, then opened her eyes, realizing someone had actually spoken the words to her. Sean stood before her, looking down and smiling, his dark eyes catching the flickering light from the overhead lamps. He took her hand and gently pulled her to her feet.

"I thought you were asleep for a moment," he said. "But you must have been having a wonderful dream, with that smile on your face."

Just then, the music slowed, and the violin began the elegant strains of "The Tennessee Waltz." Sean put his arm around her waist and grasped her hand with his. He pulled her close and began moving in a small circle around their table. He drew her with him in a steady, rhythmic waltz. Kirsta inhaled deeply, her cheek nestled in the hollow of his shoulder. She smelled his cologne and felt the stubble of his new beard against her face as they danced.

As his body moved against hers, she seemed to fit perfectly into his arms and had no trouble following his lead. She could feel the muscles in his thighs move against the thin fabric of her skirt, and somehow knew without thinking which way he would move next. Though it was impossible, Kirsta was so comfortable in his arms, dancing this way, that she could almost convince herself they'd done this many times before.

When the dance ended, Sean leaned his head back to look at her. He touched her hair. Then his eyes narrowed and a smile curled his lips.

"I know something you'd like," he said, and led her by the hand through the dining rooms into the warm damp air outside. He opened the door of his car for her, and she slid in. When he started the engine, Kirsta finally spoke.

"Where are we —" she began, but Sean raised a hand to cut her off.

"Shh," he said. "You'll see."

Silver moonlight danced across the ripples as Kirsta stood on the wooden dock, waiting for Sean to drag the canoe from under the tarp. Tendrils of mist rose from the waters to disappear in the night air. Two night birds whistled to one another far above her — lovers, she thought, trying to find their way back to one another.

A small breeze rippled through the Spanish moss hanging like tangled hair from the trees, and Kirsta trembled slightly. She didn't feel chilly, though — just the opposite. Her skin felt so warm she was almost feverish. Every nerve seemed exposed, and each sensation exaggerated. She heard a small splash nearby, and turned to see Sean steadying the canoe in the dark waters.

"Henry won't mind me using this," Sean said, helping Kirsta into the canoe. "This is his favorite fishing hole, and he showed me once where he keeps the canoe hidden."

"Do you fish, too?" asked Kirsta.

"Not as much as I used to." Sean used the paddle to propel them away from the dock. "Henry and I have spent a few mornings out here, though, competing with the 'gators for catfish."

Kirsta straightened on the seat and glanced nervously around them, trying to see into the shadows. "Are there really alligators out here?"

Sean laughed. "Sure, but you don't need to worry about them. There's plenty for them to eat in these little bayous, and 'gators are naturally pretty timid. They'll stay far away from us. It's just the film makers who'd have us believe in the fierce monsters of the swamp who crave human flesh. Actually, the mosquitos are more likely to give you a problem than the poor old 'gators."

Kirsta relaxed again, and even trailed her fingers in the warm water after a moment. They passed closed water lilies and patches of marsh grass growing along the edges of the water. A fish jumped from the bayou to plop back in with a small splash. Something fluttered past them through the mist. Kirsta breathed deeply the lush, exotic scents of the night.

Sean stopped paddling after a while, and pulled a thin mat from the bow of the canoe. He put it by his feet and motioned for Kirsta to move over near him. She slid down, leaning against his legs, and they watched a large bird fly across the narrow inlet.

"Night egret," Sean said, watching it go. "We must have disturbed it. Maybe it has a nest around here somewhere. Probably trying to draw our attention away from its young."

"There's a lot of activity out here at night," Kirsta mused, snuggling comfortably against him. "I wouldn't have expected so much going on. At least we're the only people out here right now."

"Actually, we're probably not."

Kirsta looked around. "I don't see anybody else."

He chuckled. "You wouldn't. Lots of Cajuns leave lines out here on the bayou, and since it's not quite legal, they check them at night. But you can relax — they're pros at avoiding company. And they'll stay far away from us."

Sean's hand rested on the back of her neck, and gently massaged the muscles at the base of her skull, beneath her hair. She sighed and leaned her head sideways onto his knee. The muscles of his thigh tensed for a moment as she did, then he relaxed. She felt a ripple of pleasure in her stomach as she realized she had the same effect on him that he did on her.

"This is perfect," she murmured. "I think I could stay here on the water forever."

"Mmm-hmm." Sean stroked her hair, then leaned forward and kissed her cheek. His hand moved down her arm, and he took her hand, linking his fingers through hers.

Kirsta started to speak, but he silenced her. "Sh," he whispered. "Listen. Hear that bird over to the left? That's a Chuck Will's Widow. They say that anyone who hears the widow sing at night will see the face of someone who needs to contact them."

Kirsta lifted her head and strained her ears. From somewhere far to the right, through the dense leaves and the Spanish moss, drifted soft clear musical notes. In the pale rippling light of the moon on the mists, she thought it was the saddest sound she'd ever heard.

"I hear it," she whispered, her voice shaky with emotion. "But I don't think anyone's —"

Kirsta froze as she watched the mists beside her swirl up from the water as though a breeze had whipped through them. They then seemed to coalesce into the oval shape of a face — a woman's face, Kirsta was sure. She felt all the emotions she'd felt throughout the evening — all the wonderful excitement — darken and turn to terror. The eyes beneath the pinned-up hair bored into her own, pleading with her to do something. But Kirsta had no idea what.

Then the mists cleared, and the face disappeared as suddenly as it had come. Kirsta tried to tell herself it had never been there at all, that it was just an illusion caused by the mysterious atmosphere of the swamp and Sean's story. But she knew better.

"Kirsta?" Sean's voice sounded far away. "Is something wrong?"

"No," she lied, unwilling or unable to describe what she'd just seen. "I just got a chill, that's all."

Sean chuckled and kissed her cheek again. "Someone walking across your grave, huh?"

He ran his fingers down her arm and she trembled. "You have goosebumps," he said. "You're cold. Maybe we should head back home now."

Kirsta nodded and said nothing, watching the thin strands of mist reaching like fingers around them in the darkness.

"Blond," David said without thinking.

Then he remembered — Kirsta's hair was auburn, not blond. And it wasn't that long. She might not even be able to use the combs. Why had he chosen such an unlikely gift for her?

He shrugged. Maybe he'd have Kirsta grow her hair longer, so she could put it on top of her head with the combs. Maybe he'd have her lighten it, too. She'd probably look good as a blonde.

David smiled as he left the store. His quest had begun.

CHAPTER NINE

That night, snuggled into her bed back in the cabin at Lost Oaks, Kirsta dreamed again of the blond woman. Once more, she saw what was happening through the eyes of the other woman, and was helpless to stop herself from acting out the story she was trapped in.

She wasn't in the bedroom this time, but walking into a large barn behind the topiary maze at Lost Oaks. It was obviously sturdy and cared-for, its huge beams meeting tightly, all the boards upright and firm. Her eyes were still adjusting to the dimness inside after the bright afternoon light. The air was stuffy and terribly hot, and her dress felt damp and suffocating. The high lacy collar was a noose tightening around her throat. She reached behind her to loosen some of the buttons.

She was looking for something or someone, and walked past the stalls of horses, patting them reassuringly on their noses and peering past them into the dark shadows. Some of the horses snorted their annoyance when they nuzzled her hands with their big soft lips and found no carrots or apples there.

She went back to the door and glanced all around the front of the barn, but nobody appeared. Nobody was within sight, even behind the house all the way across the field. She returned to the musty darkness inside and called softly.

"Andrew?" Nobody answered. She felt the woman's stomach tighten in fear. Was she afraid of Andrew, Kirsta wondered. But that didn't seem quite right, either.

She climbed up a stack of hay bales on the far side of the barn, nearly reaching to the boards that loosely formed the floor of the loft above. She peered around the barn again, searching for something. Particles of hay and dust mingled with tiny insects in the stray beams of sunlight poking through openings in the barn walls. Kirsta felt the woman's disappointment mingle with her own frustration, not knowing what she was looking for.

Suddenly, a hand reached from above and behind her, grasping the bare flesh at the back of her throat. Another hand went around her mouth. The hand smelled faintly of straw and animal hide. The woman gasped through her nostrils, fighting instinctively against the male fingers trapping her.

"Shh, it's me," a voice whispered urgently in her ear.

She stopped struggling, her hands reaching up the arms to touch a face rough with whiskers. She forced herself to relax, and the hand over her mouth eased away. She stood on trembling legs and turned to face her assailant.

He was of medium height, and dark. His short beard was untrimmed and dark eyes glittered in the dim light. He put his hands beneath her arms and lifted her easily into the loft beside him. She was still trembling as he stroked her hair, brushing straw from it.

"Please don't frighten me so," she sad, her voice still hoarse with fear. "I feel such fear, such danger when we're together."

He reached behind him for something. "I'm sorry, my darling," he said, handing her a long-stemmed red rose.

"Oh, it's beautiful," she said. "It's perfect."

He leaned toward her. "Your beauty flaws it," he whispered, his lips brushing her ear and sending ripples through her. "I love you. I would never do anything to make you unhappy."

She turned her face toward his, and smiled. "I know," was all she said, or had time to say. He covered her mouth with his, pressing against her lips with bruising power. Yet she dropped the rose and put her hands behind his head, wrapping her fingers in his dark hair and tried to pull him closer yet. She moaned softly in the back of her throat.

His hands went to the shoulders of her dress and began drawing the sleeves down. She felt the air ripple along her skin as the dress parted, and she squirmed against him deliciously. He lifted her in his arms and laid her down gently on a rough wool blanket beside him. He pulled the front of her dress down and then the straps of the chemise she wore underneath. He kissed the naked flesh between her breasts and she felt his rough whiskers scrape her skin. The sensation made her gasp and she pulled his face to hers again, drawing his lower lip between her teeth and biting it gently.

His fingers kneaded her breasts and squeezed the hardened nipples. He moved between her legs and lifted her skirts slowly, easing his hands up her legs as he did. He kissed her inner thighs and she felt her hips rise toward him. He moved his head upward, and the rough tickle of his beard against her soft flesh nearly drove her mad. She whimpered quietly.

Then he moved himself upward and pulled at the buttons of his trousers, and finally he was inside her, thrusting himself into her. And she thrust back, wanting him more than she'd wanted anything before in her life, crying out softly in the ecstasy of the moment. Kirsta felt the waves of release from inside the woman's body and yet was separate at the same time.

Afterward, they lay entwined together on the rough wool blanket, touching one another with feathery fingertips. Kirsta thought she heard something below them, a door closing or a heavy footstep. Obviously, the woman had heard it too. She raised her head slightly, holding her breath.

"Shh," she whispered, and placed her fingers over the man's lips. He froze, watching her face. They waited an eternity in the stifling heat of the barn, still clasped in one another's embrace, neither daring to even breathe.

But the sound was not repeated, and she gradually allowed herself to relax. "I'm sorry," she murmured, "I suppose it was one of the horses."

"Don't apologize," he said, his breath hot against her naked breast. "We always have to take great care to avoid discovery."

She rose to a sitting position, straightening her clothes. She discovered the rose crushed into the blanket, and a wave of terrible sadness flooded over her. The whole world of love and loss seemed concentrated into the battered blossom before her. She wanted to mention it to Andrew, but words failed her.

"I'd better leave," was all she said. "I'm not sure when he'll return from his errands. I believe it'll take him a while, but it isn't wise to play with fate."

She stood and walked carefully across the floor of the loft to the large open window. A kitten chased two chickens across the dirt in front of the barn, and a dog barked from beyond the maze somewhere.

"There's something calm and familiar about this place," she said, trying to pull her hair back into its silver combs, "I've often come up here searching for solace, but I've never been able to find true peace. Until now."

She turned back to him, and they quickly embraced again. He helped her down onto the hay bales. She slid to the floor and looked back up to where he stood, but he was already hidden in the shadows.

"I'll be back later with some food," she promised, dusting the straw from her dress and hair. Then she turned back to the bright light beyond the open door.

Kirsta woke late, twisted in the sheets and drenched in sweat. She remembered her dream vividly, and wondered about its significance. She realized she must be more caught up in the atmosphere of the area than she'd thought. Her body tightened in response to the memory of passionate sex in the loft and she smiled to herself as she adjusted the shower. Her date with Sean must have had some affect on the dream, too, though she was surprised she hadn't dreamed about him instead of the dark-eyed stranger. Her dreams seemed to be living a life of their own.

She pushed the erotic thoughts from her mind with some effort of will; she couldn't allow herself to be distracted by such thoughts today. She simply had to get some work done. Her father had always stressed "business before pleasure," and she'd tried to abide by those words, even though he was no longer around to impress. The trouble with David Belsen had made concentrating on business nearly impossible the last few months. Kirsta was determined to prove herself competent once again. And mooning over Sean McLeod was not the way to do that.

The rest of the day, Kirsta immersed herself in her work as she sat alone in the small study room at the Allindea Public Library. She refused to permit her mind to become cluttered with confused emotional meanderings about Sean McLeod, although she knew Sean always lurked just beyond the edge of her consciousness.

She concentrated instead on the early French and Spanish settlers who traded with the Houmas and Tunica Indians and founded the two parishes that bordered these twists in the Mississippi River. Some of the best land in West Feliciana Parish was still unsettled woodland, particularly places the Indians had considered haunted. West Feliciana Parish was just north of Pointe Coupee Parish, where Allindea nestled among the creeks and bayous, hiding from the world that raced past on Highway 61 between Baton Rouge and Natchez. Kirsta made a note to herself to try to find some of those 'haunted' spots.

Kirsta's interest was especially piqued by the mention of Yankee spies who found sanctuary in the homes of sympathetic Confederates during the Civil War. A few made it back home after the war, but many were hanged on the plantations, either during legal executions or by vigilante groups who patrolled the smaller towns. Kirsta wondered whether any spies had stayed around Allindea.

Later in the morning, Kirsta realized she was famished. She eagerly ate a delicious catfish 'po-boy' sandwich at "Auntie Em's," a little cafe across the street from the library. She'd decided to avoid the Allindea Inn, hoping she wouldn't run into Celeste Wallace again. The restaurant was surprisingly busy so early in the day. Reviewing her notes, Kirsta tried to ignore the whispers and curious glances of the local residents. Once, Kirsta even caught the waitress peering over her shoulder to read what she'd written at the top of one photocopied page.

Kirsta finished her lunch and returned to the library as soon as possible, glad to escape the feeling of sitting in a fishbowl. She quickly became immersed in her work, and didn't glance at her watch again until the young blond librarian peeked in the door sometime later. After catching Kirsta's attention by coughing softly, she pulled at a lock of unnaturally yellow hair and smiled apologetically.

"I'm sorry, miss, but the library closes at five," she said. "You're welcome to leave your books on that table over there, if you're planning to come back tomorrow. I'll make sure nobody disturbs them."

"Thanks, but I'll keep my things with me," Kirsta said, standing stiffly. "I'll probably do some work back at Lost Oaks tonight."

"Oh, you're staying at Lost Oaks?" The blond woman asked.

"Yes. Have you ever been out there?"

"No," the woman answered slowly, looking with renewed interest at Kirsta. "I'm rather a newcomer here myself. But I've heard the plantation's beautiful. I've always meant to get out there for the birding."

"The birding?" Kirsta gathered up her notebooks. "Is that some kind of hunting thing?"

The blond woman turned out the light and locked the door behind them as they left. "No, nothing like that. It's actually a day in the late spring when hundreds of birds settle into the big live oak tree in the front lawn. They're obviously passing through to their summer home, but it's very strange. They don't go anywhere else, and they only stay one night."

"What kinds of birds?" Kirsta asked as they walked to the front door.

"I don't really know, but they're all the same kind of black birds. It's the same every year. Actually, it always happens near the beginning of May — should be any day now. You'll probably be here for it."

Kirsta thanked the young woman. She hurried out to the car, silently chiding herself for losing track of the time. Now she would have to rush to get back to Lost Oaks. She'd hardly have time to freshen up before dinner. She cursed its faulty air conditioning again, and vowed to refuse to pay the full rental fee when she returned it in Baton Rouge. Even with the windows open, Kirsta felt her sundress dampen as the heat radiated from the plastic seat covers. She wiped a trickle of sweat from her forehead and watched for the nearly-hidden sign she'd had so much trouble spotting two nights ago.

Kirsta sighed with relief when she finally turned into the drive. She peered into the lengthening shadows of each curve and shook her head, realizing she was hoping to catch sight of Sean. Less than seventy-two hours, and already her brain was swirling with conflicting emotions. She'd left Pennsylvania partly to escape a relationship that had promised to ruin her life. And here she was, attracted to a man who might be no better — and could be perhaps more threatening in his own way — than David Belsen.

Would she never learn? Or, Kirsta wondered miserably, was there something about her emotional makeup that drew her to dangerous men? She would have to be very careful from now on. Then the memory of the night before washed over her like a warm tide and she was in Sean's arms again, floating along the floor at Mistmere, listening to the music in her heart as well as the music from the trio in the other room.

She wished she'd had more experience with dating and relationships. Kirsta's mother had died when Kirsta was a teenager, and Hank Linden had been forced to raise his daughter by himself. Kirsta would be forever grateful to him, but his despair at his wife's death had given him an excuse to turn his attention from Kirsta to alcohol. His insistence on academic achievement and Kirsta's sense of responsibility for him had left very little room for social experiences.

David Belsen had been her first serious romance, and she'd been seduced by his charm and California-surfer looks. She'd wanted to give up some of her responsibility, to let someone take care of her for a change. So she'd given her trust to David. There'd been something a little strange about him, some secret in his past that he kept hidden. But naively Kirsta had found this even more intriguing. Too late, she'd learned that the secret was no more than a sadistic streak, probably fostered by his cruel, overly-possessive mother.

Now, here she was in Louisiana, completely unprepared to deal with a man who, she had to admit, she found more attractive than any man she'd ever met, including David. A man she should probably give a very wide berth in order to preserve her peace of mind. Sean McLeod had secrets of his own, and if she'd learned anything from her experience with David, it was that secrets could be deadly. Yet there was something about Sean that drew her inexorably to him, like … like a moth to a flame? she wondered.

Kirsta peered into the large tree in the center of the front lawn as she drove past the main house, but didn't notice an unusual number of birds in it. She pulled the little car into the space near the house, and carried her briefcase and burlap satchel through the late-afternoon haze to her guest cabin. She had half an hour to shower and dress for dinner. She dropped her study materials next to the laptop computer on the coffee table, and noticed a single, perfect red rose in a delicate china vase in the center of the table. Daphne must have put it there for her when she made up the bed.

Smiling at the woman's thoughtfulness, Kirsta grabbed a Coke from the refrigerator before stepping into the bathroom to rinse off. The cold liquid felt great against her hot throat. She set the Coke can and a small tub of rose-scented dusting powder on the little wicker stool next to the sink. Then she turned on the hot water.

The bathroom quickly filled with steam as Kirsta undressed. The humidity allowed the air to absorb none of the moisture, and Kirsta could barely see the mirror across the room. She stepped into the tub and let the hot water rinse the perspiration and grit from her. She hoped it would wash away some of the exhaustion she felt, as well. She really should have planned enough time for a short nap.

Suddenly, the surrounding waves of steam seemed to ripple as though a breeze moved through them. Kirsta knew she had closed the bathroom door behind her, and had not opened the window next to the mirror. She had the same unsettling feeling she'd had the night before, that someone else was in the room with her, lurking just beyond the opaque shower curtain.

Kirsta cowered backward against the tile wall, holding her washcloth like a useless shield before her. Cold droplets of condensed steam from the tiles trickled down her back. She shivered, strained to see something, hear something, anything that would tell her who stood just beyond the thin plastic barrier. She fought down her panic. It must be Daphne. She probably came down to the guest house for some reason, and Kirsta didn't hear her knock over the sound of the shower.

Kirsta took a deep, shuddering breath. "Mrs. Woodring?" she called out. "Daphne? Is that you?"

She strained her ears to hear even the softest answer above the shower. She prayed for the familiar bright chatter of her hostess to answer her questions, both spoken and unspoken. Because if Daphne wasn't out there, Kirsta couldn't imagine who else might be lurking in the swirling steam.

But no one answered. The only sound was the hiss and gurgle of the water around her. Finally, Kirsta reached out and turned off the water. She heard nothing in the sudden silence. The small movement seemed to have broken through some of her terror, though, and she pulled back a corner of the shower curtain and peered out. Steam still swirled around the bathroom, but no one was there. Kirsta gasped in relief and sat on the edge of the tub as her legs buckled beneath her. She rubbed at her temples and shook her head.

Her nerves must be on edge from lack of sleep. These old houses and cabins were full of cracks and crevices to let breezes in. That's what had moved the steam. There had probably been nobody there at all, just the imaginings of a tired, overworked mind. Kirsta rose and quickly toweled herself dry. She couldn't wait to escape the claustrophobia of the damp bathroom. She decided she'd try to simply relax for the rest of the evening, and enjoy the dinner. She wouldn't think or worry about her problems until after she'd gotten a good night's rest.

As Kirsta opened the bathroom door, she remembered the can of Coke she'd set on the wicker stool before stepping into the shower. When she turned to get it, she froze. The can was on the stool where she'd left it. But the scented dusting powder was dumped in and around the sink, its cardboard tub overturned in the far corner of the room. Kirsta's fists clenched in the thick towel she held, and her teeth ground together.

There had been someone in the room with her. Someone who didn't like rose-scented dusting powder. Kirsta trembled violently for long moments, terrified to open the bathroom door. She desperately needed to see whether someone was on the other side, waiting for her. Anybody who would be lurking around in the bathroom certainly meant her no good. But what if there was someone? What would she do?

Kirsta glanced around the little room, searching for something to use as a weapon. The steam was clearing, but she saw nothing that would do her any good against an intruder. Deciding to make a break for the door if anybody was there, Kirsta suddenly realized her clothes were in the other room. She'd never felt more naked. She wrapped the towel around her and tucked the edges together as securely as possible. She drew a deep breath and opened the door.

The cabin was empty. She grabbed a poker from beside the fireplace, swiping it beneath the bed and in the closet. But she'd known the moment she left the bathroom that she was alone. The door was securely bolted and the screens on the windows hadn't been tampered with. Nobody could have entered.

And yet somebody had been there, she was sure of it. She didn't know how it was possible, but it was true. She could have accidentally dumped the powder out herself, she supposed. But something wouldn't let her believe that. Eliminate the impossible, someone had once said, and what's left, no matter how improbable, was the truth. Kirsta dressed quickly, unable to still the shuddering chill that gripped her.

Despite the heat and humidity, it took her a long time to warm up.

CHAPTER TEN

David Belsen had been driving forever, it seemed. He'd quickly lost all concept of time, heading west on Interstate 70 into the setting sun after stopping at the antique store and buying the combs for Kirsta. He smiled as he remembered how he'd taken care of Harrison Kahn. He'd taught Kahn a lesson about fooling around with women who didn't belong to him — a permanent lesson.

The long stretches of undulating pavement across Ohio had eased the redness from his mind until nothing remained but soft greys. The gently unfolding dark farmlands had seemed endless, until David felt as though the night and the road entered his soul and he merged with them. By the time he had reached Louisville, there was nothing left inside him but hard cold and darkness. Once he'd found route 65 near dawn, he had pulled into the corner of a roadside rest and slept for a couple of hours. The sounds of semis roaring to life had awakened him at nine, and he'd started on his journey again.

Now he was headed west again, along the two-hundred mile stretch of route 40 that connects Nashville with Memphis. He would soon be home. At least, the home his mother knew for most of her life. He felt the coldness inside him grow heavier as he thought of visiting her grave. But he knew she would understand when he explained.

The grey ribbon of highway slid beneath the tires of David's car as he left the miles behind. A golden sun still hovered behind the tops of the tall pine trees ahead, burning into his eyes like a laser. The low hum of the engine reminded him of his mother's voice when she sat by his childhood bed, singing him softly to sleep.

David had thought a lot about Mother since leaving Pennsylvania, about her love for him and her belief in his powers. He'd made a terrible mistake, choosing Kirsta over his mother, he knew that now. But Mother would forgive him when he proved his love to her by finding Kirsta and making her the kind of woman Mother would have wanted her to be. Kirsta would thank him, too, once she understood.

He hummed along with the road, a sad, lyrical old Civil War ballad his mother had taught him:

"Dearest love, do you remember,

when we last did meet,

how you told me that you loved me,

kneeling at my feet?"

David pictured Kirsta kneeling at his feet, her head resting on his knee. He saw himself reach a hand out to stroke her soft blond hair — no, her hair was darker than that, wasn't it? He shook his head to clear it and wiped his hand across his eyes.

When he looked up again, his car had swerved across the center line and into the path of a mini-van determined to pass him. The driver sounded his horn angrily and waved a fist in David's direction. Shaken, David ignored him. He'd have to concentrate better or he'd have an accident. Maybe he should have something to eat; he'd been driving all day and had stopped only a few times for doughnuts and coffee. He couldn't remember the last complete meal he'd had. A sign flashed by for a home-style restaurant at the next exit, and David pulled onto the ramp.

The restaurant was filling quickly, but David found a seat at the counter. The bulging trucker on the next stool didn't give David a second glance, but continued shoveling mashed potatoes into his mouth. David avoided looking at him as he studied the menu.

"Special tonight's hot meatloaf sandwich with home fries."

David glanced up to see where the soft nasal voice came from. A plump waitress in a black skirt and stained white blouse stood before him on the other side of the counter, a black cloth cap perched precariously on her pale hair. She blinked rapidly as she waited for his response. David thought she looked like a dishevelled chickadee.

"Special sounds good," David said, handing her the menu. "And a large cup of black coffee."

"You got it, honey."

She bent over to tuck the menu into its metal brackets, giving David a glimpse of the cleft between her large breasts. Was she trying to catch his attention? David glanced at the pink nametag beside the material straining to contain her bosom — Tami.

"Thanks, Tami," he said.

She looked confused for a moment, then tapped her nametag and smiled. "I always forget I'm wearing this," she said and headed back toward the kitchen.

David watched her walk away, certain her hips swayed more now than they had earlier. Yes, she was definitely interested in him. Women simply couldn't resist him.

A minute later, Tami returned with the pot of coffee and a large styrofoam cup. "Our coffee cups are all the same size," she said, "but this will hold more. You can have as much as you want. Just whistle."

She smiled at him again, then turned to the trucker as he ordered an apple dumpling for dessert. David drank deeply of the bitter, steaming coffee and savored the way it burned going down.

Just whistle. David recognized the disguised innuendo. He pictured Lauren Bacall's whorish expression as she licked her lips and told Humphrey Bogart to "just put your lips together and blow." Mother was right — women were whores, just waiting to get their hands on a man, willing to do anything to snag one.

Well, not all women, he silently corrected himself as he watched Tami wiggle back to the kitchen. Mother certainly hadn't been like that. And Kirsta could still be saved, he was sure of it. She'd shown a spark of decency. She just needed to be reminded of her inner voice. And David Belsen, Avenging Angel, was exactly the person to show her the way.

Tami was back in a few minutes. "Your dinner will be right up," she chirped to David, holding the coffee pot toward him. "Meantime, can I do you again?"

David felt his crotch tighten at the blatant sexual reference. However, he would not succumb to her advances. He must be true to his quest.

"No, you cannot 'do me,'" he muttered through clenched teeth. "I'm not interested in your slutty come-ons."

Tami stepped back as though he'd attacked her physically. "Hey, mister," she said, her brows knit in apparent confusion, "you look tired. I just thought you might want some more coffee, that's all."

The big trucker stopped eating his apple dumpling and turned to look at David.

"I'm not that stupid," David laughed coldly. "I know what you're after. I can recognize a whore when I see one."

"I ... I don't know what you're talking about," Tami stammered. "I didn't mean ..."

Her voice trailed off as the trucker hauled his bulk from the stool. He towered over David.

"I think it's time you left, chum," he said quietly, wiping his hands on the faded blue expanse of his jeans. "The coffee's on me."

David's stomach lurched at the size of the man, yet he protested weakly. "I haven't had my dinner yet."

The trucker grabbed David's arm in one meaty fist and hauled him from his seat. "Well, you'll get it somewhere else if you're smart. Now scram."

The trucker shoved David so hard toward the door that his shoulder hit painfully against the metal frame. When he found his balance, David glanced around. Nearby, people were beginning to notice that something was going on. Tami had her hand over her mouth, and David knew she was hiding a laugh.

He wanted to go back, wipe that grin off her face, but realized it might not be a good idea to draw attention to himself in case the authorities from Pennsylvania were looking for him. He pushed through the glass doors to walk on trembling legs toward his car. His hands were shaking so badly by the time he slid behind the wheel that it took him three tries to get the key into the ignition.

David continued driving west toward Memphis. The sun was lower now, silhouetting the pine forests against a mustard sky. If he hadn't been worried about drawing attention from the police back in Pennsylvania, he'd have shown them who's boss. He replayed the scene in the restaurant over and over in his mind until he got it right. He would have told Tami and the trucker to get stuffed and stalked out on his own steam. He was, after all, the Avenging Angel.

Better yet, he'd have brought the knife into the greasy spoon, so he could teach them both a lesson in humility. He felt the red glow pulse inside him until it warmed him again and stilled the trembling. They'd have taken him seriously then, not just smirking behind his back. And they'd have let him eat, he thought as his stomach complained loudly. In fact, they'd have pleaded with him to take whatever he wanted, if he'd just let them live.

David smiled, and the red glow was still with him less than an hour later when he pulled into the parking lot of the Mt. Vernon Gardens Cemetery near Bartlett, just northeast of Memphis. The sun was nearly down now, hanging like an overripe persimmon in the west. Everything was bathed in its light, but David felt as though it were he and not the sun turning the world red.

David got out of his car and stretched. He hadn't been back to the little house in Bartlett since he'd left for college, more than ten years ago. Standing in the cooling air, it seemed a lifetime ago to David. He had spent hours roaming among the tombstones as a boy, playing soldiers by himself or hide-and-seek with Mother on her days off. She'd often shown her son the little plot at the edge of the cemetery where she'd be buried one day. He'd always hated seeing it, imagining his life without her, stranded among strangers. But now he silently thanked her for making it so easy for him to find her.

David walked the familiar roads and pathways until he found the little metal plaque embossed with her name and the dates of her life. He suddenly wondered who had made all the arrangements. Probably the local attorney who had sent him the telegram about her death and the check when her will was probated.

David felt a pang of guilt and promised himself to see about the purchase of a stone when he returned — if he returned — from his mission to the south. He decided he and Kirsta would make a pilgrimage here every year to visit her and make sure the grave was taken care of. He crouched down, and touched his fingers to her name.

"I won't forget you, Mother," he said aloud.

"I know you won't, Davey."

He wasn't surprised to hear her voice. Nor was he shocked to see her standing stiffly about five yards from him when he looked up. It seemed perfectly natural that she should be there talking to him beside her grave. She wore the dark, high-necked dress she always chose for important occasions, with the small watch pinned to her shoulder. A light breeze blew, but the wisps of hair that escaped her straight grey braid never moved.

"You were right, Mother," David said, his voice trembling a bit. "I'm sorry I doubted you. Women are awful, like you said, and I'm not sure I can handle them all. Especially Kirsta."

"Of course you can, Davey." She sniffed in annoyance. "They're just women. They're not special like you. Nobody is special the way you are."

He felt tears running down his cheeks and realized he was crying. How long had it been since he'd cried? He couldn't remember. He hoped Mother wouldn't notice.

"But I'm so tired, Mother," he said. "I'm not sure I'm thinking straight. And I'm a little —" he hated to say it, but spat it out before he could change his mind "— afraid."

A breeze chilled him and Mother trembled angrily. "You're going to have to pull yourself together, David," she said. "You are not afraid. Of course you're thinking straight. You're finally standing up for yourself and doing what needs to be done. You just aren't used to having so much power."

"Do you really think so?" David didn't care that his voice was full of tears. "You're not angry with me?"

"Of course not." Mother's voice softened, just a touch. "How could I be angry with my little angel?" Then she was firm again. "But stop that whimpering. You have to prove yourself now. Grow up and act like a man, not a little boy."

"I know," he sighed. "And I am, I did. I showed that Ginny person I was a man, didn't I? She won't be trying to keep secrets from me for a while."

Mother didn't say anything, but he thought she nodded.

"And I did the right thing with that pig Harrison Kahn." He laughed, remembering. "The Avenging Angel took care of him and his fornicating ways. Kirsta will be proud of me now."

"Is Kirsta the only one you want to please?" Mother's voice was little more than a whisper in the purple air, but David heard her clearly.

"Of course not, Mother." His guilt rose in his throat like bile. How could he be thinking of that bitch now? "I want you to be proud of me, too. In fact, you're the most important one."

He waited, but she didn't answer for a long time. Then she said, "I wasn't very proud of you back at that diner on route forty, was I?"

He put his head down, resting his face on the metal plaque. It felt like an icy kiss against his cheek. "No, Mother," he muttered miserably.

"You know you have to stand up for yourself. You can't let them get the better of you again, can you, Davey?"

"No, ma'am."

"That's good, little angel. Now Mother can be proud of you. Now mother can rest in peace."

David stood up exultantly. On trembling legs he walked through the gathering darkness toward his mother. He wanted her to hold him in her arms, to cuddle him and tell him she still loved him. But when he got there, he found nothing but a scrawny shrub, shaped vaguely like a woman.

Was this what he'd been talking to all this time? Was his mother's voice nothing but his own imagination? David felt a violent chill, then laughed out loud. Of course not — he'd never let his mind play tricks like that. Mother had certainly been there for him, just like she always had.

Now David would make her proud of him.

CHAPTER ELEVEN

By the time Kirsta reached the back porch steps of the main house, she could already hear the warm, homey sounds of people chatting inside. She recognized Daphne Woodring's voice and assumed the others must be Henry Patton and his sister Etta. Their two voices were so similar, she couldn't tell which was the one she'd heard two nights earlier, when she'd stopped to ask for directions at Henry's gas station.

Kirsta paused with her hand on the screen door latch as she remembered Henry's warning that night that she reconsider her accommodations, that Lost Oaks was a "strange" place. At the time, she'd thought he was either a bit off-balance or pulling her leg. Now, in view of her experiences these past few days, Kirsta wondered whether she should have given his advice more serious consideration. She tried to shake off her sense of foreboding as she pulled the screen door open and entered the house.

Daphne, Henry and Etta were seated in the living room. Overhead, a chandelier shed a dim warm glow; Kirsta decided its brightness must be controlled by a rheostat. The flickering light of candles played like pale fingers on their wine glasses and the tops of the huge open windows that led out onto the front veranda. Mirrors at the bottom of the massive sideboard reflected the light back into the room, and Kirsta wondered why a piece of furniture would have a mirror so low to the floor.

As if reading her mind, Daphne rose from the brocade loveseat and crossed to her. "Kirsta, so nice to see you. I see you've noticed the petticoat mirrors. Everyone wonders about them when they first see them. Of course, women who wore long skirts and several layers of underthings had to have some way to check on their modesty when entering a room. Also, lamps placed on those low shelves gave more light to the uneven places on the floors."

She took Kirsta's elbow and steered her across the room. "Now, I'd like you to meet Etta and Henry Patton — though Henry said you two have already met, informally."

Henry rose from his chair, and Kirsta smiled and shook hands with both of them. Remembering Henry's crooked arthritic fingers, she was careful not to grasp his hand too hard. However, his grip on hers was surprisingly strong and firm. Even though Daphne had told her that the Pattons were twins, Kirsta was startled by how much they looked alike. Both were tall and lanky — obvious even when they sat side-by-side in the matching high-backed upholstered chairs. They each had the same long, equine features, even down to matching wrinkles and crow's feet. Etta's hair was wrapped around her head in long braids, and the white wispy ends fluttered at the edges in the same patterns as Henry's hair, like steam rising from a kettle.

Henry bowed when he shook Kirsta's hand, then sat back down. His sister just nodded and smiled. Kirsta noticed she unconsciously rubbed her knees as she sat, and recalled Daphne's comments about Etta's arthritic legs.

"Why don't you sit over there by the windows?" Daphne suggested. "There's a nice breeze coming in through the screens, and you can smell the honeysuckle. Better than any potpourri or air freshener."

Henry waved an arthritic knuckle in the direction of the windows. "Just you watch out for them guillotines," he warned. Kirsta halted and looked at him uncertainly.

"Guillotines?"

Etta clucked her tongue. "Don't pay him any attention, dear," she said. "Henry's always trying to give people a hard time. Those windows open wide enough for a grown man to walk through — used for doors as well as windows in the old days. But they don't hold very well, and if one fell down as someone was walking through …" She winced dramatically. "Well, that's why they called them guillotine windows."

Kirsta glanced up and realized the heavy drapery valance hid more window than she'd realized. At the far corner of the room the front door stood open and a few purple clouds drifted beyond the branches of the trees out front. A sweetly-scented breeze wafted through the screens and tickled the nape of her neck. Kirsta closed her eyes, at the unexpected image of Sean's fingers moving across her bare skin in the canoe the night before. Suddenly, the warm evening grew even closer, and she realized Sean was missing.

"Won't Sean be joining us for dinner?" she asked Daphne, trying to keep the disappointment from her voice.

"He went out earlier today, and didn't think he'd be back in time," Daphne answered. "He said to deliver his apologies."

Kirsta realized she should be relieved; she'd been dreading as well as anticipating another confrontation with Sean this evening. She wanted some time to sort out her emotions, to give herself a chance to be objective about her feelings.

Yet, after the closeness she'd sensed the night before at Mistmere, she felt let down, as though his absence were intentional, directed at her personally. Kirsta grew annoyed at her overly-emotional reaction. She was, after all, a grown woman; she knew Sean's interest in her was probably no more than that of a polite host. She muttered something in reply.

Daphne held up her wine glass. "I broke out another bottle of Fruit de Coeur," she smiled, "since you enjoyed it so much at dinner the other night. Can I get you a glass?"

Kirsta cringed at the sight of the dark crimson liquid. She recalled vividly watching herself paint that letter "I" on the snowy field of Daphne's tablecloth two nights before, as though watching someone else's hand move in a dream. She shook her head and swallowed drily.

"No," she answered, "no thank you. I think the wine might have been partly what kept me awake that night. I know it sounds strange, but alcohol does that to me sometimes. I want to make sure I get a good night's sleep again tonight. I have a lot of work to do tomorrow."

She recalled her erotic dream, and blushed, as though the others could read her mind.

"Oh, my dear," Daphne said sympathetically. "I suppose that's my fault. I wouldn't have given you the wine with such a heavy dinner if I'd thought for a minute…"

Kirsta patted her hostess on the shoulder. "Don't be silly. It's not your fault. And the dinner wasn't heavy at all; it was delicious. I think I was just … over-stimulated from being in a new place and the excitement of starting to work. I should have known better myself."

"So tell us about your work," said Etta Patton. "I'm dying to hear all about it. Henry and I have always been interested in local history. There are lots of fascinating things that have gone on here, more than most people imagine — even the local residents. I understand you're doing some research about the Civil War. Are you writing a book or a magazine article?"

Kirsta explained her research job briefly. She ended by saying, "I … needed to get away anyway, so I told Harrison I'd be happy do it for him."

Kirsta hoped nobody noticed she faltered at her own reasons for wanting to leave Pennsylvania. She was suddenly glad Sean hadn't been there; somehow, she felt sure he'd have noticed. She still wasn't prepared to dwell on her darker reasons for leaving Pennsylvania — not even to herself.

Etta leaned forward in her chair. "What exactly are you researching for this colleague of yours?"

"He's writing a book about the effects of the Civil War on the lives of people living on plantations. He asked me to research the chapter about Louisiana plantations, using Pointe Coupee Parish and West Feliciana Parish as examples."

Henry Patton asked, "How well does something like that pay?"

"Henry, don't be rude," his sister chided.

"I'm just askin'," he sighed. "She don't have to answer."

"That's all right," Kirsta said. "Harrison said he'd cover my expenses, and pay me for my work. Plus I get a share of the royalties when the book is published. It shouldn't take too long; the publisher is quite anxious to get the final draft of the manuscript."

Kirsta didn't add how much of a hurry she was in to get the income from this job.

"Well, I'm sure you'll find some useful information in the Allindea library," Etta said. "Unfortunately, many of the records from these local plantations have been lost because of damage done by the Yankee soldiers and carpetbaggers who came through here. But Henry and I have collected a good bit of information about that period that might be helpful, if you'd like to come over sometime. We promised Daphne we'd bring some with us tonight, but to be honest, we weren't sure what kinds of things you'd be interested in."

"I'd love to see whatever you have," Kirsta said quickly. "I got quite a lot of information at the library today, but private collections sometimes contain much more in the way of local flavor — gossip, local legends, that kind of thing."

Then Kirsta recalled what the librarian had said just before locking up that afternoon. "Speaking of local legends," she said, "I understand there's some kind of bizarre phenomenon that occurs out here on the plantation. What's it called — the birding?"

"Oh, that." Daphne chuckled. "I suppose it is kind of bizarre. At least, nobody's been able to explain it so far. But it's been happening for so many years — since at least the Civil War — I guess I'm used to it. I forget it's all that unusual."

"Tell me about it," Kirsta urged.

"Not much to tell, really. A bunch of black birds — crows or ravens or something — flock in by the hundreds every spring and roost in that old oak out front. They only stay a day or so, then move on."

"It must be loud, with all those birds out there."

"Well, most of the time it is," Daphne agreed. "All that twittering and cackling. But that's one of the odd things. About four o'clock in the afternoon, all the birds stop everything they're doing and get silent for about fifteen minutes. Then they start up again, and everything's normal."

"That's really weird," Kirsta said. "And nobody's ever been able to expain what's going on?"

Etta said, "The family brings in naturalists every few years or so to study them, but nobody's made much sense of it."

Henry leaned forward in his chair. "Bunch of bull about electromagnetic fields and phases of the moon and sunspots. Damn fools, if you ask me."

Etta threw an annoyed glance at her brother. "Well, we weren't much help on that," she said to Kirsta. "What other kinds of things are you looking for?"

"I'm especially interested in diaries and journals written by local survivors of the Civil War, if you have anything like that."

"Sure, we have a few of those lyin' around," Henry said, nonchalantly, "but there's some other stuff I expect you'll find even more interesting."

"Really? What kind of stuff?" Kirsta asked.

"Oh, I don't know," he said vaguely, "just … stuff."

Kirsta looked over at Henry Patton, and saw his eyes were fixed hard on hers. She squirmed uncomfortably in her chair. Was he making some kind of joke? It didn't appear so, but Kirsta felt he expected her to respond somehow. She had no idea what he wanted. She also realized with a start that Henry Patton wasn't at all the dumb down-home boy his laid-back manner led people to believe he was. His facade was obviously intentional, and she wondered what other surprises this enigmatic man held in store.

"Oh, Henry, stop being so goldarned melodramatic," Etta sighed. "Don't mind him, child. He likes to get everybody all riled up for nothing. But he's all smoke and no fire."

Henry snorted loudly. "Am not."

"You two," Daphne laughed, standing. "Always, bickering. It looks like we'd better head in for dinner before World War Three erupts."

She headed through the French doors into the dining room, and the others rose to follow. Henry helped Etta to her feet, and she walked very slowly, very stiffly at his side, though she held her back straight. Kirsta lagged behind, brushing imagined dust from her skirt so they wouldn't feel rushed.

As Etta and Henry disappeared through the doorway, Kirsta heard a noise out on the veranda. Peering out into the gathering dusk, she thought she glimpsed movement toward the corner of the house, as though someone had just darted away from the far window. Who on earth would be skulking around out here in the shadows, she wondered, watching them as they chatted inside?

Kirsta hurried to the screen door and jerked it open. She went out onto the wide wooden porch. A mockingbird fluttered from the railing with a loud squawk. Kirsta tried to tell herself that the bird was all she'd seen, but she wasn't convinced.

She crept around the corner of the house, keeping close to the wall. Nobody was on the veranda, but honeysuckle and yew shrubs crowded the narrow wooden steps leading down to the lawn. Someone could easily be crouched there even now, watching her every move. Kirsta shuddered as her eyes strained to penetrate the lengthening shadows. She rubbed her hands along her upper arms to get rid of the goosebumps, sorry now she'd worn a dress with thin straps instead of sleeves. Someone had been out there — she was sure of it. Should she tell the others?

Daphne interrupted her thoughts by calling to her from the dining room.

"I'm out here," Kirsta called back. She went inside to find Daphne standing in the doorway of the dining room, wiping her hands on her apron.

"What on earth were you doing out there at this hour?" Daphne asked. "You can hardly see anything now. Is something wrong?"

"No. I thought I'd … I'd like to get a breath of air," Kirsta finished lamely.

She wondered why she'd bothered to lie. If there were a burglar or peeper out there, she should tell someone. But deep down she knew that what she'd glimpsed hadn't been a burglar. Nor was it a peeping Tom. There had been something familiar about the tall, slim figure she'd glimpsed moving into the shadows. Kirsta's mind refused to consider the alternatives, and she gladly hurried back into the living room, closing the screen door firmly behind her.

"Sean just got back," Daphne said, as they walked into the dining room together. "He went upstairs to change, but he'll be right down to join us. You just sit over there on the far side of the table, and I'll set a place next to you for Sean, if you don't mind."

"That'll be fine."

Kirsta couldn't imagine spending the whole dinner with Sean at her side, watching her with those pale, bottomless eyes, remembering the last time they'd dined in this room, possibly waiting for her to do something bizarre again. But she certainly couldn't ask Daphne to put him somewhere else. That would seem rude — and to be honest, part of her didn't want to sit anywhere else.

She sat across from the Pattons, and forced a smile, determined to pay attention to the conversation until Sean decided to join them — and even after he sat down, if that was at all possible.

"Heard anything from Stuart lately?" Etta asked as Daphne set a tureen on the table. Daphne shook her head and frowned.

"Not a word. But then I don't expect to hear from him, either. I've given up trying to reconcile them; he sends Sean a Christmas card and a check every year, and that's it."

Henry snorted. "Some father. That boy might's well be an orphan for all the attention he gets from Stu. You can bet his little French floozy and her kin don't suffer that kind of neglect. He pays plenty of attention to them."

"Now, Henry," Daphne said, gathering soup bowls from the sideboard. "You know Stuart. Running from trouble's always been his way. And I'm sure Antoinette's not a 'floozy.' She's probably a lovely woman. We just never got the chance to get to know her."

"Well, that don't make it right. That boy needs a daddy. He's gotten downright … peculiar since the accident. He oughta just throw that money back in Stuart's face and be done with it."

Daphne sighed, "Sean's not that kind of man. He still has feelings for his father — though I'll admit it's beyond me to understand why."

Kirsta realized the conversation was headed in a very personal direction, and the others seemed to have completely forgotten about her in their concern over this Stuart person. Could this be Sean's father they were discussing? She cleared her throat gently to remind them of her presence.

Etta looked across the table. "Well, we certainly are airing our linen, aren't we? Poor Kirsta probably thinks we're a family full of crackpots."

"Not at all," Kirsta said quickly. "Until now, I hadn't realized you're all related, though."

"Oh, yes," Etta waved her hand. "You can't spit in Allindea without soiling a relative. There are really only six or seven different families around town. Daphne's grandma and our grandpa were first cousins. So that makes us, let's see …"

"She don't care about the particulars, Etta," Henry grumbled. "Enough to say Stuart and Sean are our kin."

"Stuart is Sean's father?" Kirsta asked.

"Estranged father might be a more accurate way of putting it."

Kirsta turned as she recognized the deep, quiet voice behind her. Sean stood in the archway that led to the stairs, his face inscrutable in the dim light. He wore a pale blue shirt open at the throat beneath a cream-colored linen jacket. The color of the shirt made his eyes look like deep pools of azure water. Kirsta forced her eyes away, feeling as though she might drown if she looked into them for long. She struggled to control her breathing.

"Sean, I didn't see you standing there," Daphne said. "Why don't you sit down? I made chilled cucumber soup this afternoon, if you'd like some. Seems there's no end in sight to this heat and humidity, and I thought a cold soup might take the edge off."

Sean looked toward the table, and Kirsta thought she saw the rippling shadow of a frown briefly cross his face when he noticed the empty chair next to hers. But he crossed and sat, his movements slow and graceful. Kirsta inhaled deeply the musky scent of him and squirmed in her chair, almost afraid he'd touch her, causing the deep tremors she'd felt the night before at Mistmere.

At the same time, she prayed for contact, even if it was only by accident. Maybe she would brush her fingers against his as she passed him a plate. Kirsta couldn't believe she was having these flights of fancy. She wondered how Sean would react if he knew her thoughts. She wanted to believe he'd be pleased, or at least flattered, but she feared he'd be appalled and see her response to him as inappropriate.

"I hear there's a storm heading this way," Daphne said, breaking the brief silence as she ladled the soup into the bowls and passed them around the table. "Weatherman says it'll probably hit either tomorrow night or the day after, depending on how long it takes to cross the Texas plains."

Etta nodded. "I didn't see the weather report today, but I knew something was on its way — my legs have been acting up all day." She rubbed her knees and frowned. "Probably be a doozy, when it gets here. My knees never lie."

"I noticed it in my hands, too," Henry agreed. "Like someone squeezin' my fingers too tight."

"It's certainly warmer down here than it is back in Pennsylvania right now," Kirsta said. "Usually in late April and early May, it's just beginning to warm up enough some days to go outdoors without a heavy coat."

Sean said, "Tourists always complain about the heat." Kirsta felt her face grow hot. He still considered her to be just another tourist.

Daphne said, "I don't think Kirsta's complaining. She was just making a comment, Sean."

Kirsta began, "Yes. I certainly didn't —"

"Sorry. I've been edgy all day; it must be the heat." Sean's voice was quiet, but Kirsta could hear the tension in it. So, she thought, sometimes the local residents are as cranky from the heat as the tourists. She considered mentioning the fact, but decided now wasn't the time.

Another silence hung over the table as the five ate their soup. Even the sounds of spoons against the china seemed somehow muffled. Sean shifted in his chair, and Kirsta felt his knee rub against hers. She waited for him to move it away, but he didn't. She glanced sideways. It might have been her imagination, but she thought she saw him smile slightly as he lifted his spoon. Kirsta left her leg where it was and continued eating the cool soup, though she barely tasted it anymore. Her attention was solely on the side of her leg that pressed lightly against his, on the almost intolerable warmth radiating from his presence beside her.

Finally, Etta spoke as Daphne cleared the table. "That soup was delicious, Daphne. I still want that recipe. Sean, your mama always used to fix cucumber soup for family picnics, didn't she?"

"I don't remember, Etta." Sean smiled sadly. "I was only nine when she died; there are a lot of things I just can't remember about her."

Henry said, "I remember at one picnic she told me the recipe was passed down in the McLeod family. She was joking about how Stu wouldn't let her give the recipe to anybody. Said he was worse than an old biddy sometimes."

Henry nodded as the pictures ran through his mind. "We were sittin' down by the pond that day, throwin' stale bread to the ducks. That was the same time she told me about the ghost."

"Ghost?" Kirsta asked. She felt Sean tense up beside her, but she leaned forward. "What ghost?"

Henry frowned at Daphne as she brought in plates filled with chicken, stuffing and green beans. "You mean you haven't told her about Andrew yet?"

"Andrew?" It took Kirsta a moment to realize why the name sounded so familiar; Andrew was the name she'd been calling out in her dream the night before. She marveled at the odd coincidence.

Etta put her hand on Henry's arm. "Henry, don't be talking out the top of your hat now."

Sean said, "Yes, Henry, there's no point in —"But Henry waved a crooked hand at Sean and spoke loudly enough to drown him out.

"Daphne, tell this girl about the infamous ghost of Lost Oaks. You do it right now, or I'll have to do it myself — and you know what a damned rotten liar I am."

Daphne clucked her tongue and looked apologetically at Sean, but Kirsta thought she saw the corners of his aunt's mouth twitch, fighting a smile. She'd obviously been waiting for just such an opportunity.

"Well," she began, "the story goes that this Yankee fellow, Andrew Lucas, was hiding out in this area near the end of the Civil War. Emotions were running hard against spies and such. He knew if he got caught he'd probably be sent east to Andersonville prison, and he didn't want to end up there — which was smart, because not many people returned from Andersonville.

"Anyway, he had to get home to St. Louis or someplace because he'd found out that his wife and little boy had been killed in a carriage accident up that way. Somehow found his way to Lost Oaks, and hid out in the barn for a few days, eating what vegetables he could steal from the garden at night and scavenging scraps from the leavings up at the main house. Nobody knew he was there for days.

"But one night, the mistress of the house couldn't sleep and was out strolling along that very walk you use each day to come up here."

Daphne pointed dramatically toward the back of the house. Sean sighed and leaned back in his chair, raising his eyes to the ceiling. His aunt ignored him and continued.

"She must have heard something, because she went into the barn, where they say he — forced himself on her. Fortunately, her husband found them before he could kill her, and called for help. By the time the others got there, he'd subdued Lucas by hitting him on the head with a broken wagon spoke. They tied Lucas up and hanged him the next day."

Henry nodded and said, "And ever since then, this Lucas fella's been tryin' to avenge himself. Visitors are always complainin' about hearin' noises and seein' strange things."

"What kinds of things?" Kirsta asked.

"Nothing really terrible," Daphne said quickly. "Shadows and misty faces at night, things like that. Once when they were teenagers, Sean's cousin Jo found a rose on her pillow. Anybody could have put it there, of course, but nobody ever admitted to leaving it."

"Of course they didn't," Sean said, exasperation dripping from his voice. Kirsta felt his knee shift away from hers beneath the table.

111

"Aunt Daphne, everybody wants to perpetuate the family ghost. Every respectable plantation has to have at least one ghost. I remember trying to scare the cousins with spooky stories and ghostly sounds when we were kids. It was lots of fun. But the truth is, I've lived here my whole life and have never seen anything. I just don't believe Andrew Lucas's spirit moans through these rafters, crying out for revenge. The whole thing's ridiculous."

"I don't know about the ghost part," Kirsta said, "but if that story is true, it's an example of the kind of thing I'm looking for in my research. Would there be any more information about the Andrew Lucas hanging somewhere? Maybe in the Allindea library?"

"Probably not," Etta said. "It's not likely to have been in the papers. But we might have something about that in our files. What do you think, Henry? You remember anything like that in those old papers?"

He squinted up at the chandelier for a moment, considering. "I don't know," he said slowly. "Could be. Why don'tcha come on over tomorrow morning and see what we got?"

Kirsta smiled. "Sounds great. Thanks."

Etta said, "Make it the afternoon, Kirsta, if you don't mind. That way, I can sort through some of the files and save you a bit of time. And I can get the house straightened up — Henry's a bit messy, I'm afraid."

"Am not," Henry muttered. "I know where everything is. You always have to mess up my stuff, tryin' to get it clean. Then I can't find the nose on my face for a week."

"Afternoon's fine, Etta," Kirsta said quickly. "That'll give me time in the morning to do some preparation and make notes on what I want to look for. But don't clean up on my account. I'm no stickler for neatness — except in my work."

"Plan on spendin' some time, honey," Henry said to Kirsta. "I think we'll have a lot to talk about."

Kirsta saw him glance hard at Sean, and she had the feeling Henry had more on his mind than Civil War history. She suddenly felt a chill trickle along her spine; she wasn't at all sure she wanted to hear what he had to tell her.

CHAPTER TWELVE

After dinner, Sean offered to walk Kirsta back to her cabin. She hesitated, remembering the awkwardness of their parting the night before, after her strange experience during the canoe ride on the bayou. She'd been unable to tell him about the face she'd seen in the mists, the tragic face that reminded her of the one she'd seen in the steamy mirror her first morning at Lost Oaks. That morning was only two days ago, and yet it seemed months had passed since.

Worse was her disappointment when he left her there alone at her cabin. But he'd grown quiet on the ride back to Lost Oaks, and she could only assume he'd misinterpreted her reaction on the bayou. He probably thought she'd reacted badly to his kiss, but she couldn't find the words to explain.

Now, when he asked whether she'd like some company on the dark paths to her cabin, she was unable to say no. They walked slowly through the warm hazy evening, and he rested his arm on her bare shoulder as they strolled beneath the low branches of an oak tree. Kirsta shivered involuntarily at his touch.

"Cold?" he asked.

Kirsta's voice caught. "No. Actually, I think it's rather warm tonight."

She hoped he wouldn't ask why she shivered. He didn't, but his fingers moved a little on the back of her neck. Kirsta began to wonder whether he could sense her thoughts. Was she that transparent? Or — she almost didn't want to dare hope — was it possible he felt the same tension, like a coiled spring deep inside, ready to snap at any moment? Sometimes, Kirsta thought, Sean seemed like a caged tiger, but tonight she sensed none of that edginess, that explosive energy just beneath the surface.

"I hope you weren't too bored tonight," he said.

"Bored? Not at all, I had a lovely time. Why would I be bored?"

"Well, you know," he shrugged, "dinner with the relatives. All that chatter about my family — and those ghost stories. It gets old pretty fast."

Kirsta smiled. "I like a good ghost story as much as the next person," she began. She hesitated, then plunged ahead. "And the fact is, I found the family part fascinating. It made me realize how much alike we are."

Sean stopped walking for a moment and looked at her. His face caught the rays of the small porch light she'd left burning at the cabin, and the yellow glow was trapped in his full lips and the creases of his long thin face. He stood so close she felt his breath on her cheeks.

"And just how are we alike, you and I?"

She had a little trouble catching her breath, but spoke in a low, firm voice. These were things she needed to say, even if they were difficult.

"The first thing is, my mother died, too. I was nearly eighteen when her car skidded on the ice and slammed into the side of a truck, but I know just how empty your life can feel after something like that."

"And the second thing?" Kirsta felt his hand move on her shoulder, stroking it gently, soothingly.

This part was even more difficult. "The second thing is, I don't have much of a relationship with my father, either. I haven't heard from him in more than three years. Not a Christmas card, not a check, not a word."

"I'm sorry, Kirsta." Sean's voice made the familiar words sound sincere. She saw her pain reflected in his eyes, and was grateful.

"Don't be," she smiled sadly. "He began drinking after Mom died, and I moved away from home as soon as I could. I tried to start up the relationship after college, but it was useless. By then he found the bottle more interesting than he found me."

Sean bent to kiss her softly then, and pulled her to him. Kirsta was so startled by his action, she made no response other than a gasp. He leaned back against the rough bark of a tree and drew her with him so that she leaned against him. She inhaled the musky scent of him.

Sean raised his face and gazed up into the twisted branches above them. Bullfrogs twanged softly down in the dark waters of the pond. His voice was soft and sad when he spoke.

"My father pulled away, too," Sean said. "He disappeared emotionally after my mother died, though he was still here physically. Then shortly after the accident — the one that killed Edwina and Andy — he left for Paris with Antoinette. I got home from a business trip and there was a letter from him in the mailbox. He was sorry, but he needed to do this, and so forth and so on."

"That must have been a blow," Kirsta said, reaching out to touch his hand. He shrugged.

"I suppose it would have been if we'd been closer. But he'd been emotionally absent for most of my life, and had moved to Baton Rouge when I got married. That's where he met Antoinette. He sends a sizable check each year in his Christmas card. At first, I was furious, and just wanted to send them back. But then I realized that giving me money is the only way he knows to make up for our lost lives together. I started a bank account for Lost Oaks, just in case our finances ever look too shaky. That way I'll never have to sell it all. Fortunately, so far, I haven't had to touch that money."

"It would be terrible to lose all this," Kirsta said peering around her into the soft shadows, as though she could see the plantation around her. "Lost Oaks is a wonderful place. I'm sure your father's happy you're doing that."

"I don't know," Sean admitted. "I've never told him. We don't talk, or even write letters. But I've let go of most of the anger. I hope he's found some happiness now, or at least some peace. I really do."

Neither said anything else for a long moment. Then Sean put his arm back across Kirsta's shoulders, and they walked in silence the rest of the way to the cabin. Kirsta's heart beat like jungle drums in her ears, and her lips ached for the touch of his again.

As she unlocked her door, Kirsta heard herself ask, "Would you like to come in?" She'd had no intention of saying it, but was glad she had.

Sean smiled. "For a nightcap, you mean?"

Kirsta felt her face grow warm, and thanked the darkness that he couldn't see her blush. "Well, I don't really have anything for a nightcap, but I could fix us a cup of tea."

Sean stepped very close to her and put one warm palm against the side of her face. "I'd love to come in," he said, his voice hoarse. "But I don't really want a cup of tea."

They stood looking into one another's eyes for a long moment, then Kirsta grasped his hand and backed slowly into the cabin. Something in the back of her mind whispered to her to let him leave, that this was all wrong, a mistake. But she knew there was no going back now; she had to have him at any cost.

Sean followed, his hand still on her cheek. Then his fingers slid around to the back of her neck, and entwined in her hair. He drew her toward him as he touched his lips to hers. This time the kiss was long and firm, and she felt his tongue burn across her lips. Kirsta wrapped her arms around his neck, pushing the door closed behind him.

Sean lifted her body against his, and she felt his hardness against her. She moaned into his mouth, wanting to melt into him, to become a part of him forever. He moved forward and laid her gently on the quilted bedspread. He slowly drew the thin straps from her shoulders and pulled down the top of her dress, cupping her right breast in his hand. He encircled the stiffening pebble of her nipple with his lips and flicked it lightly with his tongue. The sensation was electric. Kirsta moaned again and tangled her fingers in his thick black hair, dragging his face back up to hers. She pulled his tongue into her mouth, devouring it, savoring the taste of him.

Sean stood up to remove his shirt, and Kirsta thought she heard a small cough or gasp. In the few stray beams cast from the porch light through the curtains, Kirsta thought she saw him wince. His shoulders hunched for a moment. Then he straightened again, and pulled his shirt over his head without even unbuttoning it. He stood bare-chested for a moment by the side of the bed, just staring down at Kirsta.

The light rippled along Sean's chest muscles and forearms as he stood between her legs, but he remained mostly in shadow. Some trick of the light made him appear almost to flicker, like a shadow himself. Kirsta strained her eyes to focus. She suddenly felt she needed see him more clearly. Then he moved again, and descended back onto her, kissing and licking her hot skin as he pulled her dress further down, exposing her belly.

His hands were rougher now, kneading at her thighs and buttocks through the thin material of the dress. His mouth and tongue strained to devour her breasts. She could feel the edges of his teeth against the tender flesh. He seemed more forceful than he had a moment ago, as though the act of removing his shirt had somehow increased his sense of urgency. Sean's hand slipped beneath her skirt and along her bare legs. Kirsta tensed and clenched her teeth, in exquisite anticipation.

But there was an inkling of fear, too. She wanted Sean to make love to her, more than ever, but something deep inside her was whispering dark messages of warning. Something wasn't quite right, but she didn't know what it was. Kirsta told herself it was just her ridiculous fear of rejection, her inexperience. She thrust the notion away and forced herself to concentrate on Sean, on the moment.

As his fingers edged up her thighs, she gazed into his face. Beyond the haze of her need for him, Kirsta was dimly aware that Sean seemed … different. He appeared — unbelievably — to have gained weight; he actually felt heavier on her than he had a moment ago. She realized it must be her imagination, but the thought was unsettling, and she fought to ignore it. Kirsta pushed these distractions away and concentrated on the wonderful sensations in her breasts and belly. She wanted only to revel in their discoveries of one another's secret places.

Kirsta opened her eyes to look into his, and her breathing stopped. Sean's eyes were blue, icy pale blue, she was sure of it. But the eyes she looked into now were dark. The light, she told herself, it must be a trick of the light. But Kirsta couldn't escape the feeling that she was making love to a stranger. His fingers touched the edge of her panties. Kirsta drew her head back to get a better look in the scant light from outside … and didn't recognize the man on top of her.

He had dark hair like Sean's, but the face seemed shorter, the nose broader, the chin less angular. Kirsta blinked several times. Sean's face appeared to flicker in and out of focus, and he closed his eyes as his hand gripped the flimsy material between her thighs. He tore it from her and flung it aside.

Suddenly, something crashed against the wall above the bed, showering them with water and bits of ceramic. Kirsta felt Sean gasp, and he jumped up from her. He stood over her a moment, trembling violently.

"What was that? Sean, are you hurt?" Kirsta's voice quivered with all the emotions churning inside her. "Are you all right?"

"I … I don't … Oh God, oh my God." Sean covered his eyes with the heels of his hands, digging his long fingers into his hair.

"What's wrong?" Kirsta felt panic squeeze her stomach. "Are you all right? Do you need help?"

Sean didn't answer, but opened the door of the cabin and hurried out into the night. Kirsta rose shakily from the bed, pulling up the top of her dress. She stood by the door watching him stagger toward the main house until the shadows hid him from her. Then she went back inside, locking the door and leaning against it. She turned on the light.

Kirsta checked the bed to see what had crashed against the wall and rained down on them. She felt her skin grow clammy. Tiny, colorful bits of china littered her pillow, and fingers of water were trickling down onto the headboard and soaking into her pillow fast. A single red rose lay amidst the rubble on the clean linens.

How could the vase Daphne had left on the coffee table flown across the room to shatter against the wall? Kirsta measured the distance with her eyes as she lifted the rose from the satin embroidered pillow cover — ten feet at least. Had someone moved it from the coffee table and set it precariously on top of the headboard, so that it fell when Sean lay on her?

But that theory raised even more questions: who could have done that, and why would they bother? Maybe Daphne had been here again this evening, but when? And why? Or had Sean moved it when they came into the cabin? She forced her mind back, but could only recall the feeling of his hands on her body, his lips on hers, the way she'd wanted him.

The memory of Sean's fierce passion caused Kirsta's hand to clench involuntarily, and she felt a sharp pain. One of the rose's thorns had pierced her palm, drawing a small drop of blood.

"Damn," Kirsta muttered, sucking at the cut.

She quickly dropped the rose into the wastebasket by the fireplace, as though the flower itself were somehow responsible for what had happened. This was all just too much. There had to be a simple explanation — there had to be. She'd ask Daphne about it tomorrow. She got a dishtowel and began picking up the tiny pieces of broken vase. Her mind wouldn't — couldn't — erase the image of Sean, bolting through the door.

What had happened to Sean? He'd changed so suddenly, so completely in a matter of minutes. Had Kirsta done or said something to cause it? And what about the way he seemed to transform physically? Of course that wasn't possible, but why would her mind play tricks like that? Too many questions. Kirsta just couldn't understand what was going on. She felt tears sting the corners of her eyes, and fought to keep from crying. Damn it, she wouldn't let another man cause her that kind of pain, the way David had.

When she'd gotten herself under control again, she finished cleaning up the mess. After she changed the sheets, Kirsta lay in bed, replaying the scene with Sean over and over in her mind. She was sure she'd never get to sleep, agonizing over exactly what had happened in her room that night. But sheer physical and mental exhaustion took over. After twisting about in the sheets for several minutes, she drifted into an uneasy sleep of violent, disturbing dreams, dreams she couldn't quite recall the next morning when sunlight sneaked between the curtains.

Kirsta drank her coffee slowly and nibbled half-heartedly at the cranberry muffins Daphne had left in her little refrigerator. She felt nearly as tired sitting there in the hazy early-morning light as she had the night before. She glanced at her laptop computer and briefcase, still side-by-side on the coffee table. She should probably do some work before going over to the Pattons' house, but hardly had the energy to begin.

118

Kirsta stared at the coffee table for a long moment, frowning. A shudder passed through her, but she forced the growing knot of fear back. The vase and its rose had been there yesterday when she'd gone to dinner, she was sure of it. And she hadn't moved it. The questions began again, unbidden. How, then did it come to be shattered more than ten feet across the room? A dark thought crossed her mind — could someone else have been in the cabin with them last night, someone who didn't want to see them in the throes of passion?

This last thought chilled her more than the others. A picture of David's face leapt to her mind, contorted with anger and uncontrolled violence. But that was impossible — she remembered locking the doors before she left for dinner, and she'd had to unlock the front door to let herself and Sean in after dinner. David didn't even know where she was.

But she rose and checked the windows quickly. None of the panes were broken, none of the screens appeared tampered with. Kirsta drew a deep breath and forced herself to relax. She'd long ago stopped believing in the bogey-man, but nobody else could possibly have been in there. There was some other rational explanation, one she just hadn't considered yet.

Kirsta shook her head in confusion and grabbed her sketch pad and a charcoal pencil. Maybe a stroll around the plantation would clear her thoughts — or at least distract her from her problems. Sketching always relaxed her when she was tense; the concentration distracted her from troubling things. Kirsta quickly dressed in denim shorts and a yellow pullover shirt, and stepped into her sandals. The temperature was already rising, and the humidity was at least as high as it had been the night before. She'd enjoy the fresh air before the day became unbearable, and hope the Pattons' house was air conditioned.

Kirsta wandered aimlessly along the flagstone path toward the house, stopping occasionally to begin a rough sketch. She sat on the stone bench by the pond, watching the ducks paddle through the marsh grasses. The rising sun began to warm her face, and beads of perspiration crawled along her temples.

After a while, Kirsta decided to find someplace with more shade. She stood and looked around her for a spot she'd find comfortable. A bluebird flew past her toward the topiary maze, it's rust-colored breast bright in the shadows. Kirsta recalled Sean's comments about an abandoned barn behind the maze, and decided to investigate. She left the path, and headed in that direction.

As she rounded the corner of the tall hedges outlining the maze, Kirsta caught sight of some rough boards, nearly hidden by tendrils of climbing vines and weeds. That had to be the remains of the barn. She thrashed further through the tall grasses, slapping at mosquitos as she went. Several trees protected the area from the morning sun, and Kirsta smiled, sure she'd find both shade and some interesting subjects to sketch.

The walk over was a struggle through briars and waist-high spears of grass, but on closer inspection, her suspicions proved true. The huge wooden barn had been almost completely buried beneath twisted masses of leaves and interlacing vines. She ran her hand along the rough, weathered grey timbers. The boards appeared structurally sound, and no part of the building had collapsed or crumbled, but Kirsta knew better than to go inside. No matter how safe it looked, it could be hiding countless pitfalls and dangers. Her parents had warned her over and over about going into abandoned buildings when she was a child, especially if nobody knew where she was.

Kirsta backed away for a better perspective and stood in a small patch of sunlight, squinting at the old boards. She thought she'd just catch her breath for a moment, then find a good place to sit and draw. She was just so dreadfully warm, she could hardly think straight. The barn doors had fallen off or been removed, and the dark opening shimmered in the heat as she stared. She remembered her dream from two nights before, the sensual dream of the man with dark eyes and untrimmed beard who took her in the hayloft. Her thighs ached as she felt again his rough whiskers against her soft flesh.

Kirsta's eyes felt tired and heavy, but she couldn't seem to blink. The darkness looked so cool and comforting; it almost seemed to beckon her inside. She found herself listening for something, but she didn't know what. The noises of the crickets and birds chirping to one another all around her faded away in the hazy light, and yet her senses seemed almost unnaturally acute. She felt as though her skin were on fire, from the inside. Kirsta stood rock-still, listening, watching, waiting. But she had no idea what she waited for.

Suddenly, Kirsta remembered Daphne's conversation at dinner last night. When she'd told the story of Andrew Lucas, the Yankee soldier who'd been hanged at Lost Oaks, she'd mentioned this very barn as the place where he'd raped the mistress of the plantation. And Sean had said his great-great grandfather had imprisoned his wife here. Could it be the same woman? It was too cruel to believe.

And it seemed impossible for this old building to hold any such grim memories, with the morning sun flickering around it and shadows dancing gently along the sturdy boards. No place in the world could be as welcoming as this antique barn; no violence could ever happen here. This was a place of peace and love, of ecstacy and fulfillment.

Then Kirsta recalled her daydream near the pond. When was that? Days ago? Months ago? It seemed a lifetime ago in this heat, this buzzing haze inside her head. She tried to focus. This barn was where she'd felt the exultation of desire, before those terrible wrong hands encircled her throat. This barn was the center of a different kind of maze, something told her; it held answers to puzzles. She knew she must go inside now. Something — someone was waiting for her. She took one hesitant step forward, then another.

The specks of light flickering between the leaves seemed to separate from the shadows and dance before her eyes like pale fireflies or will o' the wisps. Kirsta felt herself drift into the light. Her arms and legs floated deliciously in the warmth of the morning and the soft buzzing inside her head grew louder, sounded like voices whispering or chanting all around her. She felt as though someone — a woman? — were trying to speak to her over the voices, but she couldn't understand what the voice was saying.

She thought she felt someone touch her hand, put something into the palm. She was too warm, too tired to look down. She kept her eyes focused on the bright darkness of the doorway before her, on the voices all around her.

Suddenly, a black fox leaped through the open barn door past her to disappear into the thick grass. With a violent effort, Kirsta jerked herself backward, away from the barn. She'd been almost inside the door. Suddenly, the birds began singing again and the crickets and cicadas buzzed around her as they had before. What had possessed her to think she should go inside a dangerous place like that? The word possess stood out in her mind. That's how she'd felt — possessed, by something or someone, who had wanted her to enter the barn. But why? What was happening to her?

As Kirsta stood in the grass, trying to focus her thoughts, she realized she held something. Glancing down, she saw a piece of soft stone in her hand; one edge was newly worn away. Confused, Kirsta looked around to see where it might have come from. Her eyes rested on the wide boards before her. Scratched onto the rough surface in large, awkward letters were the words:
KIRSTA GO HOME.

CHAPTER THIRTEEN

Kirsta dropped the rock as though it had burned her hand. She spun around and looked wildly about. She had the feeling someone was watching her, but saw no one. She must get a grip on her emotions. The fact that she'd half fallen asleep and written this message to herself only proved how much she needed to put the past few days into perspective — and get some sleep.

She rubbed her eyes and ran her fingers through her hair, trying to calm herself. But the uneasy feeling of not being alone stayed with her. It must be this place. She had to get away from this decrepit old barn as quickly as possible; something about it was affecting her strangely. She hurried back through the high grasses to the main house, then around the house to the front veranda. Collapsing onto the shaded front steps, Kirsta leaned back against one of the tall wooden supports. She closed her eyes, willing her breathing to slow.

The rippling shadows cooled her, allowed her tortured breathing to calm as she tried to rationalize the bizarre feelings she'd experienced a few moments ago near the barn. She'd been overheated, of course, and still hadn't gotten a good night's sleep. Her emotions were raw from the break-up with David and she'd been inundated the past few days with facts and legends about this fascinating, beautiful region, not to mention her strange experience at the chapel yesterday. No wonder she was on edge and ripe for self-delusion. She'd have to get some rest soon so she could sort out what was actually happening around her and what she was manufacturing in her own mind.

As Kirsta opened her eyes again, her attention was drawn to the huge live oak in the center of the front lawn. Tiny slivers of sunlight sparkled through the grass around it like golden coins, and its branches reached out in beautiful irregular arcs. A perfect subject for her sketchbook. Kirsta lifted the pad and charcoal slowly, still feeling a bit light-headed. But she began drawing quickly, her hand moving almost of its own accord around the rough paper. Kirsta barely glanced down as she immersed herself in the angles and textures of the ancient tree. She quickly turned the page and began another drawing without even looking at the first.

Kirsta lost all sense of time and place, so focused was she on her sketching. Sometime later, she vaguely heard the grandfather clock chime in the McLeod's living room. The sound seemed to come from a vast distance, breaking into her reverie. Looking at her watch, Kirsta was amazed to see the hands overlapping just below the eleven. Nearly three hours had passed since she'd left the cabin. It seemed like just over an hour. Where had the time gone?

Kirsta rose from the porch steps stiffly. She wasn't sure how long she'd sat there, but her head was clearer now, and she felt ready, even eager, to tackle some research work, despite the muggy weather. She closed her sketchbook and headed back to the guest house. She had plenty of time to shower and grab a light lunch — maybe some fruit and yogurt — before heading over to the Pattons' house.

The Pattons' yellow house, much smaller than Lost Oaks, was nearly hidden by the honeysuckles and wild rose bushes that clustered protectively around it. Kirsta parked beneath the branches of an old dogwood tree so the sun wouldn't heat up the car too much, and walked up the gravel drive. Two rattan rockers with matching cushions sat on the screened-in porch, and a light breeze tinkled through ceramic butterflies hanging from nylon threads. This house looked more homey, even more friendly than the main house at Lost Oaks, but Kirsta felt none of the sense of familiarity she'd felt on first sight of the McLeod's house.

Etta opened the door before Kirsta had a chance to ring the bell. A charcoal-grey cat rubbed itself against the old woman's ankles, peering at Kirsta suspiciously from behind its mistress.

"So glad to see you," Etta smiled, stepping aside to usher Kirsta in. "Hope you don't mind cats; Indigo here always has to greet our visitors. Then she'll ignore you."

A tremor crawled across Kirsta's flesh at the mention of the cat's name. Indigo. Why did that sound so disturbingly familiar? Kirsta knew very few people who owned cats; she was sure she'd never heard the name before.

Before Kirsta could respond, however, Etta continued. "Henry's in the living room. But I made some mint iced tea this morning, if you'd like a glass before we get started. My mama always said it's a sin to work before relaxing and cooling off a bit."

"That sounds wonderful." Kirsta followed her hostess through the hallway into the kitchen. She stooped to stroke the soft dark fur as the cat purred loudly. "Where did you ever come up with such an unusual name for your cat?"

Etta shrugged. "I don't know. Henry named her, I think. She's really his cat. Showed up on our doorstep about four or five months ago. Let's see … that's right, it was January first, to be exact. She's been here ever since. You must be a real cat person — she usually won't let strangers touch her."

January first. That was the night Kirsta had run from David's apartment, never to return. She felt the heat press in on her for a moment. Coincidences, so many coincidences. Too many? If she were a more superstitious person, Kirsta thought … Then she shook her head and rose. Suddenly very thirsty, she gratefully accepted the glass of tea from Etta.

They walked through an archway into a large, airy living room. The furnishings of the Pattons' house were much more serviceable than those in Sean McLeod's home. The screened windows were wide open, but ceiling fans turned slowly in both the living room and kitchen, creating a comfortable breeze.

Henry sat on a heavy green sofa against the far wall, surrounded by stacks of old magazines, folders and scrapbooks on the floor and the coffee table in front of him. Some of the papers looked as though the slightest touch would cause them to crumble to dust. He glanced up as they entered, and rose, knocking a pile of magazines over. Ignoring the small avalanche, he beckoned to the women.

"Bring some of that tea over here, Etta, before I dry up and blow away. I'm bone dry."

"I've already got one for you. Just you hush up now." Etta handed her brother a tall glass, and they stood in comfortable silence for a moment, sipping beneath the low, rhythmic hum of the overhead fan.

The living room opened into a small office space, where every available surface was covered with mounds of papers and books. Kirsta's enthusiasm flagged a bit as she looked around. It was obvious Henry couldn't possibly find anything in this confused mess of paper. On the other hand, it would be rude to leave too soon. She shrugged mentally, resigning herself to a wasted afternoon of idle chit-chat and half-remembered family stories, most of which she would be unable to use in her research.

Etta patted the sofa beside her as she sank onto one of the cushions. "Sit down, dear, and tell us about your visit so far."

Kirsta sat. "What would you like to know?"

She noticed that Etta and Henry exchanged a brief look. Then Henry cleared his throat softly and smiled at Kirsta. "Truth is, we were wonderin' whether anything ... unusual's been goin' on over there lately."

Kirsta was confused. "Unusual? In what way?"

"Just strange, that's all." Henry's smile faded. "Something that might have scared you a little. Something to do with Sean?"

Kirsta sat back, startled. How could they possibly know about the things that had been happening, the way Sean had run from her room the night before? She realized that was impossible, unless Sean himself had told them, and she was sure that hadn't happened. On the other hand, if they knew something, why would they ask her?

"I'm not sure what you're talking about," she said cautiously.

Etta sighed and sipped her tea. Finally she said, "This is ridiculous, Henry. Let's just be honest and come out with it."

"All right," he said, "that's probably best. Truth is, we've been worryin' about Sean our own selves lately. The boy's got some problems, and we're concerned about him."

Etta nodded vigorously. "He's been acting a bit ... peculiar this past month or so. Started right around the beginning of April, as I recall."

Kirsta frowned. April first was the day her travel agent had first told her about Lost Oaks, but there couldn't be any connection. "What started?" she asked.

"Well, he seemed to change," Henry answered. "He's always been a quiet boy, a little moody, especially after the accident. You know about the accident with his wife and Andy?"

"Yes, a little," Kirsta admitted, cringing inwardly at the mention of Sean's lost love.

She felt a bit embarrassed by the conversation and thought she should change the subject. She glanced around the room, as if that would help her find a new topic. She wasn't at all sure she wanted to hear what the Pattons had to tell her. This was Sean's private business.

On the other hand, anything about Sean fascinated her. She couldn't stop thinking about him, and ached to learn anything and everything people had to say about him. Before she had a chance to respond further, Etta jumped in.

"We both noticed how withdrawn Sean became after Edwina and Andy died," she said, "and we promised Daphne we'd try to help him get over the loss. We began spending as much time as possible with him — inviting him for dinner, meeting him for lunch, stopping by Lost Oaks as if we just happened to be in the neighborhood. I don't think he was fooled, though."

Henry snorted. "That wouldn't fool anybody. Place is so off the beaten track, you'd have to be crazy to be in that neighborhood accidently."

"Anyway," Etta continued with a stern glance at her brother, "we noticed that Sean acted oddly when we were at the plantation. Sometimes, he'd hardly speak, and then other times, he acted as if he barely knew us."

"It was real weird," Henry agreed. "But even weirder was what I found in his room last night when we were over for dinner."

Kirsta felt a cold creep into her spine. She didn't want to ask, but heard herself say, "What did you find?"

"Now, understand, I don't normally go creepin" around in peoples' private business," Henry began. "But last night, while we were waitin' on you, Daphne couldn't find the phone book and asked me to see if Sean had left it in his room. He has his own phone in there. Anyway, when I went up, I saw some photos all cut up into little pieces and scattered around the floor."

"Tell her what they were pictures of," urged Etta. Kirsta wanted to stop them, but couldn't find her voice.

"Well, I tried to piece them together," Henry continued, "but I couldn't figure out much except they were copies of old photos and paintings — real old, like the middle of the last century."

Kirsta heard a tinkling noise, and realized her ice tea glass was trembling in her hand. She placed it on the coffee table, careful not to spill any. She stared at the beads of condensation trickling slowly down the sides.

"Why would he do that?" she asked, her voice steadier than she expected it to be.

"I don't know," Henry said. "Unless it has something to do with the ghost."

Kirsta glanced up quickly, hoping to see him grinning at her mischievously. But his face was grim.

"Henry." Etta's voice was stern. "No need to scare the poor girl."

"I'm not tryin' to scare her," Henry said, then turned back to Kirsta. "No matter what the boy claims," he said quietly, "the ghost is real. I've seen it my own self."

"You saw the ghost of Lost Oaks?" Kirsta whispered.

Etta sighed. "Henry's always been interested in old legends and tall tales. It's made him a little superstitious."

He shrugged. "At least, I think I saw it. Couple weeks ago, just after closin' time at the station. I'd promised Daphne I'd drop some bread off, and couldn't get away earlier. She and I were jawin' on the veranda there, and she told me you'd made reservations. She was all excited and makin' plans about what she needed to do before you got there."

Kirsta smiled a little, picturing Daphne's nervous excitement at the prospect of their first guest.

"She told me Sean had just gotten home, and to tell the truth, he wasn't all that keen on the idea of rentin' the cabin to strangers. Anyways, after she said goodnight, I glanced around and saw something by that big old live oak tree right in the middle of the front lawn. The more I stared, the more it looked like a man, hangin' by the neck from one of them big branches."

Kirsta gasped, remembering her strange vision two days earlier, just before she'd become lost in Witchman's Woods.

Henry continued. "I rubbed my eyes and looked away, and it was gone. But I know what I saw — it's no damned dream or hallucination — no matter what anybody says."

He looked meaningfully at Etta, who blushed and cleared her throat. They both looked at Kirsta expectantly.

She wondered whether to tell them the things that had happened to her the past few days. But what had happened? she asked herself. Just a few incidents of delusions produced by too little sleep, an overactive imagination and emotional upheaval. Let's face it, there was nothing to tell, though she felt stomach clench at the thought of Henry seeing the same thing she'd seen in Witchman's Woods.

Kirsta forced a smile. "I appreciate your telling me this," she said, "but I haven't seen anything like that. I will keep my eyes open, though. And I'll be sure to let you know if anything strange happens."

Etta and Henry exchanged another look and he shrugged. "That's good, you do that. Then we might's well get on to the business at hand."

"Maybe we should move out to the back porch, Henry," Etta said, looking at Kirsta. "I think our guest looks a bit peaked from the heat."

Kirsta smiled gratefully. "I could use a little fresh air."

As they stood, Henry pulled some books off an armchair nearby, and Kirsta winced to see a few brown-edged pages slide from one. He picked up a packet of crumbling envelopes, tied with a ribbon that looked as if it might have been green at one time. He handled the antique papers roughly, as though they'd just been written and held no importance to anyone.

"I found some old letters in one of those cupboards," he said, motioning for Kirsta to walk through the kitchen. "I knew there'd be something besides rust flakes and dust puppies in one of them old drawers."

They went out the back door and sat in white wicker rockers on the back porch. Morning-glory vines clogged the trellis, so that most of the wide porch was in shade. Hummingbirds and bees droned softly at the blossoms.

"Let her look at the letters, Henry," Etta said quietly. "She should read them for herself." He handed the packet to Kirsta.

"Who wrote them?" she asked.

"Lots of people," Henry answered. "But the important thing is, they were written to Sean's great-grandpa, Owen McLeod. He's the son of the woman Daphne was tellin' you about last night."

"Woman?" Kirsta tried to recall the conversation of the night before. "The one who was raped by the Yankee soldier?"

"That's the one." Etta nodded. "Only it looks like maybe she was a bit more of a participant than everybody thought."

"Are you suggesting she wasn't raped?"

"Well, read them for yourself." Etta gestured at the packet, and Kirsta untied the frayed ribbon carefully.

"I put the important ones on top," Etta said. "You can read the others if you like, but those first three are from Owen's aunt in New Orleans. This aunt was his mother's only sister. Apparently, young Owen had a falling out with his daddy, David McLeod, when Owen's mother died. He was very young — no more than twelve — when it happened. He must have blamed his father somehow for his mother's death. As you'll see, there was no love lost between the aunt and David McLeod."

David, Kirsta thought. Was there no end to these strange coincidences? She opened the first envelope. "Dearest nephew," it began, "I read with sympathy your recent letter. I can hardly bear the thought of your desperate anguish at this terrible loss. If I hadn't this injury to my knee, I'd have certainly been up to attend the funeral and bring you back to New Orleans with me. It won't be long now, the doctor says — you must be patient.

"Your father has not told you the entire truth, I'm afraid. You may indeed suspect his complicity in your poor mother's death, but there will never be proof, so you must put aside these speculations. They will prove more harm than good to you. There are things you should know, but these are not to be written of in letters, where prying eyes can find them. When we are together again, my darling boy, I will speak, though the subject be difficult and the telling painful."

The second letter was dated nearly six months after the first. The paper the letter was on had several irregular creases, as though the letter had been crumpled and then straightened. There was no postmark on the envelope, just the handwritten words: "Master Owen McLeod, Personal." The letter had been sealed with red sealing wax.

"My sweet Owen," it began, "You could be right in suspecting your father is intercepting your mail. You must try at all costs to get down here. This infection keeps me bound to my bed, often delirious with fevers. I know your father forbids our communication, but I fear for your safety if you remain there longer. I remember times your mother ran to me for asylum from him. I've always felt something about the area around Lost Oaks causes exaggerations in people — good is better, bad is worse. Maybe the Indians were right to avoid the place.

But I could never convince your poor mother to remain here with me when she came. I told her of my fears, but she turned a deaf ear. I think your father had some strange hold over her. He does have a charisma. But now your reports of his nocturnal wanderings through the house, calling to your dead mother, frighten me. I worry his sanity may be slipping.

"No matter what he says, believe me when I say your mother was never a murderess. She could not have killed poor Andrew Lucas nor had him killed. Nor was she a harlot. She was a fine, beautiful woman. But this subject is not fit for paper. It can only be spoken, in words that are gone as soon as they leave the lips. You must be told." The letter was signed "Auntie."

Kirsta opened the next letter, a growing sense of dread creeping over her. She sipped her tea and slapped at a mosquito, wishing now she'd stayed inside. At least in there a fan kept the air moving.

This letter was dated a week after the previous one, in a different hand — bolder, masculine. The letter was very brief, expressing regret that Owen's aunt had died peacefully in her sleep, during David McLeod's visit with her. Her fever had diminished, and she was slowly gaining strength, but obviously her heart had been affected, and had given out suddenly during their private conference. She had left Owen a bit of money and some jewelry.

Kirsta put the letter down. "I'm not sure I understand all this," she said after a moment. "I can see it's possible that Owen's mother was having an affair with Andrew Lucas, but other things are also possible. I don't really see how you came to that conclusion."

"Rumor," Henry said simply.

"Rumor?"

"Well, I wanted to show you the letters first — just the facts, you might say. Now for the other stuff. You know how families are, they tell stories to each other about each other all the time. Well, the stories passed down about Owen's mama go something like this: her parents married her off to David McLeod as partial repayment of a debt they owed him. He was definitely a charmer — blond and handsome — but it seems he was also a mite touched, or maybe he drank a bit. Anyway, he had a hell of a temper. Couple of times, she ran home to her folks in New Orleans, but they always sent her back."

Etta broke in. "Against the advice and wishes of her sister, to the aunt's credit. She'd always warned the family about David McLeod, but nobody would listen."

Henry continued. "Then this Yankee fella Lucas hears his wife and son were hurt in an accident back in Memphis, and he deserts his post in Georgia to go home to them. He makes his way to the Allindea area and hides in the old barn at Lost Oaks. Well Owen's mama finds him half-dead out there, and takes pity on him. She brings him food at night, and they end up fallin' in love and … doin' what comes naturally. Unfortunately, David walks in on them one night, and drags the Yankee out. David's screamin' rape and traitor and I don't know what all to high heaven. He has his wife locked in the barn, and takes poor Andrew Lucas off to be executed."

"Without benefit of judge and jury, I suspect," Etta added grimly. "Blood was pretty hot back then against northerners."

Kirsta sat back for a moment, letting the story sink in. The cat rubbed against her legs, then jumped into her lap. She scratched it softly behind the ears.

"That's an amazing story," she said finally. "What was her name — David McLeod's wife, I mean?"

Henry glanced at the cat, purring loudly in Kirsta's lap. "Name's Indigo," he said.

When Kirsta returned to her cabin later that afternoon, she lay back on the bed, a damp washcloth across her forehead. The day had grown very warm, and there was a heaviness in the air that pressed in on her head like a helmet. She needed to sort out all the stories and events concerning Lost Oaks, but found it difficult to think. Rivulets of water trickled down the sides of her head to soak into her pillow, but she remained still, trying to concentrate on what she'd found out that day.

After the Pattons' revelation about Indigo McLeod's death and her possible relationship with the Yankee soldier Andrew Lucas, Henry had grown strangely taciturn, even a bit irritable. Kirsta had the feeling he had more to tell her, but he claimed he was too tired for any more "rumor-mongering." Kirsta had chatted politely with Etta for another half-hour or so, asking about her baking and quilting, but Henry had buried himself in a *National Geographic* magazine and ignored them both.

Kirsta had driven home the long way, past the Allindea cemetery, with its mossy weathered tombstones, many tilted at crazy angles. The stone chapel adjoined the iron fence on one side, and a shaded lawn stretched away on the other. Kirsta had recalled her strange experience in the chapel two days earlier, and slowed the car. It was difficult to believe anything so bizarre could take place in such a tranquil setting.

As Kirsta felt the pillow dampening beneath her, she wondered whether Indigo and David McLeod were buried in the Allindea cemetery. And what about Andrew Lucas? Did they send his remains home — wherever that was — or bury him somewhere around Lost Oaks, too? She made a mental note to check on that.

Footsteps approached the cabin's front porch. Kirsta prayed Daphne wasn't coming down to invite her to dinner. She simply wasn't up to changing her clothes and making polite conversation tonight. She would have to think of some excuse that wouldn't sound too rude.

The footsteps stopped at the bottom of the porch steps, and paused. Kirsta realized she was holding her breath, listening. It seemed a long time before the person outside stepped onto the porch, and when it happened, Kirsta realized it couldn't be Daphne. These steps were heavier, more decisive — a man's steps.

Sean, she thought. Please, God, let me be wrong.

As she whispered this silent prayer, a knock sounded on the door and Sean called her name softly. She moaned softly into her fist. The last thing she wanted right now was to face him after the way he'd run from her room the night before. He surely had his reasons, but Kirsta wasn't ready to hear them. She knew it must have something to do with guilt over his late wife Edwina, and Kirsta realized she'd rather not hear him discuss his passion for another woman.

Then there was the strange, frightening moment when she'd thought he changed. She didn't want to think about that, either, at least not after her afternoon at the Patton's house. Kirsta sighed. Maybe if she didn't answer, he'd think she was out somewhere.

"Are you all right, Kirsta?"

Damn, she thought. Sean had obviously heard her light moan through the thin boards of the wall behind her. She couldn't pretend not to be there.

Kirsta rose slowly, the washcloth dropping to the floor beside the bed. As she bent to pick it up, she noticed Sean's shirt next to it, partially covered by the long dust ruffle. Kirsta grabbed it; obviously this was why he'd come. She quickly ran her fingers through her hair and opened the door. Sean stood on the small porch, a large picnic basket in one hand. He frowned at her, studying her face.

"Are you okay?" he asked again.

"I'm fine, thanks. It's just the heat." Kirsta held the shirt out, trying to be polite and calm. She hoped he didn't notice that her hand trembled slightly.

"This must be what you've come for," she said. "It got covered somehow. I'm sorry I didn't notice it earlier; I would have dropped it off."

Sean looked blankly at the shirt for a moment, then took it from her. "I wondered —" he began, then stopped and looked into Kirsta's eyes. "We need to talk."

Kirsta shook her head. "No, really," she said quickly. "No explanations are necessary. I understand completely. It was just one of those things."

Sean dropped the basket heavily to the porch and grasped her shoulders with both hands. The shirt was still gripped in his right hand, and the cotton collar fluttered against her cheek. Kirsta noticed he wore the same musky cologne she'd smelled the night before.

Sean's hands were surprisingly strong, clutching her arms, and his pale eyes flickered with a dark fire. Kirsta felt panic grip her throat, as she remembered seeing that same look in David's eyes whenever he grew angry with her. She thrust the terrifying memory back. Sean was different, he had to be, she told herself silently.

"But I don't understand," he muttered between clenched teeth. "That's the problem, don't you see? Look, Kirsta, we have to talk about this — I have to talk about this. Or I don't know what might happen."

Kirsta felt her heart stop as his fingers dug into her flesh and his eyes burned into hers. She twisted his hands away with a quick upward thrust of her arms. Fighting an all-too-familiar need for flight, Kirsta backed toward the doorway of the cabin, ready to lock herself inside at the least threat from him. The blood pounded in her ears and her headache throbbed at her temples like fists beating against her skull. She thrust away memories of David Belsen as she tried to regain control of the situation.

"Sean, what's the matter with you?" she gasped.

After a moment, Sean seemed to collapse within himself. The cruel fire faded from his eyes. Then he shook his head. "I'm sorry, Kirsta," he said quietly "but that's exactly the problem. I don't know what happens to me sometimes. Please, give me a chance to explain, to make it up to you."

Kirsta felt her heart warm again as she studied his face closely. He seemed so confused, so vulnerable. She wanted to hold him in her arms and comfort him. She wanted to see the Sean who'd kissed her while they danced at Mistmere.

"I don't know," she began slowly, "There's too much going on here. Maybe we'd better —"

Sean pointed to the basket. "Look, Aunt Daphne packed you a picnic dinner when she realized you'd been gone most of the day. She figured you'd fallen asleep and sent me down here to leave it on the porch for you. I happen to know there's enough food in here for a small army. I wonder if — would you be willing to give me another chance while we try to make a dent in it."

Kirsta wanted to say no. She knew there was something dangerous about this tall dark man before her, this man who'd just squeezed her arms so tightly she could still feel his fingers against her flesh. But there was something else there, too, something that reached into her soul and touched her with warmth and longing. His eyes pleaded with her, and she knew then she couldn't deny him. Not yet, anyway.

"I have to confess I'm a bit hungry," she admitted. "Where should we eat? Inside?" She pointed at the doorway behind her.

Sean shook his head again, and a look flickered across his eyes — anger? fear? Then it was gone again so quickly Kirsta wasn't sure she'd even seen it.

"Let's get away from this place," he said. "Sometimes I feel as if Lost Oaks is smothering me. All that history. There are lots of nice shady spots around Allindea where we can have a picnic. I'll let you decide. We'll just drive around until you see one you like."

Kirsta remembered the grassy lawn beside the old cemetery chapel and mentioned it to him. "I don't know whether anybody would object," she added, "but it looked so cool and comfortable in there under the trees."

"That's a great idea," Sean agreed, grasping the basket and ushering Kirsta off the porch toward his car. "I know the caretaker; in fact, I think he's a distant cousin. I'm sure he won't give us any trouble."

It wasn't trouble from the caretaker I was worried about, thought Kirsta. But she said nothing.

CHAPTER FOURTEEN

David pulled the rusted grey minivan into the parking lot of a truck stop along route sixty-one, just south of Vicksburg, Mississippi. He turned off the motor, but continued to sit behind the wheel for a long time. His whole body ached, every exhausted, cramped muscle crying out for both rest and exercise at the same time. His eyelids felt like sandpaper scraping across his eyeballs each time he blinked.

The sun was still at least an hour from setting, but David knew he had to get some rest. He closed his eyes and tried to remember what had happened during the last twenty-four hours. The daylight time flew past, like a rerun on high speed tape, clear and crisp. He'd found a wooded stream at dawn near a little town along route one called Christmas. He'd immersed himself in the chilly water, and scrubbed hard at his naked flesh with pine branches and marsh grass until he felt raw and clean. He'd enjoyed watching the mists rise off the Mississippi, so he'd continued following route one south along the river until it joined route sixty-one about twenty miles north of Vicksburg.

But the long dark hours before that, the time before he acquired the grey minivan, were less clear. David caught only glimpses at first, until he forced himself to breathe deeply and relax. Then the night exploded into his consciousness like a dark meteor hurtling through his brain.

He saw himself sitting by Mother's grave last night, waiting for her to come back, but she never did. The temperature had dropped sharply after the sun went down, and the wind picked up, sending icy needles through his thin shirt. When he'd finally glanced at his watch, it was well after midnight.

David couldn't believe it; it hadn't even been six o'clock when he'd stopped. Surely, he'd only been in the cemetery for an hour or so. Then he had understood: time was meaningless for someone who'd gone beyond mere humanity. The Avenging Angel had no use for clocks. With fingers stiff and trembling with cold, David had unstrapped the leather band of his watch — the expensive watch Kirsta had given him for his last birthday — and left it there on Mother's grave. It would serve as a symbol only she could understand.

He'd driven south for a long time last night after his visit with Mother, her voice still echoing in his mind as the pavement flew past beneath him. He was still in the white car then, the car that contained the life of the old David Belsen. As the darkness engulfed him, he began to realize that these things, even this David Belsen, held the Avenging Angel captive in the wrong life, like a cocoon traps the emerging butterfly.

He had to find a way to break free, to escape his prison of powerlessness before he could ever be strong enough to show Kirsta how much she really loved him. He drove south through the night. As the square numerals of his dashboard clock showed him that it was almost three in the morning, David had finally found a gas station still open along route sixty-one just south of Lyon. He'd decided to fill the tank, in case he had trouble finding another station before he ran out of gas. He'd pulled next to the self-service pumps and climbed stiffly from the car. His fingers had fumbled with the gas cap before he could get it open, then he'd placed the nozzle into the opening and flipped the lever to start the gasoline flowing.

On the other side of the pumps he'd noticed an old grey minivan. The driver had his back to David, but something about the set of the shoulders, the blond hair, had attracted David's attention. There was something familiar about this man. David had shifted slightly to get a better view without being seen himself, and had peered between the supporting metal posts as the van's driver replaced the gas nozzle.

At first the man hadn't appeared particularly interesting. But as David watched, his vision had seemed to blur for a moment. He'd wiped at his tired eyes with one hand, then looked at the man again. Now each feature, each line and crease, even every pore seemed crystal clear beneath the fluorescent lights. He had only a glimpse before the man turned away again, but it was enough. David stepped back involuntarily, feeling as though his heart had stopped beating. He was looking into his own face.

David heard the hose clunk as the gas stopped flowing, and jerked the nozzle from his tank opening. He quickly replaced the cap as he watched the man with his face pay the attendant through a slit in the front of the glass booth. David pulled bills from his wallet, barely glancing at them in his hurry. As he'd thrust the bills at the attendant, the grey minivan had pulled slowly onto the pavement, heading south.

Diving back into his white car, exhaustion forgotten for the moment, David ignored the gas station attendant's shouts about taking his change. He had to follow the minivan. He hadn't worried about being diverted from his journey to find Kirsta, suspecting this was part of the greater plan. He'd known he was right when he'd gotten close enough to the vehicle to read the license plate: KL1-1NO. It was a sign to the Avenging Angel. "KL", of course, stood for Kirsta Linden. And Kirsta had left on January first, thus "1-1."

But the last two letters were the most significant, he'd gradually realized. The word "NO" obviously meant that Kirsta should never have left him, but that was only the surface meaning. There was another level of meaning in that awful two-letter word, glowing hotly in the beam from his headlights. David understood he must not continue south in his present condition to find Kirsta. He had to shed his old life and start over in a new and better form. And in order to do that, he must destroy the old David Belsen.

The minivan had traveled south for a few miles, then pulled onto a narrow road heading west. The sign said the road led to Rena Lara. David had smiled then, and continued following, sure that he'd done the right thing. The road was narrow and little-used, just the sort of place he'd been looking for.

The minivan had slowed suddenly, and David slowed as well, keeping some distance between them. After another mile or two, the van had pulled over to the side of the road, onto the berm. Confused, David pulled up behind him. Should he get out to see what the problem was, or wait until the man drove on? David's palms had grown sweaty as he tried to figure out what to do. He'd squirmed in an agony of indecision as he heard Mother's voice again, telling him to grow up and act like a man, to make her proud. How, Mother, he'd begged her, how do I do that?

A moment later, the decision had been taken from him. The door of the van had opened, and the driver got out, tucking his keys into the pocket of his worn jeans. David's innards froze as he watched the man walk back along the road toward him. As the blond man entered the glow of his headlights, David squinted. The man was his height and weight, but wasn't his nose much longer than David's, his eyes wider-set, his lips thinner? David had blinked hard and when he'd looked up again, the features had rearranged themselves again into David's face. Yes, he'd been right the first time.

As the man approached, David's fingers slid around the handle of his father's knife. He rolled down his window. The man with David's face had leaned one elbow on the roof of David's car and stood stiffly for a moment before speaking. He bent only slightly at the waist, hardly glancing at David.

"You followin' me, mister?" the familiar stranger had asked, his gravelly voice heavily laced with a southern drawl. He turned his head and spat into the road next to the front tire.

Instead of answering, David had thrust his right hand through the window, plunging the knife into the man's belly, until only the handle protruded. He gave it a sharp twist. The man had backed away a couple of paces, a look of almost comic surprise on his face, and tried to pull the knife out. But David forced open his car door, knocking the man to the ground. Then he grabbed the knife himself and set to work.

Some time later, David had gotten the man into his car, propping the corpse behind the wheel. He'd removed the gas cap and repeatedly stuffed several shirts into the small opening with a stick so that they were soaked with gasoline. These he then tucked around the stranger, leaving a dry shirt dangling from the door. After he'd shut the car door, David realized he'd left the minivan's keys in the pocket of the man's jeans. With a grimace, he leaned into the open window. The strong gasoline fumes mingling with the stench of blood and death nearly made him retch, but David had gritted his teeth and jammed his hand into the man's pocket, grabbing the keychain. It was sticky with drying blood.

When he'd reached across the man's body to get his map of Louisiana, his father's hunting knife and the bag containing the silver combs he'd bought for Kirsta, David had felt the stranger's blood soaking into the front of his shirt. Only then had he realized he was covered in blood. No matter, he thought, he was shedding this whole life — he might as well start with these clothes.

David had checked the back of the van to see whether the driver had left a change of clothes. He'd found a duffel bag, cooking equipment and a sleeping bag. Apparently, the man had been planning to spend some time in the vehicle. Good, thought David. Then nobody would be looking for him.

David carefully put his wallet, the map, knife and combs in the glove drawer of the minivan and started on the engine. He pulled forward another twenty yards or so, leaving the engine running while he undressed. He emerged from the van naked, and carried his clothes back to the little white car. He pulled a lighter from his pants pocket and stuffed the soiled clothes into the open window.

Then David had stepped away from the car containing his life and his past — and the dead body that was now David Belsen — and flicked the wheel of the lighter. He touched the flame to the shirt still dangling from the car door, and ran toward the van. As he'd reached the door, he turned to see his life explode in flame. Even from this distance, he could feel the searing heat. David had raised his face to the dark, moonless sky and howled as he felt the power enter him.

He'd watched the car burn, trying to glimpse his own cremation within, but the flames quickly obscured the blackened figure in the driver's seat. As black smoke rose like a huge bird into the blacker night sky, David had imagined the elements of his past incinerating: the books from classes he'd taken and classes he'd taught, cassette tapes, clothes. The trivial minutiae that had never really defined him, ceased now to matter at all.

David Belsen, who had been abandoned by his mother and his lover, existed no longer. This moment was the birth of a new David, whose mother would always be proud of him, and whose woman would love him forever. He would keep the name David, which held connotations of Biblical strength and holiness and honor. But Belsen was a weak name, the name of a father who left nothing of himself behind except a book and a knife. David would find another name to make himself complete. Until then, he would simply be David.

He climbed behind the wheel of the minivan, still naked, and pulled back onto the road. He savored the feel of the rough fabric against his back and buttocks. Nobody had passed in either direction since he'd turned onto this road, so he wasn't worried that the car would be found before it burned itself out. In any case, if anybody from Pennsylvania were looking for him, they'd find his corpse. His power was nearly complete.

After a while, the small road had ended at the little town of Rena Lara. Route one headed south, so David had decided to follow it until he found a place to clean himself. He drove beneath streetlights through the centers of towns, never worrying once about anyone bothering him. He'd known he was invincible, and kept his windows wide open to feel the chill night air against his sticky skin. When he'd found the town of Christmas, he'd known it was time to look for a place to clean up. And after he'd baptized himself in the little stream, he'd taken some jeans and a tee shirt from the large duffel bag in the back of the van. They had fit him perfectly, as he'd known they would. After all, they were David Belsen's clothes.

A rap at the van's window startled David into consciousness. His hand twitched to the right, reaching for the hunting knife beside him; too late, he remembered putting it into the glove drawer with the map and silver combs. Stiff muscles creaked in his neck as he turned his head to the left. He squinted his eyes against the bright sunlight.

A squat, middle-aged woman peered in the window at him. Her pale eyes were magnified by thick glasses and her lips protruded in a worried pout, giving her a strong fishy appearance. David was immediately repelled. He didn't want to open the window, but she waggled her finger at him, indicating he should roll it down. David started the engine and pressed the button, lowering the glass a few inches.

"You okay?" the woman asked, her voice hoarse and too loud.

David didn't answer immediately, and she asked it again, speaking very slowly, as though he were an imbecile.

"Are ... you ... okay?"

"Fine," David muttered.

"Wally and I are parked right there," she pointed to a motor home two spaces away. "We saw you pull in a couple minutes ago, and it looked like you passed out. I got worried. You still don't look so good."

"I'm fine," David repeated. "Just tired, that's all." He looked away, trying to end the conversation without drawing too much attention to himself. However, his mind was whirling. A couple of minutes? Is that all the longer he'd been parked here? It seemed like hours. His own change was obviously affecting even the passage of time.

Instead of leaving, the woman only moved closer, practically pressing her fish-face against the glass.

"You know, heart attacks are one of the biggest causes of highway accidents," she continued. "Wally and me saw a guy having a heart attack on I-eighty one time. His car was weaving across the road so much, we thought he was drunk at first. When we figured out what was wrong, we called the police on the CB. Saved his life," she finished proudly.

David sighed. "That's great," he said, turning off the engine again. "I'm just a little tired and hungry. I was about to get something to eat in there." He started to open the door.

"Well, that's good," the woman said, backing away. "You got to keep alert, you know."

Just then, a man's voice bellowed from behind her. "Marge, are you just gonna flap your damn gums all day, or are we gonna try to make Memphis by dark?"

David felt a twinge of pleasure as Marge flushed in embarrassment and hurried back to the waiting Wally. He watched the motor home pull away, then opened the door wider. He was already here, so he might as well go inside and grab a sandwich and some coffee.

After the bright sunlight outside, the interior of the truck stop seemed dark and cavernous. The large front portion housed the cash register and a gift/news/souvenir stand. Confederate flags of all sizes were either tacked to the walls or drooping from thin wooden dowels. Girlie magazines topped the magazine racks, their immodest covers delicately hidden by brown wrappers. Hundreds of bells, thimbles, mugs and ashtrays all displayed either the ever-present Confederate flag or some painting depicting the quintessential Mississippi, often a Gone-With-the-Wind-type plantation scene.

David felt claustrophobic and confused amid the clutter. The place seemed noisy and hectic, though very few patrons actually wandered the narrow aisles. As he ducked sideways to avoid colliding with a rack of promotional beach towels, David backed into something that fell to the floor with a clatter. It sounded like canon fire to him, and he whirled, expecting someone to come running to see what he'd done. But nobody seemed to notice; even the gum-popping blonde at the cash register hardly glanced up.

David looked behind him. A plastic elephant's foot lay sideways on the floor, ten or fifteen souvenir canes and walking sticks poking from its opening like snakes escaping a log. David righted the ridiculous container and began replacing its contents. Suddenly he stopped. In his hand he grasped a polished black cane topped with a silver globe. He straightened slowly, bringing the cane closer to his face. It was beautiful, he thought, completely out-of-place in this tacky gift shop. David cupped the globe in his palm, and tapped the end of the cane lightly against the linoleum. It was the perfect height for him. He'd always wanted a cane like this.

He moved to the opposite wall, where he examined himself in a long, narrow mirror. The glass was tinted some pink or sepia color, lending David the look of an old photo or daguerreotype. He straightened his shoulders and leaned one hand lightly on the head of the cane. He smiled. All he needed now, he thought, was a white summer suit and hat.

He carried the cane to the cash register, his hunger momentarily forgotten in his quest to make the treasure his. He paid the cashier and hurried out to the waiting van, laying the cane gently across the passenger's seat, where he could see it as he drove south.

CHAPTER FIFTEEN

As Sean drove his red sports car along the road toward Allindea, Kirsta watched him from the corners of her eyes. He said very little, apparently concentrating on driving, though they passed very few other cars. The road seemed nearly empty. Kirsta was sure the chapel and cemetery would be deserted as well. They would be alone for their picnic.

Kirsta wondered whether she was being foolish, letting herself give Sean one more chance to chip through the wall she'd built around her heart. She didn't want to give another man a chance to hurt her the way David had. Surely, Sean could never do anything so cruel. But in the same moment, she recalled his roughness the night before and the way his fingers bruised her arms just a few minutes ago.

And now she was letting him drive her to a secluded spot for a picnic. Kirsta suddenly shuddered slightly at the irony of picnicking near a cemetery, especially with someone who'd made threatening gestures. What ever had made her suggest it? She wished she knew the area better, and could have made a more appropriate suggestion.

In a few minutes, Sean pulled the car onto gravel behind the cemetery. The sun hung low, casting hazy golden beams through the branches of the trees as he spread a blanket on the grass and motioned for Kirsta to sit. Crickets chirped softly in the weeds growing between the wrought iron fence posts behind them. Kirsta breathed deeply, inhaling the sweetness of the evening air.

Sean opened the large wicker basket and began removing the contents: two foil-wrapped halves of chicken, fragrant with the odors of pungent herbs and spices; a plastic container of wild rice and mandarin oranges; another container of marinated green beans; a large piece of chocolate torte — and a bottle of Fruit de Coeur.

When Sean put down place settings for two, including wine glasses, Kirsta couldn't help grinning. "So this dinner for two was a last-minute brain-storm, huh?"

He grinned back, and Kirsta was startled by the almost childlike joy on his face. She saw none of the brooding, haunted look she'd come to find so familiar back at Lost Oaks.

"Okay," he admitted, "I have to confess that when Aunt Daphne asked me to deliver the dinner, I was hoping you'd invite me to join you. But, I think she had the same idea, because I saw her sneak a second wine glass in the basket when she thought I wasn't looking."

Sean pulled the cork from the wine bottle and handed it to Kirsta as he served heaping portions of food onto the two plates. She hesitated a moment, remembering the last time she'd drunk it, but everything felt different this evening ... right, somehow. She ignored the unpleasant memories and poured the wine into their glasses.

As they ate, the golden shadows lengthened and the calls of the birds changed from busy daytime chatter to the melancholy trills and warbles signaling the coming darkness. Kirsta watched Sean carefully, but saw no sign of the tension she'd thought was a natural part of his demeanor. Even his movements — gestures, facial expressions — were more fluid, less anxious. Kirsta leaned back against the trunk of a tree and began to relax.

"This was a wonderful idea," she murmured over the rim of her wine glass. "I don't think I've ever felt so peaceful — or at least not for a long time."

"Me too."

Sean offered her a piece of the torte, but Kirsta groaned dramatically and waved it away, patting her stomach to show how full she was. He shrugged.

"You know," he continued, "I've always loved Lost Oaks — it's my family's home, and I grew up there. But lately, well, I think I'm happier when I'm away."

Kirsta stretched. "Actually, I've noticed that. But I don't think it's really so surprising, do you? Considering everything."

"What do you mean, 'considering everything?'"

Kirsta hesitated, but felt so comfortable with Sean at that moment — even more comfortable than she had the night they'd danced at Mistmere — she knew she could say anything to him.

"Well, let's face it, you're obviously still affected by your wife's and son's deaths. It's a terrible trauma to lose people you love that much. And the

house at Lost Oaks is a constant reminder of your joys when they were alive —
and therefore, of your grief."

He was silent for a long time. Kirsta began to wonder whether she'd gone
too far.

"Is that what Aunt Daphne told you? That my life with Edwina and Andy
was joyful?"

"Well, not in so many words, I suppose. But she implied that you and
Edwina were so wrapped up in each other that you lost contact with most of
your family. Deep love has that effect on people sometimes."

Kirsta felt a sudden sharp ache deep inside, and wished she'd known a
passion like that, too. For the first time, she was startled to realize she'd never
experienced complete and total love for another person.

"I suppose it must have looked like that to other people," he mused,
pulling a pink flower from the grass and rolling the stem between his fingers.
The sinking sun shone in Sean's eyes as he looked at her, and they glowed an
eerie orange. Unsettled, Kirsta looked away.

"The truth is much different," he said. "At first, I suppose I thought I loved
Edwina. She was sophisticated, elegant, the perfect hostess to the kind of
clientele I wanted to entertain. But Edwina had another side, a side I never
saw until after the wedding."

He stopped speaking and lay back on the blanket, his head near Kirsta's
shoulder. He absently pulled the petals off the pink flower as he resumed.

"Edwina had a vicious streak, and a tongue to match," he said. "She knew
just where to cast her barbs to do the most damage, and shot straight and
deadly when she wanted to hurt someone. Of course, I was her target most
often, being the most convenient. I stopped inviting people over for fear she'd
turn on them. But that made it even worse."

"How?"

"I was gone more often then, and Edwina became jealous of my job,
accused me of cheating on her. I stayed home as much as possible, but we
needed some kind of income. I refused to live on my father's money unless I
became desperate. I tried to be a good husband to Edwina, to make her happy.
But she grew more and more distant. Maybe I should have realized it wasn't
my fault, that she had deeper problems, but I didn't, not then. Not until it was
too late.

"Edwina had been married for a short time once before. Andy was her
child from that marriage. About two years after she and I were married, Andy
came to live with us — he was about four then. Something seemed to snap in

Edwina. I think she couldn't stand not being the center of my world anymore. The doctors called it schizophrenia and said she should be institutionalized. Whatever it was, I turned my business over to someone else while I stayed at home until I could find a place for her. I was afraid for Andy, to tell the truth."

"Did she ever … hurt him?"

When he shook his head, a lock of hair fell across his forehead. Kirsta wanted to brush it away, but couldn't risk disturbing him. She waited, and finally he began again.

"I don't think she ever hurt him, not physically, but she never paid attention to him, either. She just lost interest in him as soon as we brought him home from the airport. She simply ignored him when he cried, as though she couldn't even hear him. It nearly drove me crazy, too, to think she was actually able to tune him out completely. I tried to befriend him, but he never warmed up to me at all, just wanted to be with his mom.

"Anyway, somehow Edwina found out about the place I'd found for her, a home for disturbed people down near Baton Rouge. The day before I was supposed to take her there, she jumped on a plane with Andy, and headed up toward Memphis, where her parents still lived. I don't know what she planned to do once she got there. But I never found out, because the plane crashed into the Mississippi during a freak blizzard."

He turned toward her, leaning on one elbow, and in the dim purple glow — all that remained of the sunset — he touched Kirsta's lips gently with one finger. She trembled at the sensation.

"So you see," he said sadly, "my memories of Edwina aren't exactly what you'd call joyous. In fact, I still cringe whenever her name is mentioned — more from the time she was here than the fact that she isn't anymore. But I've missed Andy more than I'd ever have expected, considering how he felt about me."

"So that's why you don't like to talk about her," Kirsta said, amazed by his revelation. "It brings back all those awful times. That's why you seem so tense sometimes. And here I thought —" she stopped, unsure how much to say.

"You thought I missed her," he said, his finger trailing down her chin to her throat, "and couldn't stand the thought of replacing her with someone else."

"But that's not why I'm always tense these days," he continued, his voice rougher now, almost a whisper. "It's because sometimes I do things I wouldn't normally do, things that I'm not even thinking about doing. It's as though someone else is doing them, someone else inside me. I know it sounds crazy, but that feeling of being two people has been with me for several months now."

"Did you ever talk to anybody about it?"

"Once." He paused. "I talked to my family doctor about it, and he sent me to a psychologist in Baton Rouge. I went a few of times, but he couldn't find anything wrong. He said it was probably just a delayed trauma reaction to the accident, that I'd get over it in time."

His finger traced circles lightly on the upper part of her chest, where the neck of her shirt scooped low. "But now that you're here, I notice it more and more. Maybe it's because of us ... of how you make me feel. Do you understand what I mean?"

Before she could answer, he asked, "Do you suppose that's possible? Could I become worse because there's someone new that I care about? Or do I simply notice it more now?"

"I don't know the answers to those questions," Kirsta said, "but I do know that people can have profound effects on each other — for the better and for the worse."

Sean's hand stopped moving. "You sound as though you're talking from experience," he said. "And not very pleasant experience at that."

Kirsta nodded. "I just escaped from a pretty nasty relationship myself, so I have a pretty good idea of what you went through with Edwina. And I know how that kind of thing can affect how you look at people from then on. They can be very frightening."

Sean bent his head to whisper in her ear, and his voice barely audible over the whir of insects around them. "Don't be afraid," he murmured. His hand moved down to her breast.

Kirsta said nothing. She didn't trust her voice just then. Her flesh rose under his touch, and she sighed and closed her eyes. Then she felt his weight shift beside her, and his lips caressed hers. His hand slid under the hem of her shirt and pulled one breast from the stretchy cup of her bra, teasing the nipple erect. His head lowered, and he gently nipped at her breast through the thin fabric of her shirt.

Kirsta arched her back toward him, sighing. He pulled at her clothes, drawing them smoothly from her as though he'd known her body forever. And yet he explored with his fingers and tongue territory new even to Kirsta, sending fiery ripples through her again and again, building like the warning rumbles of an earthquake.

And she tasted and explored him, too, wanting the learning to go on forever, but sure she couldn't stand the anticipation another second. She slowly unbuttoned his shirt and slacks, her fingers trembling so that she could barely control them. She sucked on his earlobes and ran her tongue across his eyelids, savoring the shudder that ran through him. She rubbed her face in the wiry curls on his chest, then dipped her head lower to lick the tiny cavern of his navel.

Then he was on her and in her, filling her with himself, fitting so perfectly inside her that she never wanted to be empty again. He softly moaned her name over and over in her ear so that the sound of it blended with the sad call of the woodthrush on the warm evening breeze. They were climbing to heights neither had ever explored. And when they reached the peak together, Kirsta bit her lip to keep from crying out and felt a tear of joy trickle down her cheek.

They lay entwined on the blanket, and Kirsta wanted this moment to go on forever, this quietness, this sense of completeness. She'd never known a man could be so gentle and strong at the same time. Her own limited experience had left much to be desired — until now.

Kirsta marveled at this man beside her, whose warm breath tickled the soft hairs at the nape of her neck. This Sean was so different from the man who'd lain on top of her the night before in her cabin — gentler, more considerate, more ... real, somehow. She recalled the trick of light that had created the illusion of physical change. A shiver ran through her.

"Are you cold?" Sean mumbled into her hair.

"No," she answered, and smiled up at him, hoping he could see it in the gathering darkness. "I was just wondering whether that was you making love to me just now, or the other person inside you."

He raised his head and shook it. "No," he said quietly. "That was definitely me."

"Sean, I was just kidding," Kirsta hurried to say. "I didn't mean to —"

Sean put a finger on her lips to silence her. "I know," he said, "but I wasn't. I feel more like Sean McLeod right now than I have since ... I don't know when. Maybe since Edwina and Andy died. Maybe longer."

He pulled her face to his and kissed her softly. "Thank you," he murmured. A breeze caught the edge of the blanket and rippled it. "Maybe we should start back to Lost Oaks," he said. "Or at least get dressed. Before you catch cold."

Kirsta snuggled close to him and held him tightly. "I don't ever want to leave here. Let's just lie together a little longer."

A moment later a car drove slowly past the cemetery gates. Sean rose on one elbow and held Kirsta's shirt out to her. "Well, you may not be cold," he said, "but if we don't get dressed, we may be calling Aunt Daphne for bail money on indecent exposure charges. I think that was a police car."

They dressed quickly, and packed the picnic basket in silence. Kirsta folded the blanket while Sean put the basket on the back seat of the car. When they got in, Sean leaned over and kissed her again.

"I hope this is just the start of something," he said. "And I hope you don't finish your work too soon."

He backed the car out, and on the way back to the plantation they discussed the historical information Kirsta had found in the Allindea library.

"I'm particularly interested in the relationship between rural southerners and the Yankee soldiers who came through these communities during the later part of the Civil War," she said.

"What do you mean by their 'relationship'?"

"Well, I'm sure some southerners began to suspect that the Confederates were going to lose the war during the last few months of battle," she explained. "The effect of that would be different on different people. Some would become even more hostile, but others might recognize that it could be to their advantage to stay on the good side of the conquerors."

Sean said nothing, and Kirsta glanced at him. His face in the dim green light from the dashboard was serious, and she thought his jaw seemed set firmly. She wondered whether he'd even heard what she'd said. Then he spoke, his voice sounding a bit tired and gravelly.

"I think people in the south suffered terribly during the Civil War," he said. "They watched their hopes and dreams go up in smoke — sometimes literally — when the Yankees came through. Around here, things weren't as bad, because the battles were being fought further to the east, but ... well, I know the war caused some tragedies around here, too."

They were passing Henry Patton's gas station, and Kirsta remembered her visit to their house earlier in the day. She turned in her seat to face Sean. "Sean," she asked, "that reminds me — did you ever hear about an ancestor of yours named Indigo McLeod?"

The car swerved slightly, and Kirsta gripped the dashboard. She looked at Sean, but all he said was, "Damned rabbit."

Sean didn't answer her question, and Kirsta thought he'd forgotten about it.

"Sean?" she asked. "Do you know anything about Indigo McLeod?"

She thought she saw a muscle twitch in Sean's jaw, but he looked away for a second as he turned into the drive to Lost Oaks. When he answered, he spoke slowly and precisely.

"I believe she's my great-great grandmother or something," he said. "As a matter of fact, she's buried back in the Allindea cemetery." He paused, then asked, "How did you happen to hear about Indigo?"

"I was over at the Pattons' house today, and Henry and Etta were giving me some background on local Civil War stories. When you mentioned local people suffering because of the war, we were passing Henry's place, and I remembered what they'd said about Indigo and David McLeod."

Kirsta could hear the breath hissing through Sean's nostrils as they drove along the gravel road toward his house. She thought he was breathing a bit fast, and wondered whether he was upset or angry about something. But she couldn't imagine what it would be. The warm, comfortable, loving mood of the evening seemed to have disappeared somewhere into the darkness that surrounded them. She wished she could bring it back.

"Sean? What's the matter?"

When he didn't answer, Kirsta reached a hand out and tentatively touched Sean's arm. He moved away from her. His head lowered slightly, and his shoulders hunched. His eyes were fixed on the drive. What was wrong with him, Kirsta wondered? What had she said or done to make him act this way?

Or maybe it wasn't her. Maybe it had something to do with being back at Lost Oaks. When he pulled up to her cabin, he left the motor running as he got out. He jerked open her door.

"Do you really want to know what's wrong?" he asked through clenched teeth. "Do you?"

Kirsta began to speak, to beg him to calm down, but he ignored her.

"I wish the Pattons would keep their damned noses out of our business," he growled. "That's what's wrong. The mistakes our family made more than a hundred years ago is none of their affair. They're nothing but a couple of busybodies."

"But they're your relatives," Kirsta said.

"And you're a stranger," he said. "What makes you think you have the right to come clawing through the past, opening up old scars, hurting people?"

"I … I'm not trying to hurt anyone," Kirsta stammered, confused and a bit frightened by his sudden change. "I just thought you … I thought we —"

Sean slammed the car door. "You didn't think at all," he said. "That's the problem. You're looking for history, are you? Well, you'd better be careful, or the history you find might wind up being more than you bargained for."

He whirled before she could answer, and jumped back behind the wheel. The tires spat dirt behind them as he spun around and headed back to the main house.

Kirsta stood on her porch, shivering in the warm night, for a long time after he was gone.

Once inside, she undressed slowly and took a long, hot bath, soaking in the steamy water. She was exhausted, and yet knew she'd find little rest tonight, after her emotional roller-coaster ride with Sean. He was so complicated, he really seemed to be two different people at times.

Was the man who had kissed her gently and made love to her in the sunset the same man who had gripped her arms so fiercely in the afternoon and said such angry things just an hour ago by the front porch? She'd never be able to finish her work here if she allowed herself to get caught up in such turmoil.

Kirsta sighed, allowing the heat and moisture to work on her tense muscles. She leaned her head back against a towel she'd folded onto the edge of the tub, covered her eyes with a damp washcloth, and closed her eyes. The warm water eased itself into all her secret places, and she felt as though she were floating. She forced all the stress and confusion away, concentrating on the crickets and the steady, slow drip … drip … drip from the faucet.

After a time, the sounds seemed to synchronize with her pulse and breathing, and she let her mind drift in the steam she knew was rising from the tub. She heard soft creaks and whispers from beyond the bathroom door as the cabin settled into the night, and hummed an old ballad.

"Dearest love, do you remember,
when we last did meet,
how you told me that you loved me,
kneeling at my feet?"

Kirsta smiled, recalling the last time she'd heard those words — two nights before, in the restaurant at Mistmere, while waiting for Sean to return from his meeting. She felt again the muscles of his thighs against hers as they danced in their private corner of the screened porch, and she thought she could smell the dark, musky scent of him beside her now. She ached for the touch of his hand on her skin, the whisper of his breath in her hair.

Kirsta sang the first stanza of the song softly, her voice oddly muffled in the small room. She imagined Sean beside her, singing the sad ballad with

149

her, his deep tones a perfect accompaniment to her, as she continued with the second verse:

"Ah, how proud you stood before me
in your suit of blue,
when you vowed to me and country
ever to be true."

Kirsta was surprised how easily she remembered the words of the old song. She was sure she'd never heard it before that night at Mistmere. But the warm night and her feelings about Sean seemed to bring it all back, including her fantasy. Again she was sitting on the veranda in a lacy white dress, with Sean bending over her, his face nearing hers. The crickets whirred faster, and the dripping of the faucet disappeared. Kirsta parted her lips in anticipation, as Sean pressed a rose to her breast.

"Weep not for me, Indigo, my love. Soon we'll be together, I promise."

The voice seemed so real, the words so fervent, that Kirsta tensed, dragging herself reluctantly back to the present. She waited, afraid to move, the washcloth still over her eyes. Surely she imagined the voice.

She listened, straining her ears for the slightest sound. The faucet's drip now sounded as loud as canon shots, and each creak and groan of the boards around her like thunder. Was that a door closing?

"Sean?" Kirsta's voice was no more than a hoarse whisper.

She sat up, trembling, and pulled the wet cloth from her eyes. No one was in the bathroom. She rose from the tub and wrapped a bath towel around her. She tiptoed across the floor, leaving puddles on the boards.

Nobody was in the main room of the cabin, either, and the door was still bolted from the inside.

CHAPTER SIXTEEN

She slept restlessly, though she was exhausted. In her dreams, she relived the scene at the Allindea cemetery, in all it's gentleness and passion. She was making love again, in the glow from the setting sun. Her whole being knew the joy of complete oneness with another person, and she rode again the waves of ecstacy. But when she looked up, the man above her in the dark red light had no face.

Then suddenly she was back in the apartment with David Belsen, his mood swinging from tender to terrorizing in mere moments. She lived again through that final night of violence. She heard them argue over meaningless trivia. She wanted to stop herself, take the words back this time, avoid the unavoidable. Again, she saw the familiar twitch in his jaw and heard the fury in his voice.

Helpless to change history, she watched him grip the large crystal ball of the snow globe, the tendons in his hand standing out like tree roots. In slow motion, he raised the globe over his head, and Kirsta was unable to move, her eyes fixed on the scene inside, tiny white flakes drifting around the little village, now tilted at a precarious angle. She couldn't breathe; all the oxygen seemed to be sucked out of the room.

David howled in frustration and rage, and the glass ball flew through the empty air. Only this time, Kirsta didn't duck fast enough, or his aim was better. This time, the globe was headed straight for her face. In horror, she watched her own terrified reflection grow larger and larger as the antique treasure tilted toward her. She closed her eyes, anticipating the agony as shards of glass sliced her flesh.

But the pain never came. When she opened her eyes again, she was naked inside the globe, freezing in a bitter winter wind as huge flakes of snow whirled around her. She pounded on the wall of glass frantically, begging someone to let her out. She couldn't hear her own voice in the dense air.

Then David's face was there, huge and distorted beyond the curved edge of her prison. He smiled and tapped his finger on the glass, the sound booming in the heavy air around her like thunder. She covered her ears, but David only grinned and thumped his finger harder and harder until even her bones seemed to vibrate with every thud.

She silently pleaded with him to stop. He did, then moved his face so close that she backed away to the other side of the globe. His eyes were like twin pale moons above her. He moved his lips, and though she couldn't hear the words, she knew what he was saying, over and over.

"You're mine," he said, "forever and ever. You're mine." Kirsta was glad she couldn't hear herself scream.

Kirsta woke late, feeling no more rested than she'd been when she went to bed the night before. As she slowly sat up, she noticed something red peeking out from under her pillow. She lifted the pillow gently, dread tightening the muscles of her stomach and chest. A single long-stemmed red rose lay on the white sheet.

Kirsta drew a sharp breath as she recalled the vivid fantasy she'd had the night before, soaking in the tub. Sean had given her a red rose. Where could this flower have come from? How long had it been in her bed? She leaned closer to examine the dark red petals, not wanting to touch it. The blossom looked somewhat crushed, and the edges of the delicate petals were dark and curling. So the flower must have been in her room for some time, perhaps before she went to bed.

Kirsta remembered how exposed and vulnerable she'd felt after leaving the bath. Though it seemed impossible, she'd been unable to shake off the sensation that someone had been in the cabin with her. She had turned off the lights quickly and crawled, exhausted, between the sheets. She'd lain awake a long time, listening to each chirp and creak, wondering whether the intruder was returning. No wonder, she thought, that her dreams had been so disturbing.

It was certainly plausible that Daphne had put the rose in the room while Kirsta and Sean were on their picnic earlier. She could have brought it with her when she left the breakfast rolls in the refrigerator. Kirsta smiled. That's exactly the kind of thing the old dear would do. Maybe it slid off the pillow when Kirsta sat on the bed to undress for her bath, and she never noticed it until now.

She realized there might be another explanation. It was one Kirsta didn't want to consider, but recalling her dream about David, she knew she had to face it and put it behind her. What if David had followed her down here and was trying to drive her crazy, like that old film *Gaslight*, where Joseph Cotton tries to drive Ingrid Bergman insane?

Kirsta shook her head as she straightened the sheets and quilt. Why would David do something like that? His style was certainly more blunt than sneaking around trying to frighten her. If he still wanted Kirsta, he'd simply walk in someday and grab her.

Kirsta clenched her fists at the thought, then pushed it away. David didn't even know where she was; only Harrison Kahn and Ginny knew. Suddenly, Kirsta remembered Daphne's message that Ginny had called her. In all the confusion, she'd completely forgotten to return the call. Kirsta shrugged; if it had been important, Ginny would have called again. Kirsta made a mental note to call her friend later that day.

Then she decided she'd mention the flower to Daphne later in the day, if she found an opportunity to do so in a way that didn't draw too much attention to it. That way she'd be sure.

Kirsta showered quickly and dressed in pink shorts and a white eyelet lace tank top. Then she set out a cup and teabag, sitting at the coffee table to go through her notes while waiting for the water to boil. She nibbled on a pecan roll as she scrolled through the random pages of information she'd entered on her computer. She read the same passages over and over, trying to concentrate on her work. She sighed and glanced out the window.

The sky was overcast, though the air was still and dense, hanging over Kirsta like a hot wet blanket. She wished the storm the Pattons predicted at dinner would hit, lifting this barometric weight from her shoulders. But she also realized that for her, the heaviness came from inside as well as outside. She had fallen in love with Sean. There was no use trying to deny it anymore. He was gentle and kind and loving — he'd proved that over and over during the few days she'd been in Louisiana. And last night, when they made love beneath the oaks in the cemetery, she had been sure that he loved her, too. His voice, his face, his touch — everything about him shouted his love for her.

But he'd been so abrupt, even angry, by the time they'd returned to Lost Oaks, he'd been like a different person. The teakettle screamed for attention, and Kirsta poured the steaming water into her mug. Maybe the caffeine would perk her up.

A different person. The words jumped into Kirsta's mind again. Even Sean had admitted he felt like someone else when he was on the plantation. What could that possibly mean? she wondered. Sean had said that sometimes he felt as though there were someone else inside him. Was it possible that something unnatural — even supernatural — was going on here? Apparently that's what Henry and Etta Patton believed, with all their stories about the ghost of Lost Oaks.

Kirsta looked out the window and watched the old goose chase a dog near the pond. She'd never believed in ghosts and goblins, even as a child. Her father had always said that her "common sense" was one of her best traits, so she'd cultivated that, scoffing at any suggestion of the occult or mysterious. Her explanation was always to remind everyone that rockets and televisions were considered science fiction not long ago, and primitive people still ran screaming during eclipses.

It was more likely — and certainly easier to believe — that Sean was suffering from some kind of mental aberration following his wife's and son's deaths. Kirsta asked herself whether she was really ready to get involved with a man who had such serious problems. Maybe she should just get on the next plane and return to Pennsylvania now, leaving Sean and this beautiful, mysterious place behind her forever. But Kirsta knew she couldn't do that. Not only did she need the money this job provided, but she needed to stay away from David as long as possible. He had to understand she wasn't coming back to him. David would come to his senses if she gave him enough time, she was sure of that.

And Kirsta had never run away from her problems. Of course, she'd left when David threatened her, but that was just common sense. In fact, she probably should have left that relationship as soon as he'd shown signs of instability, rather than stay out of some misguided sense of loyalty. She took a long drink of the hot tea, and felt it relax and strengthen her as it went down, as though she'd imbibed some kind of magical potion of wisdom. She knew what to do.

She would remain here at Lost Oaks, yes, but during that time stay as far from Sean McLeod as possible. Even though her feelings for him were much stronger than anything she'd ever felt before, she mustn't let herself get drawn into the same kind of destructive, even dangerous relationship she'd had with David Belsen. Kirsta ignored the small voice that insisted she reconsider her decision, that Sean was nothing like David Belsen. She simply shook her head, pushing the contradictory thoughts away.

She straightened her shoulders and opened her notebook. The pages on top referred to her conversation with Etta and Henry Patton the day before, their stories about Indigo and David McLeod and their son Owen. Kirsta decided to find out more about the McLeods and the Yankee soldier, Andrew

Lucas. Their confrontation might be an excellent example of the kind of thing Harrison Kahn was looking for from her research. Individual stories always made theoretical texts more interesting, lent them credibility. Also, it shouldn't be too difficult to gather information about local history. If the Pattons had records, perhaps other residents did, too.

Kirsta made a list of key names and events: Andrew Lucas (hanging, wife and son killed), Indigo McLeod (possible affair with Andrew, locked in barn, buried in Allindea cemetery), David McLeod (violence, visit to Indigo's aunt), Owen McLeod. She would talk to Daphne later today to get some ideas. Unless Sean was up at the house, of course. Kirsta rose and went to the front window of the cabin. She couldn't see Sean's car through the branches of the live oaks and willows. Maybe he'd left for the day, she thought as relief and disappointment washed over her. Had he left for good? She frowned and silently chastised herself for even caring where he'd gone.

She grabbed her notebook and sketch pad, and headed up the path toward the main house. Before she rapped on the back screen door, Daphne opened it.

"Well, I'm glad you stopped by," she said, wiping her hands on her apron. "I was just slicing some cold meats for sandwiches. I was going to bring a tray down for you in a bit, in case you'd like a light lunch. But now that you're here, it saves me the trip. Are you hungry yet?"

Kirsta followed her in, automatically glancing around for signs of Sean's presence. "Is it lunchtime already?"

"Well, it's only eleven, but I don't stand on ceremony. Sean's out with a client in Baton Rouge or someplace, so it's just the two of us. If you want to eat now, it's almost ready."

Kirsta realized she was famished, and admitted it to Daphne. "It's strange, but I seem to lose my sense of time down here," she continued. "I got up at nine-thirty, and sat down to make some notes, and here it is an hour-and-a-half later."

"My mama used to say that love changed the path of the sun. Might that be your problem?"

Daphne's back was to Kirsta, but she knew what Daphne was talking about. Sean. Kirsta's face grew warm, and she didn't know what to say. So she said nothing. Daphne seemed to sense the awkwardness, and quickly changed the subject.

"Did you get hold of your friend from Pennsylvania, that Ginny girl?"

Kirsta rolled her eyes at the ceiling. "My mind," she complained, "where is it these days? No, I'll do it right now, before we eat, if that's all right."

155

"No problem, phone's right there." Daphne pointed toward the pink wall phone. "I'll cut us some fresh flowers — give you some privacy."

Kirsta smiled her thanks as she dialed Ginny's number. The phone rang six times before Ginny picked up. When she heard Kirsta's voice she nearly screamed.

"Why haven't you called? I've been nearly frantic with worry."

Kirsta shook her head, smiling. Ginny over-reacted to everything. "I'm a big girl now," she said drily. "I've traveled alone before."

"That's not what I mean, and you know it," Ginny retorted. "I'm talking about David."

Kirsta's breath seemed to stop. "What about David?"

"Didn't you get my message?"

"Well, Mrs. Woodring said you'd left a message on the machine the other day," Kirsta admitted, "but she didn't say anything about David."

"Not that message," Ginny said, her voice tight with frustration, "the other one. I talked with some man yesterday and told him to have you call right away because David was on his way to Louisiana."

Kirsta's legs trembled and she collapsed back onto a stool. "David's coming here? How did he find out where I am?"

There was a long pause, then Ginny cleared her throat. "That's not important any more," she said. "He won't be bothering you — he's dead."

The room seemed to lurch around Kirsta. She closed her eyes until the dizziness passed.

"Kirsta? Are you okay?" Ginny's voice seemed small and tinny. Kirsta forced her eyes open again.

"You'd better start at the beginning," she said carefully. "I'm not following this at all."

"David came over here the other night," Ginny began. "He wanted to find out where you'd gone, said he wanted to patch things up with you. At first, I wouldn't tell him, but then he … he was—" her voice broke.

"I understand," Kirsta said. "You don't have to explain."

"Well, I finally told him. I called you the next day, but nobody was there."

"Why didn't you call right away?"

"Because he said he'd … well, I was still afraid he'd come back. So I guess I convinced myself he really did want to patch things up. Or maybe he'd just forget about it and not bother you."

Sure, thought Kirsta. Like a cat won't bother a mouse. But she said nothing.

"But by the next morning, I realized how stupid that was, and that he might get crazy like that with you. So I left a message for you to call back. Then I read in the papers that Martin Radive had been killed."

"Oh, poor Martin," Kirsta moaned.

"Well, I remembered that David had mentioned that name when he was here, and had seemed jealous of the time you spent in Martin's house. I think he believed you were having an affair or something. So I called the police, then I called you again and left the message with that man. I told him to have you call me right away. I said, "Tell her David is on his way.""

Kirsta realized Ginny must have spoken with Sean. Why, then, hadn't he given her the message?

Ginny was still talking. "Anyway, like I said, the danger is over. The police called me just a few minutes ago to say they found David's car along some side road in Mississippi. Apparently, there'd been a fire and the car was completely destroyed."

"With David inside."

"Yes," Ginny said quietly. "He was still behind the wheel." Kirsta said nothing for a long time. "Are you okay?" Ginny asked.

"I think so." Kirsta sighed. "I'm glad he didn't find me, but to burn up in a car ..." She shuddered.

"I know what you mean," Ginny said. "Nobody deserves that. But at least you know you're safe now."

"Yes." But somehow Kirsta didn't feel safe. She inhaled deeply, trying to still the trembling. She knew her nerves were still reacting to the news that David had been following her, that her security, possibly even her life, had been in jeopardy. It would take some time for the other news, the news that David was gone, to sink in.

Kirsta and Ginny spoke for a few more minutes, and Kirsta promised she'd call again in a few days. When she hung up, she leaned back against the wall and closed her eyes again.

She heard a soft cough and opened her eyes. Daphne stood in the doorway, frowning at her, several yellow roses clutched in her hand.

"Is everything all right, dear?" she asked.

Kirsta nodded and forced a small smile. "Just some bad news about the death of ... a friend."

"I'm so sorry," Daphne hurried over and touched Kirsta's shoulder. "Will you have to go back to Pennsylvania?"

Kirsta thought about that, then shook her head. "No. There's nothing I can do now."

"Well then, let's fix that lunch. Maybe getting some food in your stomach will help you feel better." Daphne put the roses into a glass vase.

"You just might be right," Kirsta said. "I am hungry. What can I do to help?"

"Grab us a couple of napkins and some silver from the chest, will you dear? I think we'll eat out on the veranda — try to catch whatever breeze we can. I'll set up a fan out there to help. It'll keep the bugs away, too."

By the time they'd finished their sandwiches and fruit salad, Kirsta's spirits had risen. Though she'd felt a momentary pang of disappointment that Sean had left the plantation, she quickly convinced herself it was for the best. She didn't have to keep an eye out for him all day, trying to avoid him. She could relax.

"By the way, Daphne, thank you so much for the picnic dinner you sent down last night," Kirsta said, trying to keep the memories of Sean's naked body from her thoughts. "And the rose. Touches like that mean so much."

"You're welcome, dear," Daphne said, then her brow furrowed. "But I don't remember putting a rose in the basket."

"No, not in the basket," Kirsta said, feeling a dark premonition. "I'm talking about the rose in my room, on the bed, last night."

Daphne looked blankly at her for a moment, then shook her head. "I don't know what you mean. I didn't put a rose in your room — though that's a nice idea. I wish I had thought of it. Maybe Sean put it there."

Somehow, Kirsta didn't think so. She considered continuing the query, but decided she didn't want to explain to Daphne why she was sure Sean wouldn't have left the flower.

"Anyway, the dinner was delicious," she said. "I'd spent the morning wandering around the plantation and sketching, and didn't have time for much lunch before going over to the Pattons' house."

"I didn't know you were an artist, too," Daphne said, pushing her chair back from the table. "So many talents."

"I'm not much of an artist, really. I just find that drawing things helps me see them better, notice details I might otherwise miss."

"That's a good idea; I'd never have thought of it. Would you show me the drawings? I'd love to see them."

"Of course." Kirsta grabbed her sketchpad. "As long as you don't expect much. I haven't even looked at them myself since I did them."

Daphne took the pad from Kirsta and opened it to the first page. From her position opposite, Kirsta couldn't see the drawings herself, but remembered the places as Daphne exclaimed over them.

"Oh, these of the pond are lovely. I never realized how the light looks on the water in the early morning. I'm always checking out the flowers and animals. Charcoal helps you to see things in a new way, doesn't it?

"And here's that old barn out back. I hope you didn't go inside." She glanced up, then lowered her eyes again. "I'm not sure it's safe in there. Old boards and rusty nails and hornets' nests, you know."

Kirsta remembered her strange experience at the barn, and wished she'd erased the writing on the boards. She thought she saw a shadow of something flicker across the woman's face — something that had nothing to do with the dangers she'd listed. But it was gone so quickly she wasn't sure she'd seen it.

"No, I stayed outside," she said. She decided to take a chance. "But I drew that picture later, on the front steps. I felt … odd when I was out by the barn."

Daphne didn't look up. "Hmmmm." She quickly turned the page. "Well, there's no point taking chances when you —"

Daphne froze as she looked at the picture before her. The color seemed to drain from her face, and Kirsta thought she seemed to age. Was she having a heart attack or stroke? Kirsta rose from her chair, wondering where to find the number for a doctor or the ambulance.

"What's the matter, Daphne? Are you all right?"

Daphne looked up at her. "I'm fine," she said shakily. "I was just startled by this drawing of that old tree, that's all. The others are all so realistic, so pleasant. I hadn't expected you to add things to them. Especially not something this disturbing."

"What are you talking about?" Kirsta crossed to see what the woman was looking at. She, too, froze at the sight of the drawing before her.

The ancient live oak in the center of the front lawn filled the page, each long twisted branch carefully delineated with firm strokes. One particularly heavy branch reached out about ten or fifteen feet from the ground. The limbs below it had either broken or been cut off, leaving lumpy scars on the trunk. From this branch dangled a terrible burden. A man's body hung limply at the end of a rope. His arms were tied behind his back, and his head cocked to one side at an impossible angle. The same vision she'd had in Witchman's woods.

"I don't understand," Kirsta whispered.

She had no memory of drawing the dreadful scene. She couldn't imagine why she would do such a thing. The sight of the poor wretch brought such a sense of awful despair and longing to her heart that, without thinking, she reached out and tore the page from the pad.

Beneath it, was another sketch of the same scene from a different angle. In this version, the viewer was closer to the hanged man. Rips and gouges in his dark clothes showed clearly, and his face was now visible. His eyes stared upward through the long dark bangs, as though looking for a sign from God, and his tongue protruded from the side of his mouth. Even in death, Kirsta could see how handsome he must have been. There was something familiar about the features, though she was sure she'd never seen the man before.

"How did you know what Andrew Lucas looked like?"

Daphne's question broke the spell the drawing had on Kirsta, and she moved away a few steps, as though the distance would make it less real.

"Andrew Lucas?"

"You remember, he's the Yankee soldier I said haunts this place. That's exactly what he looked like. Let me show you."

Kirsta followed her into the house. Daphne opened a drawer in the heavy sideboard and drew out a large frayed scrapbook with crumbling pages of black construction paper. The spine was tied with faded ribbon. Daphne opened the book, and carefully turned the pages until she found the one she wanted.

"I don't know who took this photograph, but the writing on the back says 'Andrew Lucas, May 5, 1865.'"

The photo had yellowed with age, but clearly showed a handsome young man in a tattered dark uniform standing against a hedge. Some distance behind him could be seen the front of a two-story barn. Lengths of rope stretched across his broad torso, holding his arms behind his back. He scowled angrily from the center of the photo, his thick dark hair nearly covering one eye.

Close behind him and to one side stood another man. The second man was only partially visible, most of his face and half his body outside the edge of the paper. But Kirsta could still make out the arrogant sneer that lifted the corner of his mouth. She held the photo closer.

"You're right," she said, "this man in front certainly looks like the one I drew. Wait a minute. What's this?" She pointed to the photo.

"Oh that's the window in the top of the barn. For a time, there was a second story room in the loft that seasonal workers used when they stayed here. Supposedly, that's where Andrew Lucas took Indigo McLeod when he raped her. Only the lower story of the barn is left now — the second story was torn off long before I was even born."

Kirsta tapped at the photo again. "But look at the window. Doesn't it look like someone is there?"

"It could be, but my old eyes aren't very good anymore." Daphne opened another drawer and found a magnifying glass. She handed it to Kirsta.

Kirsta focused the thick lens over the little square window, and gasped. She saw a woman leaning against the glass, blond curls awry around her face. This part of the photo was slightly blurred and a bit grainy on magnification, but certain things were obvious, nevertheless.

The woman's hands were behind her back, and her arms tight against her back as though she were bound. But it was the eyes that chilled Kirsta. Pale eyes screamed in desperate impotence above the rag that stretched tightly across the woman's mouth.

CHAPTER SEVENTEEN

Kirsta sat for a long time in the grass by the pond that afternoon, thinking about Indigo and David McLeod and Andrew Lucas. She had to sort out what she knew from what she imagined or hoped the situation was. Apparently, Indigo had loved Andrew; there was nothing remotely like rape involved in their relationship from what she could tell. Even her dreams told her that, if dreams could have any informative value.

And what about her dreams, she wondered. Were they simply her projections of what she suspected or wished had happened, or were they something more, some kind of message from the past? Was it possible that Indigo was trying to tell Kirsta the truth about her life with David McLeod and Andrew Lucas through her dreams? But why? Did she want to set the record straight, after all these years? That just didn't seem plausible — why choose Kirsta? Why now? If these nightly visions were more than just dreams, there must be a better reason than that.

Of course, the record did need straightening. The only source of the rape story was David McLeod, who must have caught them together and realized their true feelings. His volatile personality couldn't handle the jealousy, and he conveniently had Andrew hanged as a spy and rapist — while Indigo watched helplessly from the barn window, unable to stop him. Of course, nobody would doubt David's story, especially if his wife weren't there to stand up for her lover. Once Andrew was dead, there was no point in Indigo telling the truth. Who would she tell? She probably realized that her peace and safety depended on keeping David McLeod happy.

What a sad story it was. Kirsta thought it was no wonder she'd reacted strongly to it — so strongly that she'd have nightmares and daydreams about it. But what about the other things that had happened — the things that she couldn't blame on dreams? What about the words she'd scratched on the barn wall, the spilled dusting powder while she was showering, and the voices and visions she'd experienced at the cemetery chapel? And what about Sean's abrupt changes in mood — even in appearance?

Kirsta rubbed her eyes, trying not to think about these disturbing incidents. There must be some logical explanation, she told herself, there simply had to be. Kirsta didn't think she was losing her mind — she was fairly sure she'd know if that were happening. She just hadn't figured it out yet. Or if these were truly supernatural events, then she would have to accept that and carry on with her work. There didn't appear to be any immediate danger. And who ever heard of anyone being injured by a ghost? Frightened, yes; even scared to death, probably — but not directly harmed.

She lay back on the thick grass and closed her eyes against the grey clouds. Dragonflies flew past her face, their helicopter wings buzzing hotly in the still, damp air. Kirsta's mind drifted through the afternoon like a rose petal on the rippling water beside her. She imagined herself back in the cemetery, with Sean drowsing beside her. She felt again his hands on her breasts, his lips against hers. Her flesh tingled at the memory; she felt his tongue move softly along her face.

Suddenly, she realized fingers were actually stroking her cheek. Kirsta opened her eyes and sat up quickly, covering the place with her hand as though she'd been stung. Sean knelt beside her, his dark eyes fixed on hers.

"Sean." Kirsta's voice cracked. Her heart hammered in her throat. She didn't want him to know how he frightened her, peering at her so intently. She wasn't sure what emotion she read in that gaze.

Kirsta tried to grab hold of her emotions, though her heart pounded violently. She blinked hard to thrust the erotic memories of the night before from her mind. So much can change in one twenty-four hour period, she thought. So much can change in an hour.

"Why didn't you give me the phone message from Ginny?" she asked him suddenly.

"Phone message?" He looked genuinely confused. "I don't remember any message."

"She said she spoke with a man, and asked him to tell me that David was coming for me."

A muscle twitched in Sean's jaw and his eyes narrowed. "David?" he asked. "Damn him. What does he want with you?"

Kirsta was confused. Had she mentioned David's name to Sean? She couldn't remember.

Then Sean said quickly, "What I mean is, who's David?"

"It's just somebody I knew," Kirsta said in exasperation. "The point is, why didn't you tell me about it?"

"I didn't take the message," he said. "Daphne's had some painters working in the office the last few days. Maybe one of them took it and forgot to say anything to her."

"Maybe." But Kirsta wasn't convinced.

"Look, we have to talk, Kirsta." Sean's gaze never left hers. "How about in your cabin?"

"Sean, I'm not sure that's a good idea," she said. "I've had a very trying day. I think we both need some time apart to … to evaluate what happened yesterday."

Sean's eyes blazed with anger. "Evaluate? You sound like a damned accountant."

He pulled back slightly and took a deep breath. "Okay, I'm sorry. I understand how you feel. I really do. That's why I want to talk. If you don't want to go back to your room, then let's just take a walk. Would that be so terrible?"

Kirsta hesitated, trying to focus her thoughts. His overwhelming presence made concentrating extremely difficult. As long as they kept things on a non-romantic level — if that were possible — it would probably be all right.

She nodded. "Okay, a walk sounds like a good idea. Maybe the exercise will get my mind off this heat."

"It always gets like this before a big storm. It's like you're caught in a glass bubble and can't get out."

Kirsta started at the comparison, so close to her dream about David, and wondered if he'd somehow gotten the image from her mind. It seemed impossible, but she was intrigued by the possibility.

Sean stood, and Kirsta let him help her up, savoring the touch of his fingers on her arm. He was wearing jeans and a pale yellow shirt, and Kirsta watched the muscles in his arms ripple as he moved his hand to the small of her back. But the intimacy of that touch was too much — she had to keep a clear head. Kirsta reluctantly moved away slightly, and Sean's hand dropped. He said nothing. They walked along the flagstone path.

Suddenly there was a rustling and hissing behind them, and Kirsta turned to see the big old goose waddling after them. She hurried toward Sean while keeping a wary eye on Kirsta.

Sean turned too, and chuckled, reaching into his pocket. He held out a cracker, and the goose snatched it from him. She backed away with a last glance and hiss at Kirsta.

"She always wants her treat," Sean said. "I automatically grab a cracker when I leave the house."

"I don't think she likes me very much," Kirsta noted.

"She doesn't like anybody except me. But I think she's jealous of you."

"Jealous? After last night, I don't think she has anything to be jealous about."

Sean put his hands on Kirsta's shoulders and turned her toward him. "I'm talking about last night. You're trying to tell me you couldn't see how I felt when we made love?"

Kirsta felt her mouth go dry when she remembered how it was with him in the grass. "I thought I could," she admitted, "but by the time we got back here, I had another opinion."

"I know," Sean said, dropping his hands. "I want to apologize for the way I acted last evening.

"No apology necessary," Kirsta answered, hating the formality in her voice. "You were just —"

Sean put up a hand to quiet her. "You don't have to make excuses for me. In fact, there's no way for you to know what was going on in my mind, because I don't understand it myself. I'm not even sure how to explain it to you."

They strolled on in silence for a moment or two, while Kirsta let him organize his thoughts. She realized they'd strayed off the path, and were heading toward the topiary maze. She said nothing, not wanting to disturb him. Maybe, just maybe, he could make her understand, if she'd just give him the chance.

"The only thing I can figure out is that something you said on the way home set me off, made my blood boil."

Kirsta stopped in her tracks. "Look, Sean, if you're going to try to blame all this on me ..."

"No, no," he said quickly. "That's not it at all. I'm not trying to blame anybody. I'm only trying to explain something I don't understand myself. Truthfully, I don't even remember what you said after we left the cemetery. I just remember this ... a kind of heavy fog moving into my brain while you were talking. I couldn't even hear your words, but I know I desperately wanted you to stop talking."

"I'm not sure I'm following you," Kirsta said as they walked on. "I don't think I said anything that should have upset you. I was just talking about my research."

"I don't get it either," Sean insisted. "I'm just trying to be honest about how I felt. Even now, I don't know what you were talking about. I don't even remember what I said. But I do remember the awful, nearly uncontrollable anger I felt — and how your face looked when I left. Like I'd slapped you."

Kirsta nodded. "That's exactly how I felt." Confusion made her head ache. How could he be so sensitive and understanding now, after the terrible scene at her front door?

Sean turned to her as they reached the towering hedges of the maze. His eyes were kind and loving, but the haunted look was there, too. He gently put his hands on either side of her face. His touch felt wonderful; she didn't move away.

"But I'd never want to hurt you," he said, his voice hoarse with emotion. "Can you see that? Can you? You're really important to me."

Kirsta felt herself melt at his touch, and wanted to believe him, more than she'd ever wanted anything. But she tried to remember her pledge to herself, that she could not let this man into her life. He was too dangerous. She took his hands firmly in hers, and slowly lowered them.

"Sean, I don't know what to say. This is all so confusing."

He smiled sadly. "I know."

Then a mischievous grin spread across his face. He grasped her hand in his and pulled her forward, into the maze. She held back, but he drew her on.

"Come on," he laughed. "I want to see the Marryin' Magnolia with you."

Kirsta dug in her heels and Sean turned. "I don't like it in there," she said, trying to keep her voice from trembling. She felt it was important to stay calm.

"This place makes me really uncomfortable. Maybe it's claustrophobia or something, but I'd rather go back out. We could sit on the porch and just sip some iced tea and talk."

"I have an idea," Sean said, still smiling. He backed up through the maze entrance, pulling her gently forward. "When we get to the center of the maze, you climb into the tree. I used to go up there when I was a little boy. You don't have to go high; you can see the whole maze from about half-way up. It's really not so complex. Once you see it from above, you'll easily be able to figure it out."

"I don't know, Sean. I'd rather not."

But Kirsta grudgingly allowed him to lead her between the tall hedges. The dark passageways seemed to go on forever. Finally, they reached the center, where the gigantic old magnolia tree spread its branches. In the hazy light from the overcast skies, the clearing didn't seem as friendly or welcoming as it had a few days earlier, when she'd gone in with Daphne. Kirsta wished she'd been more insistent about not going in.

"See? Nothing to it. Everything's fine."

Kirsta looked at Sean, and her heart clenched. He was still smiling, but his face was flushed with excitement and his eyes held a bright, unnatural glitter. He wasn't looking at Kirsta, but at the tree behind her. He didn't seem capable of seeing anything else.

"Climb into it now," he said hoarsely.

"Sean, let's just go back," Kirsta began uneasily, as she moved past him toward the maze they'd just exited.

He clutched her shoulders in both hands and spun her around to face him. "No." He looked feverish. His breath was hot against her face.

"Climb that tree," he said. "Go on. You have to. Do it for me."

He pushed her toward the magnolia tree, none too gently. Kirsta hesitated, then reached into the branches, and began pulling herself upward. She hadn't climbed a tree since she was a child, and the activity felt awkward and unfamiliar. Her hands were clammy, and she nearly lost her footing once or twice, but soon found herself about fifteen feet above the ground.

She looked down, enjoying the perspective. She even noticed a small breeze up here that she hadn't felt on the ground. Sean's face was tilted back, as he watched her. He frowned and pressed his hands to the sides of his head, as though he were trying to keep something from escaping. He looked up at her again. The strange mood seemed to have left him, but he appeared tired, a bit sad. Despite his height and strength, he looked lonely and vulnerable standing below her, and Kirsta's heart ached.

Sean's other side seemed like a dark dream from up here. Something about the distance between them and this towering angle allowed her to recall his gentleness and kindness. She thought of the way Mr. Robbison had praised him at Mistmere. No matter what she told herself, Kirsta had to admit she loved Sean. She smiled down at him and waved.

He smiled back unsurely. "Maybe you'd better come down now," he called. "I think we should go back out."

"Not just yet," she called. "You were right. I can see the layout of the maze perfectly from up here."

Not only could she make out the path of the maze from there, but it really wasn't all that complicated. A left turn from the entrance, then a right past two openings, another left and a switchback to the clearing. She leaned back against the trunk of the tree, feeling pleased with herself and more relaxed.

Two large dark birds circled each other over the house. Like Sean and me, she thought, going around and around in the emptiness until we find each other. She liked the comparison, and felt a great joy surge in her chest. Coming in here with Sean had been a good idea, after all. She struck a coy pose.

"What was that legend about the Marryin' Magnolia again?" she laughed.

"I'm serious," Sean said, his voice tense, a bit louder. "There's something … I don't know exactly, but I feel uneasy, as if something terrible's about to happen."

Kirsta looked hard at Sean. He tilted his face upward again, till she could see his expression clearly — and she didn't like what she saw. The dark, haunted look had returned to his eyes, and his jaw moved. He seemed to be saying something, though she could hear nothing. Her stomach clenched as she turned to begin her descent without another word. She'd learned not to argue with him when he looked like that.

With her left hand, she grasped the sturdy limb above her to balance herself. Her fingers touched something smooth in the crotch of the branch. Kirsta glanced up, and spied a small wooden box nailed to the trunk of the tree.

"Wait a minute, Sean, there's something up here."

Sean didn't answer, but Kirsta tugged at the lid of the box. After a moment, it came off. She was at too low an angle to look into the box, but gingerly reached her hand inside. She pulled a leather pouch out. She wanted to open it, but decided to get on solid ground first. She tucked it into the pocket of her shorts, and continued her descent slowly, testing each branch as she went.

By the time she reached the bottom, Sean was pacing the clearing, rubbing his hands nervously together. He kept glancing around, as though expecting someone to come bounding from the hedges at any minute.

Kirsta pulled the pouch from her pocket. "Look what I found up in the tree," she said, holding it out to him.

"Never mind that," he muttered. "I thought you'd never get back down. Now, let's get out of here."

"You were the one who wanted to come here in the first place," Kirsta sighed. "You keep changing your mind; I can hardly keep up."

Sean ran a hand through his thick dark hair. "I know, I know. There's just something about being in here. It brings back bad memories, I guess. Edwina and I used to come here before we got married."

Kirsta felt a pang of jealousy and annoyance. "Well, why did you insist I climb the tree, then? It doesn't make any sense."

"I can't explain … at that moment, it seemed important to me that you do it, that's all." Sean threw up his hands in disgust. "I don't know why, okay?"

He glanced around nervously again. "Now let's go somewhere else. There's just something about this place …"

"Open this first." Kirsta grasped his hand, opened the fingers, and placed the pouch there firmly.

He stared at it as though it were a particularly disgusting form of insect. "I don't want to." His voice was raspy.

"Why not?"

"I don't know. I have the feeling it's going to be something bad, something evil, that it might change everything."

"Change what?" But somehow she knew he meant them.

Kirsta felt a chill run through her, despite the heat of the afternoon. Then she mentally shook herself. This was absolutely ridiculous. She was letting Sean's overreaction to his unpleasant memories affect her own ability to think clearly. She took back the pouch, drew a deep breath, and pulled the strings apart.

She waited, but nothing jumped out at her. She opened the neck of the bag and peered in. Something shiny glinted inside. She reached in and lifted the object out. A brooch rested in the palm of her hand, an ornate silver filigree brooch with a large square-cut amethyst. In the center of the amethyst was inlaid a silver letter "I". Kirsta felt she'd seen the brooch before, but it took her a moment to remember where. Her dream that first night at Lost Oaks — the blond woman had pulled it from her dress when her husband knocked on the door.

Kirsta had trouble breathing, and her hand began to tremble. "Sean," she whispered, "something strange is going on."

But Sean didn't answer. He merely stared at the treasure in her hand as though it were a poisonous snake ready to strike. He pushed her hand away and glared at her.

"You dare mock me like this." His voice was cold as ice, and his eyes seemed to have grown darker, the pale blue nearly violet now. Kirsta backed away, remembering the night in her cabin, when Sean seemed to have changed.

It's the light, she told herself, and realized those were the same words she'd used to explain it the first time. She hadn't completely believed it then, either. His eyes couldn't have actually changed color in moments. But she kept her eyes averted, she didn't want to look at his face again.

"Sean," she pleaded, "what are you talking about? I'm not mocking you. I'd never do that."

Suddenly, Sean lunged toward her. His fingers barely missed her wrist as she instinctively jumped away. She called out his name, knowing it was useless. He wouldn't — or couldn't — hear her now. She realized she was in danger if she stayed here any longer. Kirsta turned as he lunged again, and fled through the entrance to the maze.

Some rational corner of her panicked mind pictured the maze as she'd seen it from the magnolia tree. This was no time to get backed into a corner. She made a sharp left and plunged through the opening. Sean's heavy footsteps pounded the ground not far behind her. Then she ran past two openings to her left, praying her memory was accurate. She could hear Sean panting behind her, slashing angrily at the hedges with his hands. Then a right turn and she was out and racing across the lawn.

When she reached the cabin, she ran up the steps, flung open the door and hurried inside, slamming it behind her. She slid the iron bolt home. Leaning her back against the door, trying to catch her breath, she realized suddenly how thin the door was. If Sean wanted to break it down, he could. She waited, holding her breath, listening for the sound of Sean's footsteps on the porch, wondering what she'd do if she heard them. But they never came.

When Kirsta finally worked up the courage to peek through the curtains, she didn't see Sean anywhere. She waited a while longer, then stepped out onto the porch. The hot, still air hung over her like a damp blanket. A sparrow fluttered in the grass, looking for seeds or insects, and the old goose strutted beneath an oak tree further up the drive. Thunder rumbled quietly in the distance.

Everything seemed so normal, so mundane. And yet, Kirsta knew her world would never be the same. Lost Oaks was a part of her now, for better or worse, with its sweet scents and exotic colors — and its history. What's more, Sean McLeod had entered her, emotionally as well as physically, and she was changed forever. But something else had happened to her, too — was perhaps still happening. Something less obvious, less definable, something infinitely more frightening.

CHAPTER EIGHTEEN

The afternoon lay like a damp blanket over Allindea as David pulled the grey minivan into a space in front of the Allindea Historical Society and Museum. He wanted nothing more than to crawl into the back and curl up on the sleeping bag. But there were things to be done, preparations to be made before he and Kirsta could leave together.

He'd caught a couple hours of sleep just below Natchez, where route sixty-one narrowed to two lanes. He'd stopped to have some breakfast in Doloroso, then found an unused-looking dirt path just south of town. He'd pulled the van far enough up the bumpy trail that it wouldn't be seen from the road, and had fallen asleep in the back.

When he'd awakened an hour ago, his head ached viciously and he'd felt more tired than when he went to sleep. He'd stopped at a fast-food restaurant in Woodville to clean up and shave. The van's engine hadn't sounded right when he'd come out, and he knew he'd have to get it fixed before he and Kirsta set off for their new life. But the most important thing was to get to Allindea as soon as possible. He wasn't having problems with the van yet.

David put the silver-headed cane in the back of the van before getting out and locking the doors. He hated the thought of how stuffy the van would be when he came back later, but he couldn't take the chance of some joy-rider finding the hunting knife in the glove drawer.

David had to figure out where Kirsta was staying — some plantation near Allindea was all he could get out of that stupid Ginny. He'd suspected she'd known more, but he'd gotten tired of playing games with her. If he had to, he'd visit all the plantations in the area until he found Kirsta. He'd find her eventually — they were destined to be together, to live as man and wife.

But first he had to find the right clothes. The Avenging Angel, King David, couldn't be wed in jeans and a tee shirt, which was all the duffel bag

171

contained. He glanced up and down the street, finally seeing a sign for "The Male Bag." That sounded like a men's store, so he headed that way.

Few people wandered the streets of Allindea that afternoon, apparently preferring to stay inside their air-conditioned shops and offices. Wooden gingerbread curled and twisted like spider legs beneath the eaves of the large white houses he passed, and smaller cottages peered from behind their shrubs and rose gardens. A nice quiet little town, David thought. Exactly the kind of town he and Kirsta could settle down in. But not this one. They would have to find a different home, one where neither of them was known, where they could start new.

When David opened the door of The Male Bag, air-conditioned coolness enveloped him. It felt better than the stifling humidity outside, but seemed to aggravate his headache instead of alleviating it. David winced and gritted his teeth. He had to concentrate on his preparations.

"Can I help you, sir?" A young man smiled and walked his way. "I'm Wayne, and I'd be happy to show you anything you need."

David squinted at Wayne. "I'm looking for a white tuxedo," he said. "For my wedding."

"Excellent," Wayne said, pulling a receipt book from the inside pocket of his tailored jacket. "Now, what date is the wedding?"

David paused. He hadn't expected the question. It depended on how soon he found Kirsta, but of course, he couldn't say that. He had to be precise so as not to make anyone suspicious.

"Day after tomorrow." He tried to sound definite.

Wayne frowned. "Oh, I'm afraid we can't get a white tuxedo that quickly," he said. "We don't keep them in stock, so we'd have to special order. It would take at least a week."

Then he brightened. "But I probably have a black tuxedo your size in stock, and maybe we could do something special in the way of a cummerbund or —"

"No, it has to be white," David snapped. "White's the only color that would work." He knew this was true, but didn't know exactly why.

"Oh, I see." Wayne was frowning again and chewing on the end of his pencil thoughtfully. Both men were silent for a moment as Wayne peered around the store as though a white tuxedo might suddenly appear on the racks. Then he looked hopefully at David.

"What about a white suit?" he asked. "We do have some lightweight summer slacks and jackets that just arrived. Would that work?"

A white suit. David again saw in his mind the sepia image of himself standing stiffly, the silver-headed cane gripped firmly in his hand.

"Yes," he said slowly, "I think a white suit would work nicely. It might be just the thing."

Relief flooded into Wayne's face as he stuffed the receipt book back into his pocket. He steered David toward the back of the shop.

"I've been unpacking these, so they're still a bit wrinkled," he explained. "But the styles are the latest. I'm sure you'll find something you like."

A half hour later, David had chosen a cream-colored jacket and slacks with matching shirt and tie. "Do you have a hat to match?" he asked. "I think it needs a hat."

Wayne said he thought a hat would be too much, but David insisted. When the outfit was complete, he paid for it with cash. Wayne looked surprised, but said nothing.

"By the way," David said as Wayne handed him the receipt, "I'm looking for a friend of mine."

"Somebody from Allindea?" Wayne smiled. "It's a small town and I was born here; I probably know everybody around."

"Well, it's not really someone from Allindea," David said, glad he'd invented the story on the drive down from Vicksburg. "It's my fiancee's maid of honor. I'm picking her up and taking her on to the wedding in Baton Rouge. She's staying with friends in the area."

"What's their name?"

David knew he had to be careful here. "To be honest, I can't remember the name." He tried to grin sheepishly. "My fiancee told me, but it's been a long drive, and I didn't write it down. She always tells me I depend too much on my memory."

Wayne nodded. "My wife's always saying that about me, too."

"I do know it's a plantation just outside of town, though, if that helps."

Wayne shrugged. "I'm afraid not. There are several plantations around here. All through this area of the south, actually. Rosedown, Butler Greenwood, Catalpa, Highland — any of those sound familiar?"

David shook his head. "I'm not sure she even mentioned the name of the plantation. Do you recall any strangers in town recently? This woman is very attractive with shoulder-length auburn hair."

"Sorry, I'm afraid not. You could get a list of local plantations from Celeste Wallace at the historical society, though. She's also in charge of the chamber of commerce. Then I guess you'll have to call each one until you reach her."

"Thanks. I'll do that." David carried the suit bag out to the waiting van.

As he hung the suit on the hook behind the driver's seat, a red-haired woman opened the door of the Allindea Historical Society and stepped onto the front porch. She peered at the sky, then glanced at her watch.

David straightened up and smiled at her. "Hi," he said.

"Hi there," she waved. "I'm just trying to decide how long it's going to be until that storm gets here. I'd like to get home before it hits. I think I left my windows open."

"There's a storm coming?"

"That's what the weathermen say. I don't put much faith in them, but that sky's got a dangerous look to it. And there's a breeze picking up."

"You're probably right, then." David pushed the van door closed with his back. "I don't suppose you're Celeste Wallace?"

She tucked a stray strand of hair behind her ear and looked at David more closely. "I am. Should I know you?"

David stepped onto the porch. Despite his distaste at her sudden interest in him, he moved closer to her. "Not at all," he said. "I just got your name from Wayne, down at The Male Bag. He said you might be able to give me some information."

"I'd be happy to. What kind of information do you need?"

"I need a list of the plantations in the area which might rent rooms to guests."

"No problem." Celeste opened the large door behind her and ushered David inside. "I've got exactly what you want right here." She opened a drawer in a huge roll-top desk next to the door and shuffled through it for a moment.

"Aha! Here it is." She handed him a handful of flyers and a two-page typed list of names and addresses.

"Actually," she said, straightening the beads she wore around her throat, "if it's a room you're looking for, I have a room over my garage I rent out sometimes. The price is cheap, and I include breakfast."

David cringed inwardly, but forced a grin. "No, it's not for me. I'm trying to find a friend who's staying at a local plantation, but I can't remember the name of the place."

Celeste looked disappointed. "Oh, I see. Well, tell me what he looks like; maybe I've seen him around town."

"Actually, it's a woman. She's medium height and has shoulder-length auburn hair."

"You must mean that woman from Pennsylvania — Kristie something, isn't it?"

David's stomach lurched and he had to force himself not to grab Celeste's arms and shake her. "That's right," he said evenly. "Kirsta Linden. Do you know her?"

"She was in here a day or so ago," Celeste said. "Kind of quiet, but she seemed real nice."

David felt a bead of sweat trickle between his shoulder blades. The air in the damn museum seemed to be disappearing. "Did she happen to say where she was staying?"

"Oh, yes," Celeste nodded. "In fact, she was really interested in some of the artifacts we have from there. She's out at Sean McLeod's place, Lost Oaks."

"Lost Oaks," David said. The name of the plantation felt strangely familiar in his mouth, as though he'd said it a hundred times. But he was sure he'd never heard of it before.

"The address is on that paper I gave you," Celeste said. "You go down Main Street there and turn right at the light. That road will end at a stop sign. Take another left, and Lost Oaks is about six or eight miles from town on your left, past Henry Patton's gas station. If you want to call, you can use my phone."

"No, that's all right." David swallowed hard. "I want to surprise her. She thought I would take longer getting here."

"Okay, I understand." Celeste smiled at him conspiratorially.

"Thanks," David said, opening the door with trembling fingers. "Thanks very much, Miss Wallace."

"No problem." She followed him out onto the porch. "Hope everything goes the way you want it to," she called as he opened the van door.

David turned. "Pardon?"

"With the wedding and everything," Celeste explained."And tell Kirsta I said hello."

David waved and got behind the wheel. He started the engine, and backed out of the parking space. He started down Main Street in the direction Celeste Wallace had pointed. The air in the van was even closer than he'd feared, and he rolled down his windows. At the stop light, he glanced at the list of guest houses, and the name Lost Oaks seemed to raise from the white page.

"Lost Oaks," he said to himself. Why did that sound so familiar?

Celeste Wallace had said the owner was Sean McLeod. McLeod. David smiled, liking the sound of the name. Clouds were white, pure, distant from the corruption of the world. Clouds were close to Heaven, where the angels dwelled. It was another sign. David had found his new name — from now on he would be David McLeod.

He drove for a while, then noticed the van's gas tank was half empty. Hadn't it been filled only the night before? He'd have to get rid of this gas-guzzler as soon as possible. But for now he needed to fill it up before getting the woman. For just a moment, David couldn't remember her name. God, he was so tired. He couldn't picture her face. He concentrated, and after a moment the name came to him — Kirsta. Kirsta Linden, that was it. He sighed, relieved that he'd remembered.

They'd want to leave as soon as possible — unless they decided to stay in Louisiana, maybe at Lost Oaks. He hadn't thought of it before, but the idea of living on the plantation with his woman suddenly struck David as a very plausible one. It seemed natural, right, somehow. Suddenly, he noticed a red light on the dashboard, outlining the words "service engine soon." Damn, he thought, how long had that been on?

Down the road, he saw a sign for Henry's Gas Station. That must be the one Celeste had mentioned. He was getting close. This would probably be his last chance to fill up the tank and get the engine checked out before finding the woman. He pulled the van next to the pumps, as a young man with a greasy ponytail came out of the little building, rubbing his hands on an oily rag.

"Fill 'er up?" the boy asked.

"Yes," David said, glancing at the name stitched on the coveralls. "And Mike, I think there's something wrong with the engine. The 'service engine' light keeps coming on. Can someone check it out?"

Mike frowned. "Well, I don't know. Henry's takin' the day off, and he don't usually like me doin' garage work when he's not here."

David pulled some bills from his wallet. "I won't tell him if you won't," he said. "Could you at least check and see if it's something you can handle? Even if it's just a patch job. I really need to get it fixed right away."

Mike still wasn't sure. "I don't know how fast I'll be, workin' alone and havin' to keep an eye on the pumps."

"It's all right, I'll wait."

"Okay then," Mike said with enthusiasm. "Just pull 'er in the garage, and I'll see what I can do."

"Great," David said. "Thanks."

David drove into the garage after Mike opened the door, then carefully unhooked the suit bag. No sense in wasting time, he thought, and carried it into the restroom.

David McLeod prepared to meet his bride.

CHAPTER NINETEEN

Kirsta paced from one side of the narrow wooden porch to another. She'd come outside only after she waited for Sean's car to speed off down the driveway. Why had he chased her through the maze? Kirsta wished she hadn't panicked the way she had — surely Sean wouldn't have hurt her. He'd told her how much he cared for her. Then she remembered his eyes. It wasn't just the change in color that disturbed her, but that other change she'd seen, as though a completely different man were looking at her through them.

The rusty chains of the swing creaked as the increasing breeze moved it gently backward and forward. Kirsta grabbed it, trying to silence it. Every buzz of cicadas, every bird's twitter seemed to crawl across the endings of her nerves like tiny insects. She had to think, but the world seemed to be conspiring against her.

It wasn't just Sean's erratic moods that caused her so much confusion, though those were scary enough by themselves. It was something else, just at the edge of her consciousness, something she should see or understand. Kirsta felt as though she were building a delicate bridge over a precipice. She knew it would collapse if she didn't fit the parts together just right, but she wasn't sure she had all the pieces.

Kirsta sat on the swing and put her head in her hands. She closed her eyes, trying to concentrate. She saw again the photograph of Andrew Lucas before he was hanged. She examined the figure of the blond man standing behind Lucas — the sneering, arrogant twist of the mouth and set of the shoulders. Recognition began to dawn in Kirsta's mind. But it wasn't until she pictured again the blurred figure of the woman bound and gagged in the barn window that she finally made the connection.

These were the two people in her dream the first night. The woman's face was the same one she'd seen looking back at her from the carved mirror.

Kirsta sat up, stopping the motion of the swing. A black bird squawked in startled annoyance and flew away, but Kirsta barely noticed. She'd seen the same face at least two other times, also — in the steam of her bathroom mirror the morning after the dream and in the mists along the bayou two nights ago.

Indigo McLeod. It had to be. Indigo was trying to tell Kirsta something, she was sure of it now. And that something probably concerned Sean, though Kirsta couldn't imagine how. But she knew where she could find some information fast.

Kirsta rose and hurried to her car. As she passed the back porch of the main house, Daphne waved to her to stop.

"Will you be back for dinner, dear?" Daphne asked. "I'm afraid I have to go to Natchez soon. My sister Jezebel's feeling poorly and asked me to run some errands for her. It's about an hour's drive. I'll be out until rather late tonight, but I can leave something warm in the oven for you, if you'd like."

"No thanks." Kirsta tried to forced a smile, but it felt more like a grimace. "I'm not very hungry. I'll stop at the grocery store and pick up some cheese and crackers or something."

Daphne looked relieved. "If you're sure. By the way, I left my sister's number next to the phone. Sean raced off earlier, saying something about staying in Baton Rouge tonight. I guess he has an early meeting tomorrow morning. I barely had time to tell him about Jezzy."

"No problem," Kirsta said, feeling relief flood through her. Sean would be gone for the night. "I appreciate the thought, but I'm sure I won't need anything. I'm exhausted. When I get back, I'm going to climb under that quilt and sleep like the dead."

"Well, if you need anything at all, don't hesitate to use the phone. I hate leaving you alone like this — especially with a storm coming. I thought Sean would be here when I promised my sister I'd stop over tonight. Unfortunately, she couldn't get anybody else on such short notice."

"Don't think twice about it," Kirsta said. "I like being alone, even in storms. I know where the candles are. Don't worry about me."

Apparently reassured, Daphne smiled and turned back to the house, waving a last goodbye. As Kirsta drove down the gravel drive, she noticed a lot of activity in the tree tops. There seemed to be a lot of birds on the property today. She wondered whether that meant the birding would be soon. Something about the thought of all those birds coming for no known reason sent a chill down her spine. There were simply too many strange things happening around Lost Oaks.

Ten minutes later, Kirsta pulled into the Pattons' drive. The cat Indigo greeted her at the screen door, mewing softly. Kirsta stroked her head and wondered whether the cat were trying to talk to her, too. Etta was wiping her hands on an apron when she appeared in answer to Kirsta's knock.

"Oh, hello Kirsta. This is certainly a surprise." But Kirsta didn't think she sounded all that surprised.

"Would you like something cold to drink?" Etta offered as she opened the screen door.

"No thank you," Kirsta said, entering. "I need to ask you and Henry some questions, if he's around. And I'd like to look at some old family photos, if you have them."

Etta nodded as she ushered Kirsta through the house. "All right, dear. Henry's in the living room; he left Mike to take care of the station today. Had to get some book work done."

"Good," Kirsta said. "I hope I'm not being a nuisance."

"Not at all. We're always glad to see you."

Kirsta ran a hand through her hair and forced a smile. "I probably seem a little distracted — and I guess I am. I'm sorry to just show up unannounced like this, but I got an idea, and wanted to check it out while I was thinking about it."

Etta smiled as they entered the living room. "Of course. I know exactly what that's like. Research can become quite compelling."

She explained Kirsta's request to Henry, who nodded, but didn't rise or greet Kirsta. He didn't seem particularly surprised to see her either.

"Now, will any old photos do, or do you have something particular in mind?" Etta asked.

Kirsta swallowed drily. "Do you have any clear photos of David and Indigo McLeod?" she asked.

Etta looked at Henry. He nodded, and Kirsta thought he winced slightly as he rose to get the big scrapbook from the counter. She wondered whether the humidity was aggravating the arthritis in his hands, or whether something else was bothering him.

"I'm sure there must be some in here," he said as he began paging through the tattered book. "Etta put all these photos in chronological order a few years ago after she had her knee done and she couldn't get around much."

Etta nodded in agreement. "It kept me busy while the leg healed. Of course, I'm sure they aren't actually in strict chronological order, because many of them weren't dated, but the general periods are consistent. I'm sure of that."

Kirsta realized she was clenching and unclenching her hands, and forced herself to stop. She wanted to shout at them to hurry. Or better yet, she'd like to grab the book and find the photos herself. Not that she'd have any idea where to look, or what to look for. But the two old people seemed to move so slowly — and Kirsta was pretty sure she'd know the McLeods when she saw them.

"Here's a good one."

Henry held the book toward Kirsta. He pointed at a large photo of two people sitting on a wide veranda in matching wicker rocking chairs. The woman wore a light-colored lacy dress, and held a tortoise-shell fan. The man was dressed in a white suit and shirt, a silver-headed black cane across his lap. A large dog lay sleeping on the porch between the two chairs.

The photograph seemed a study in whiteness. Both people were blond. The woman's long hair was twisted into pale braids, a white flower tucked behind her ear, where a few curls had slipped loose. The man's hair appeared slightly darker, though obviously still blond, where it showed beneath his white hat. Even the dog was light-colored. Neither David nor Indigo smiled as they stared straight into the camera's eye.

Henry was talking as he pointed at the picture, explaining something, but Kirsta heard nothing except the roaring of blood in her ears. Not only were these the two people in the background of the photograph of Andrew Lucas, the photograph Kirsta had examined only hours earlier — but they were also definitely the two people she'd dreamed about the first night she'd spent at Lost Oaks. And something more — this was the blond woman she'd seen mourning in the chapel rectory. But the man in the photo was definitely not the man stretched out on the table. She hadn't seen his face, but he'd had very dark hair.

"What's wrong, dear?"

Etta's face frowned in concern, and Kirsta realized she must look like she'd seen a ghost. And maybe she had, she thought. She sank slowly to the sofa and tried to pull herself together before answering.

"I'll take that cold drink now," she said weakly.

After Etta had gotten them all glasses of iced tea, Kirsta spoke. "Something very strange is happening to me. But not just to me — it's happening to Sean, too. You two have got to help me sort it out. I don't know who else to ask."

Henry looked at Etta sternly. "I told you. But would you listen to me? No, I'm just an old fool. Well, now it might be too late."

"Oh, Henry," Etta seemed close to tears. "I'm sorry. I just didn't want to believe it." To Kirsta she said, "We'll do anything we can to make it right, dear."

"What are you two talking about?" Kirsta realized her voiced was a bit shrill, but she wanted to shake them both.

Etta patted Kirsta's hand. "It'll be all right, dear. Henry's been trying to tell me for weeks that the ghost is back at Lost Oaks. But frankly, I never believed in that old story; I thought he was just pulling my leg again. He's like that, you know, always playing pranks."

"Am not."

Kirsta felt as though she were about to scream. She opened her mouth to speak, but then thought the better of it. It was probably best to let them tell her in their own way, if she could stand it. Interrupting just might drag things out longer.

Etta started to argue, but Henry raised his hand to quiet her. "Truth is," he said to Kirsta, "I think the past is tryin' to move into the present somehow over to Lost Oaks. I know that sounds nutty as all hell, but it's the only thing I can figure to make any sense outta what's goin' on."

"What is going on?" Kirsta asked. "Don't you think it's about time I knew?"

"From the way I've seen you and Sean lookin' at each other," Henry said, "I sure do. It's perfectly obvious you're head over heels in love with the boy."

He looked hard at Kirsta. She was startled by his statement, but just nodded. This was no time to be coy or play games. The stakes were too high.

"Yep, I could tell," Henry continued. "I guess I been around long enough to know when two people love each other."

Kirsta felt her stomach lurch. Did that mean he thought Sean loved her as well? She didn't have time to dwell on the answer to that question or its ramifications.

"I'd like to wish you both a world of luck," Henry was saying, "but you're gonna need more than luck before this is all over. Young lady, I think you're in a mighty dangerous situation over at Lost Oaks."

Kirsta's mouth was dry. "What kind of danger?" she whispered.

Henry beat the heel of his hand against the chair arm angrily. "That's the bloody hell of it," he scowled. "I just don't know. That's why I haven't said anything about it to anybody before now. I just feel it, that's all. That boy's gonna cause you grief."

"Sean?" Kirsta tried to smile. "But didn't you just say he loves me?"

"I know," Henry said, shaking his head. "I know I did. But somehow that only makes it all worse. I can't explain it, but I just feel it in my innards that you'd be safer if he didn't care about you so much. Call me an old fool, call me nuts. Just don't ignore me."

Kirsta wanted to tell him he was crazy, or at least wrong, but she found she couldn't. She'd felt the same things herself, and now was the time to face it. The very way Sean looked at her showed that he loved her. But there was something dangerous in those looks, too, something frightening about his love.

"But why?" was all she could ask. "What's going on?"

"We don't know," Etta said. "We've been trying to figure it out ourselves, so we'd make more sense than this. If we spoke too soon, we'd sound like a couple of senile old storytellers. And then you'd never listen."

Henry added, "But from the looks of you, you've seen enough on your own to believe us."

Kirsta nodded. "Does Daphne know any of this?" she asked.

Etta laughed gently. "Poor Daphne, I'm sure we'd know if she suspected anything was wrong. She's a sweet thing, but she wildly over-reacts to everything. She probably knew you and Sean were in love before you did, because she wanted it to be true. She's been hoping he'd find somebody to settle down with again. But we haven't told her anything about the haunting. Truth is, I didn't even believe it until a few days ago myself."

"What convinced you?" Kirsta asked her.

"Sean did," Etta confessed.

"Sean?"

Etta nodded. "After you were out here yesterday, I remembered some things I thought you should know about Indigo. Henry had gone upstairs to putter around with his stamps, so I got in the car and headed over to Lost Oaks. When I got there, I saw someone kind of lurking around the cabin you're staying in, peering in the windows, listening at the door. When I got closer, I realized it was Sean. I called out to him. He came stalking over to me — stalking's the only word I can think of to describe it — and asked what I was doing there.

"Well, I didn't get too specific; I didn't want to go into all we'd talked about earlier, to be honest. He looked so angry, so ... different. When I said I wanted to see you, he became furious, and told me to get off his property, to leave you alone. He called me an old meddler — and some other things."

She paused. Kirsta said, "Well, that's rude, but it doesn't sound ghostly or —"

Etta interrupted her. "You're right. But none of that's what really scared me. It was when he talked about you. His voice changed, got … different, somehow, darker or deeper. Oh, I don't know how to describe it. And he used kind of old-fashioned language. But the part that made my hackles rise was when he called you Indigo."

Kirsta gasped, but said nothing. Etta continued, "I stopped him and corrected him, he seemed confused for a minute. Then he just said I must have misheard him. But I didn't; he'd said it twice, very clearly."

She looked embarrassed, and said, "I have to confess, I got scared then, and left. I hardly even remember the drive home."

They were all silent for a long moment. Then Kirsta asked, "What does all this mean? It's strange and frightening, but I don't really understand it."

Henry said, "Truth is, neither do we. I've wrapped my brain all around it these past days, but I can't make hide nor hair of it. Just some things seem to be important — things from the past. Like this Indigo stuff, and the way Sean's acting, and me seein' that hanged man, and the date and all."

"The date?" Kirsta asked. "What date?"

Etta said, "Today's date. Or tomorrow's. Or maybe yesterday's. We haven't been able to find out for sure, but I think it's important."

Suddenly Kirsta felt like Alice in Wonderland, talking to the Red Queen. Etta made perfect sense to herself and Henry, Kirsta was sure of it. But she made no sense to Kirsta.

Henry waved his hand impatiently at his sister. "Etta's gettin' all tongue-tied tryin' to tell you that Andrew Lucas was hanged one of these days hereabouts, back in the eighteen-sixties. That just seems important, somehow. But I'm damned if I know why."

"Henry's done some more research," Etta said, "and he uncovered some, well, startling facts. But we don't really understand where it all leads."

"I almost don't want to ask," Kirsta said, "but what kind of facts?"

"Well, let's see." Henry stood and rooted through a sheaf of papers resting on a pile of old volumes in his office. "I wrote down some notes and I know I've got them somewhere."

He held up a handful of pale green sheets. "Oh, here are those old phone bills we were lookin' for, Etta."

Kirsta groaned inwardly.

Etta motioned for him to keep looking. "Don't worry," she muttered to Kirsta, "he'll find them. He just lets himself get distracted too easily."

"Here it is," Henry called out, and brought a legal-sized notepad in with

184

him. Kirsta could see uneven scribbles all over the front, facing every direction. She wondered whether he'd be able to read his own writing.

He frowned at it and turned the notepad end-over-end several times, confirming Kirsta's fear. "Looks like nothin' but hen scratches," he scowled. "Give me a minute to translate my handwritin'."

"Can't you just remember what's on it, Henry?" Etta said after a pause. "I remember some of it myself. I could help."

"Leave me alone, woman," Henry sighed. "I almost have it. There." He pointed at the paper and grinned proudly at them before continuing, like a child who finally understands a difficult math problem.

"Thing is," Henry said, peering at his notes, "it seems there are a lot of similarities between what went on at Lost Oaks in the eighteen-sixties and what's happening now."

"Like what?" Kirsta prompted.

"Like what happened to Sean's family," Etta said. "The accident."

Henry nodded. "You remember how Edwina and Andy McLeod were killed in a plane crash a couple years ago?"

"I remember," Kirsta said. "They were on their way to Memphis, to see her parents, weren't they?"

"That's right," Henry said. "Well, Andrew Lucas' wife and daughter were killed in a carriage accident, too. That's why he was goin' home, remember. I found an old letter that says Lucas spent a couple nights in jail, but no magistrate could come to try him, so he was released to vigilantes. While he was in jail, he told the deputy about what had happened to his family. They'd been heading north along the Mississippi, when part of the road caved in. The whole kit and caboodle ended up in the river. Near as I can figure, it was right near where Edwina's plane went down in that snowstorm."

"That's incredible," Kirsta gasped.

"And that's not the half of it," Henry continued. "During the Civil War, Lost Oaks was losing money big-time, like a lot of the plantations down here. David McLeod was having a hell of a time keeping his head above water. Turns out, his daddy was overseas, tryin' to make a fortune in the furniture business — in Paris. He sent money whenever he could, but he and David didn't get along very well, so David always sent the money back."

"I don't know how much you know about Sean and Stuart," Etta said, "but the relationship is very similar."

"It's sure a lot of coincidences." Henry shook his head. "But maybe it all amounts to less than a handful of cornfeed in a silo. I just don't know. Then there's the birding."

It took Kirsta a moment to remember what the librarian had told her about the black birds that flew into Lost Oaks every spring. She couldn't find any connection with present events.

She sighed. "What could a bunch of birds have to do with all this?"

"Well, it may be a stretch, mind you," Henry drawled, "but the local Indians had a lot of legends that centered around blackbirds. The Houmas Indians thought that the land Lost Oaks sits on is haunted or something."

"Celeste Wallace told me a little about that," Kirsta said.

"You talked with Celeste Wallace?" Etta asked. "I didn't know that. Celeste certainly enjoys talking about local history."

Henry sniffed. "That damn woman's more gossip than historian," he muttered, "but the part about the Indians is true. And one of the Houmas beliefs is that blackbirds bring messages from ancestors to influence the behavior of their descendants. And another is that the birds protect the souls of the innocent at the time of death."

"I'm still not sure I get it," Kirsta said.

"Anyway," Etta pointed out, "the birds haven't even shown up yet this year.

"Yeah, you're right." He waved a hand in the air dismissively. "It's probably got nothing to do with all this. But they say the birding started somewhere during the eighteen hundreds, and it's just one more coincidence."

They were all silent a moment, and Kirsta wondered how they would react if they knew the rest of the coincidences, such as her own abusive relationship — so much like Indigo's — with a man named David. And what about all the dreams, she thought, and the voices and bizarre tableau she'd witnessed the first time she'd gone to the cemetery chapel? Could it be possible Indigo McLeod really was trying to contact her? Before today, Kirsta had never seriously considered the possibility of messages from beyond the grave. Now it seemed not only possible, but probable.

She began to realize all this might explain the significance of the letter "I" appearing over and over, and the writing on the barn wall, and her recurring visions of Indigo's face. But this only raised more questions than it answered. Why was Indigo trying to contact her? What about the roses? And, most importantly, how did Sean fit in with all this?

Kirsta wanted to ask the Pattons about all these things, but she felt so exhausted, so drained of all emotion and energy that she couldn't find the words to begin.

Instead, she heard herself ask, "Do either of you believe in possession?"

CHAPTER TWENTY

"Possession?" Etta asked. "You mean like demons and witches?"

"No," Kirsta answered slowly. "At least I don't think so. Oh, I'm not sure what I mean." She hit her fist against the sofa arm in frustration.

The phone rang. Etta stood. "I think you'd better try to explain it to us, Kirsta. But wait until you can pull your thoughts together. I'll take care of whoever's on the phone as soon as possible."

Henry frowned as he watched her limp into the kitchen. The house was so quiet Kirsta could hear the ice cubes click as they melted in the glasses. A breeze rustled the drapes hanging limply by the window behind Kirsta and she shivered at the sound.

"Storm's gonna hit tonight for sure," Henry said. "And it's gonna be a mean one."

"Why do you say that?" Kirsta asked. "The sky hasn't changed, and the wind hasn't picked up much. It could be days yet till it gets here."

"Nope, it's tonight. Etta's legs and my hands are givin' us a world of trouble today," he mused, slowly flexing his fingers. "That's why I didn't go down to the station. And the air's carryin' the scent of mud. Can't you smell it?"

"I don't know. I think so."

Kirsta sniffed. She did notice something, a musty, tangy odor. But she wasn't sure whether it was a new smell, or whether it had always been there and she just imagined it because of what Henry had said. She decided it didn't matter.

Etta returned with a plate of cookies. "Here we go," she said. "A bite of shortbread should make you feel better."

Her voice was cheerful, but Kirsta noticed a darker undercurrent. Was that a hint of worry — or fear — behind Etta's eyes?

187

"Who was on the phone?" Henry asked as he reached for a cookie.

"Daphne," Etta said. "She was just getting ready to visit her sister Jezzy in Natchez." She paused. "She called because she thought Kirsta would like to know the blackbirds are here for the birding."

Henry glanced up quickly, the hand holding the cookie frozen halfway to his mouth. Kirsta didn't like the look in his eyes.

"You don't say." His voice was little more than a whisper. "So it is happening. I'll be damned."

Kirsta tried to sound casual. "I noticed a lot of birds in the area when I left today. I wondered if they were coming in for the birding. They're only here till tomorrow, then?"

"That's right," Etta said. "Tomorrow evening they'll be gone." She took a bite of cookie. "Now, tell us your idea about somebody being possessed."

"It's not just somebody," Kirsta said. "It's Sean."

Henry snorted. "Surely, you don't think the devil's takin' Sean over?"

"No, not the devil. It's what you said about Andrew Lucas and all the coincidences."

Kirsta squirmed a little on the sofa and cleared her throat before continuing. "I think maybe Andrew Lucas is trying to take control of Sean."

Etta took a sharp breath. Henry asked, "What makes you say that?"

Kirsta said, "Well, I've seen and heard some pretty weird things myself since I got to Lost Oaks."

"Oh, you poor girl," Etta said. "I thought — I'd hoped we were the only ones. Whatever happened to you?"

"It's not really important what they were, but all the events seem to have to do with the period we're talking about. Visions of hanged men, dreams of a man and woman in nineteenth century clothing. Then there's something you said yesterday about noticing that Sean acted oddly on the plantation. I've noticed that, too. Sean even made a comment about being more relaxed when he's away from Lost Oaks. And —"

She stopped, feeling a bit guilty about revealing Sean's confidences during their picnic at the cemetery.

"And what, honey?" Henry prompted. "Don't hold back on us now. This might be important."

Kirsta sighed. "You're right. Sean made a comment last night about feeling as though someone else were inside him sometimes, making him do things he doesn't want to do. I think that might be truer than he realizes, and it might be Andrew Lucas."

She bit her lip and watched the ice floating in her tea. Each breath felt strained, as though her ribs didn't want to move. She wanted to be anywhere else, but knew this was the only place to solve the mystery of what was happening to her and Sean.

Henry said quietly, "What's the rest, Kirsta?"

She didn't look up. "I think Andrew Lucas wants to make Sean hurt me."

Etta gasped. "But why would Andrew want to hurt you?"

"I'm not sure," Kirsta admitted. "But I think it has something to do with his hanging, or with Indigo McLeod, or ... I don't know exactly. I just think I'm on the right track."

Etta clicked her tongue. "Andrew Lucas returning now because of a hanging that happened more than a hundred years ago? I'm afraid that doesn't make any sense at all."

"You said Sean called me Indigo when you spoke to him last night, didn't you?"

Etta sputtered. "Well, yes, I thought he did. But maybe he just —"

"Well, I think I've heard him call me Indigo, too. I think he's been sneaking into the cabin somehow as Andrew to ..." She stopped.

"To do what?" Etta prompted.

"That's just it," Kirsta said, standing. She paced the living room, feeling caged. "I don't know what. I'm not even sure of what I'm saying. This is all too confusing. But sometimes I think Sean even looks like Andrew Lucas."

Silence hung over the room for a moment. Then Etta's face brightened. "But if he's Andrew Lucas, then you're all right, as long as he thinks you're Indigo. He'd never harm the woman he loved. He surely knows she had nothing to do with having him hanged."

"Makes sense to me," Henry agreed, but he didn't sound too sure. He was scowling down at the notes scrawled on the legal pad.

Kirsta couldn't put her finger on it, but something told her Etta wasn't quite right. She was sure there was a piece missing from the puzzle. She kept seeing the photo of Andrew waiting for the noose, with Indigo captive in the barn far behind him. Something about Andrew's eyes ...

"You're probably right." Kirsta tried to smile. "I'm just trying too hard to tie everything together, I guess. I shouldn't have bothered you two with all this."

"Not at all," Etta said. "I'm glad you stopped by. As a matter of fact, just before you got here, Henry and I were talking about taking a drive over to Lost Oaks. We want you to come stay with us."

"Stay here?"

"Sure, why not?" Henry said. "It's not a plantation, but we've got plenty of room. We'd enjoy the company. And to be honest," he added, "we weren't all that sure you'd be safe back there with … well, you know."

"With Sean." Kirsta finished the sentence for him quietly. "That's what you mean isn't it?"

Etta and Henry exchanged an awkward glance, and he cleared his throat. Etta patted Kirsta's shoulder.

"Now, we're not talking against him, understand," she said. "He's a wonderful boy. But you said yourself he just hasn't been quite right lately. And we think that maybe you'd be more comfortable here with us for the rest of your stay."

"Who knows?" Henry said, rising from his chair. "Maybe the birding does have something to do with all this. If so, there's a good chance it'll all clear up by tomorrow night when the birds leave, and everything will be hunky dory."

"Maybe, maybe not," Etta said carefully. "But until then, you have your safety and peace of mind to consider."

"I understand," Kirsta said, rising. "And I suppose I have to agree, although I'd hate to think that Sean would ever do anything …"

She broke off, unable to finish the sentence around the tightness in her throat and chest. Her heart wouldn't let the words come.

She straightened her shoulders and pulled her car keys from her purse. "But I know I don't have anything to worry about tonight — Daphne said Sean is staying in Baton Rouge. I'll pack up my stuff first thing in the morning, and be gone before he gets back home."

As she walked to the front door, Kirsta's heart already ached from missing Sean — and the plantation. How could she ever leave Lost Oaks?

Driving back to the plantation after stopping at a fast-food restaurant for hamburgers and a Coke, Kirsta considered the irony of her situation. She'd come down to Louisiana to escape emotional turmoil and find peace, to get her life together. But the whole world had turned topsy-turvy: what was once beyond the realm of possibility now seemed perfectly reasonable. Reality and myth had changed places. It all made a terrible kind of sense.

It was incredible to think that when she finally found the man she loved more than any man she'd ever met, a man who seemed to love her in return, he was also the man who seemed capable of doing her the most harm. If she and the Pattons were right, the dangers she faced from Sean went far deeper than anything she'd anticipated. She hit her fist on the steering wheel in frustration. After all she'd been through with David Belsen, she deserved better than this.

A low roll of thunder followed her from the west as she pulled into the Lost Oaks drive. It sounded a bit louder than it had earlier, and Kirsta stopped the car to listen. The rumble wasn't repeated, but she noticed that the slight breeze had freshened. The feathery edges of the honeysuckle bush by the sign rippled as she drove by. She rolled down her window all the way. The air felt damp and delicious, and as Kirsta closed her eyes to savor it, she smelled the same musty odor she'd noticed at the Pattons' house. Maybe Henry was right about the storm.

She continued slowly up the gravel drive, suddenly feeling very lonely in the evening shadows. As she rounded the last bend, the grey house came into sight, looking dark and foreboding in the shadows, with no lights to brighten the empty windows. Even the flowers in the garden seemed to huddle together, preparing for the onslaught of the storm.

Kirsta's gaze fell on the huge live oak tree in the center of the front lawn and she jammed the brake. Though the breeze had died down for a moment, the tree seemed to move with a life of its own, leaves and branches vibrating all around it. Climbing from the car, Kirsta realized the tree's branches were covered in birds. Wherever her gaze landed, she saw a blackbird nodding or twitching or ruffling its feathers. But there was absolutely no sound — the birds were completely silent. In fact, everything was completely silent.

A terrible sense of dread suddenly overcame Kirsta. She shuddered violently. Maybe she should turn around and go as quickly as possible back to the Pattons', where security and companionship waited. She wouldn't have to spend the night alone, here where danger seemed to lurk around every corner. Kirsta was sure they'd understand, even welcome her with relief. She'd come back in the morning, or whenever the storm let up, to get her things. Or better yet, she'd pay someone to come over here and get them. Then she'd never have to see Lost Oaks again — or explain to Sean.

Never see Lost Oaks again. The phrase echoed over and over in her head as she stood by her car in the gathering twilight. She hated the thought of saying good-bye to this place forever. But when she thought of never seeing Sean again, her whole being seemed to collapse, to fold in on itself. Kirsta could hardly breathe. She clenched her eyes.

"I love you, Sean," she whispered to the darkness, "and I'm afraid I don't know how to leave you."

Suddenly, a breeze kicked up again and the birds began muttering and squawking to one another. Kirsta opened her eyes again and her glance fell on the old cook's cabin by the pond. It looked as cozy and welcoming as ever. The overpowering desire to flee disappeared as quickly as it had come.

Kirsta got back into her car and continued past the big house. She was exhausted and hungry and her nerves were on edge. Too many stories, she decided, too many strange things to sort out. No wonder she'd had an anxiety attack. She'd eat her dinner and go to bed early. In the morning she could decide what to do. Kirsta tried to ignore the aching emptiness that tugged at her throat when she thought about leaving in the morning.

Even if Andrew's ghost were haunting Lost Oaks, it only seemed to bother her when Sean was around. She had nothing to worry about tonight, since Sean was at least an hour's drive away. As long as he wasn't on the plantation, Kirsta would be fine.

As she carried the bags with her dinner into the cabin, a gust of wind slammed the wooden door open against the wall. Kirsta jumped at the resounding bang it made. Then she smiled at herself, and went back to close it. Standing in the open doorway, she thought she saw something move behind the big oak tree halfway to the house.

She froze — who would be lurking around the yard in this weather? Nobody should be anywhere near Lost Oaks except her. Kirsta squinted against the wind, her eyes watering as a fresh gust blew in. Then the old goose waddled away from the tree, muttering at leaves blowing past and hissing behind her at the tree trunk. What had possessed the poor old thing to leave her nest on such a night? Usually Sean was the only one who could get her to move. Kirsta shrugged. Maybe the birding disturbed her.

Kirsta chuckled at herself as she pushed the door shut. She'd have to get her nerves under control before the storm hit or she'd be a wreck all night, panicking at every clap of thunder. She decided to take a quick shower and eat, then get to bed as soon as possible. She grabbed her nightgown and went into the bathroom to undress.

After her shower, Kirsta opened the paper bag holding her hamburger and french fries, then got a plate and some napkins from the cupboard. The damp air seemed to have drawn the temperature down; the wooden floor felt cold under her bare feet, and she could feel the wind creep between the boards. She put the food into the microwave. Next to the microwave she noticed a bottle with a note on it: "Thought you'd like a little nip before bed tonight. Sweet dreams, see you in the morning. Daphne."

She turned the bottle around to look at the label. Fruit de coeur. Kirsta smiled at her hostess's thoughtfulness and started into the other room with her dinner. Then she stopped. Why not? she thought. A glass of wine would probably help her sleep better — might even knock her out, as tired as she was. Kirsta went back into the kitchenette and uncorked the wine bottle, pouring some into a juice glass. With a pang, she remembered the crystal glasses she and Sean had used near the cemetery, just before they'd ...

"Stop it," she ordered herself. "Just try to put it behind you." Something told her "try" was the operative word.

She put the glass and plate on the coffee table next to her computer. As she ate, she watched the sky darken beyond the pond. She thought of the beautiful red-golden sky behind the trees at the cemetery and wished for that time again. Was that only twenty-four hours ago? So much seemed to have happened since then. Her whole life had changed. One minute, her world was complete with her love for Sean and his for her. Now, only a day later, everything was over. She still loved him — she couldn't deny that, even to herself. But she had to do something. She couldn't let things go on the way they were; it was just too risky. She'd tried that with David, and it had only gotten worse.

Kirsta suddenly recalled her conversation with Ginny that morning. David — dead. Had he burned himself and his car intentionally? It was hard to imagine David doing anything like that. But then how did it happen? Kirsta knew she should be glad that he'd never bother her again, but the very thought of him left a cold spot in the pit of her stomach. Kirsta grit her teeth. It was as though he were out there, standing in the shadows somewhere watching her. She shuddered, then realized she'd combined David's horrible death with Sean's bizarre behavior lately. It was certainly more like David to act strangely.

Kirsta felt her throat ache as she thought about Sean. After reaching the highest peak she'd ever felt last night, she now had reached the lowest, darkest pit. A gust of wind rattled the pane of the window next to her, and Kirsta shuddered, pulling her nightgown closer around her legs. She could barely see outside now. Trees and bushes were just shadows rippling against the paler shadows of clouds marching across the sky. Feeling exposed and a little vulnerable, Kirsta got up and closed the curtains. She checked the mantle to make sure the candles and matches were still there.

She poured herself another small glass of wine and drank it quickly. Then she climbed into the big bed, drawing the sheets up. She turned out the light.

Pale flashes of lightning danced around the edges of the drapes, though the rumbles of thunder still sounded faint and distant. Kirsta knew she'd never get to sleep now. She decided to close her eyes and rest until the storm arrived.

When she awoke, the storm had arrived. Thunder rattled the panes of glass in the windows and wind screamed through cracks in the old boards of the cabin. Rain beat against the roof. Kirsta sat up groggily in bed. The wine had hit her harder than she'd expected. She reached out to turn on the light. Her fingers twisted the knob on the lamp, but nothing happened. She turned it two or three more times, but the room remained dark. The electricity must be out. She recalled seeing the candles on the mantle before going to sleep.

As she started to put one foot on the cool floor, a flash of lightning illuminated the room. Kirsta froze. She clearly remembered closing the drapes before getting into bed. But now the drapes had been pulled away. Feeling dread seep like ice water into her veins, she turned her head.

A man stood silhouetted against the window.

CHAPTER TWENTY-ONE

A clap of thunder shook the walls. In the next flash of lightning, Kirsta saw more. She saw the trapdoor open in the center of the floor. But this barely registered, because she also saw the man's face. She recognized him. Sean. Of course, that was why the old goose had been wandering around by the tree. Sean had been there.

"Sean?" she said, her voice trembling. "What are you doing here?"

Without answering, he moved slowly toward the bed, and stood over her a moment, not moving. Then he reached out to touch her hair. Kirsta drew away from his fingers. This was Sean — she'd seen his face. But somehow he didn't seem like Sean.

"When did you get back from Baton Rouge?"

"Indigo," he said, ignoring her question, "don't be afraid. I've come back for you."

It was Andrew Lucas speaking. She knew she had to bring Sean back from wherever he'd gone before it was too late.

"No, you're wrong," Kirsta called over the roar of the rain. "I'm not Indigo, I'm Kirsta. You're not Andrew Lucas, you're —"

He put his fingers across her lips. "Hush. You're mine again, my love. I've waited so long, so long."

He bent and pressed his lips to her. Despite her fear, Kirsta felt herself respond. She wanted to wrap her arms around his neck and surrender to the heat of his passion. But this wasn't Sean, she reminded herself. This man was a stranger who was living out some other life in some other time. Kirsta pulled back. She gripped his shoulders and pushed him away from her.

In the flickering light from the storm, Kirsta watched the lines of his face shimmer the way it had the night he'd tried to make love to her, and earlier that day in the maze. It seemed Sean and Andrew Lucas were fighting for control.

"Sean," she screamed, "don't let him win."

But it was too late. The face she loved settled into the coarser features of the doomed man in the old photos and in her drawings. The man with the noose around his neck. The kindness left his eyes, and a cold hardness remained. His lips parted in a terrible parody of a grin, and he looked through her.

Kirsta tried to pull away, but he grabbed both her hands in one of his. His strength was incredible. No matter how she struggled, he seemed to have no trouble holding her.

"All right, Mrs. McLeod," he snarled, "we'll do it the hard way, if you insist."

He reached into his pocket with his free hand, and pulled out a shiny object. A silver filigree ring, Kirsta saw. He put it on her left hand.

"Remember this, my darling?" he said. "This is the ring your husband gave you on your wedding day. 'Till death us do part — David,' it says inside. You hid it in the loft when you pledged your love to me, told him you'd lost it. Remember? Remember? Well, you betrayed me for him, so I think you should wear it again."

Kirsta renewed her struggles, but was unable to free her hands. He had her pinned against the headboard, so she couldn't move her legs or torso more than a few inches.

"Please, Sean," she begged, "I didn't betray you. Indigo didn't betray you."

He ignored her. Standing straight, he pulled her to her feet. Kirsta twisted hard and broke away, lunging toward the door. She tugged at the bolt, but it held tight. Sean leaped for her, knocking her off her feet. She grabbed at the night table to stop herself from falling, but landed heavily against the floor.

Dimly, she was aware of something small clutched in the palm of her hand. Indigo's brooch. She grasped it tighter, as though it were a talisman that might release her from this madness.

The wind was knocked out of her. As she struggled for breath, Sean pulled her arms behind her. He drew his belt from the loops of his trousers, and wrapped it tightly around her wrists. Then he jerked her to her feet.

"This is only fitting," he said. "My hands were bound, too, you know, when I was led to my execution."

"Execution?"

Kirsta tried to speak, but her lungs were still gasping for air and her head throbbed from the fall. Her voice was no more than a whisper, drowned by the storm.

He continued speaking as he opened the door. "Of course, you wouldn't know the details of my execution, would you? You couldn't be bothered to be present for such a triviality. That's how your husband put it — you couldn't be bothered."

"Sean, I don't know what you're talking about," Kirsta gasped as he dragged her out onto the porch.

Wild wind whipped her hair about her face. Her thin nightgown wrapped around her legs, hobbling her as Sean pulled her forward, his fingers digging into her arm. He shouted something at her as they staggered off the porch into the rain, but Kirsta couldn't hear his voice over the roar of the storm raging around them.

Needles of rain seemed to pierce her naked arms and shoulders in a thousand places at once, and she was nearly blinded by the water in her eyes. Her bare feet slipped and slid in the mud and wet grass as he pulled her along the path that led past the main house. Kirsta peered at the darkened windows, praying for a light to come on. What time was it? she wondered. When would Daphne be home?

"Daphne!" she called into the thundering darkness. "Please, somebody, help!"

Sean ignored her. He jerked her forward roughly. Kirsta tripped over a tree root and lost her footing, stumbling to keep up with the terrifying man who wore her lover's face. She cried out for Sean to stop, but he never paused. Kirsta could barely hear her own voice. Even if Daphne had been home, she realized miserably, she'd never have heard Kirsta's screams over the din of the storm.

They finally rounded the corner of the big grey house, so cold and imposing in the violent darkness. A bolt of lightning spat into the front lawn, not fifty feet from where Kirsta and Sean struggled on the flagstones leading to the veranda's steps. Kirsta's nostrils tingled from the scent of cordite in the air. But the acrid smell was nothing compared to what met her eyes in that brief flash.

In the center of the carefully manicured grass stood the ancient live oak. It looked like a dark god against the white flash from the lightning, huge crooked branches waving wildly about it. Blackbirds dotted the branches like strange growths. But something else burned itself into Kirsta's mind long after her retina released the bizarre image she'd just seen. Dangling from one of the branches, whipped by the storm, was a long thick rope, twisted into a hangman's noose.

"No!" Kirsta screamed into the wind, renewing her struggles. "Sean, it's me, Kirsta."

Either he didn't hear her or didn't care. He continued to drag her relentlessly across the grass toward the tree. His single-minded purpose seemed to give him superhuman strength; he drew her along behind him with no apparent effort. Kirsta felt like no more than a branch carried in the jaws of some terrible, unfeeling beast.

As they got closer, she made out the form of a stool placed beneath the branch at the spot where the noose hung. Sean wrapped one arm around her thighs and drew her up and against him. Kirsta groaned in despair at the irony of this deadly embrace. He grabbed the noose with his free hand. He placed it around her neck as he lifted her onto the stool. Kirsta felt the hemp scrape roughly at her throat. Her toes clutched at the edges of the slippery wooden surface as she tried to maintain her balance.

"Now," Sean said, glaring at her with the dark eyes of a man who died more than a century ago, "now you'll see how it feels to die alone. To have the one you love betray you at the end."

A strong gust of wind seemed to grab at her legs, and Kirsta struggled to stay erect on the narrow seat of the stool. She desperately worked her hands in the belt, but couldn't free them. She felt again the object she'd clutched in her fall against the night table, and recognized it as the silver brooch she'd found in the magnolia tree.

"Sean, please," Kirsta began, but Sean cut her off as thunder cracked like a canon over their heads. The birds rustled above her restlessly.

"Have you any last words?" he shouted into the wind.

Kirsta's grip tightened on the silver brooch, and she felt the tip of the pin prick the soft flesh in the palm of her hand. Her blood trickled warmly around the brooch, and in her mind's eye, she saw it stain the letter "I" a bright red. She lifted her face into the rain.

"Indigo McLeod," she called to the thunder and lightning, "I know you're somewhere listening. Help me. Show Andrew that you love him. Let Sean come back to me."

As the last words left her lips, another bolt of lightning crashed into the lawn, less than ten feet from where Sean stood. He didn't move. His eyes remained fixed on Kirsta's face. She clenched her eyes closed as the flash blinded her. A moment later, she heard a voice and realized her lips were moving.

"Andrew, my love," the voice said. "How could you do this?"

"Indigo," Sean gasped. "Is it — could it be you?"

Kirsta opened her eyes. She knew the voice had come from her mouth, but the sound seemed to radiate to her from outside her, like the echo of a sigh in the mountains. Though the wind and rain still raged around them, Kirsta felt nothing and heard nothing except their voices. She felt her lips move again.

"Andrew," the voice said sadly, "even now I love you. Your heart knows I could never betray you. Listen to your heart, my dearest."

Sean took one faltering step, then another toward the stool. "Why did you allow them to hang me, Indigo?" he asked, his voice trembling and hurt. "Why did you desert me?"

Kirsta's heart felt as though it would break.

"I didn't allow anyone. It wasn't within my power to stop David. And I could never desert you, my love. David found out about us; he was in the barn that last afternoon when you gave me the rose. He bound me and kept me prisoner, watching, in the loft room until after your … your execution. I tried to get to you, to save you, but it was impossible."

"You didn't choose him over me?" Sean reached one hand out tentatively and touched Kirsta's arm.

"How could I?" Kirsta felt herself answer. "Andrew, my darling, I mourned you for the rest of my life — and still do. I even saved the brooch you gave me when we climbed the magnolia."

Sean leaned his head against her thigh. Kirsta wanted to reach out to him, to stroke his hair, to comfort him. But her hands were still bound, and the rope was still around her neck.

"Release me, my love," she said. "Don't pile mistake upon mistake now. Let it be over at last."

Sean heaved a hoarse sob against her, and reached behind Kirsta to loosen his belt from her wrists. Suddenly, a white figure ran from beside the veranda. A silver-headed cane rose over Sean's head, and before Kirsta could warn him, it cracked sharply against his skull.

Sean dropped silently to the sodden earth.

Kirsta couldn't believe her eyes. David stood before her, his golden hair now plastered around his face, rain running down his cheeks and chin like tears. He wore a pale suit and shirt, drooping soggily against his body. A matching fedora lay some yards behind him, where it had blown off in the wind. David's eyes were narrow and cruel as he slowly approached Kirsta. She struggled frantically to free her hands from Sean's belt, now loosened a bit from her wrists.

"I've come for you, my darling."

David's sneer corrupted the meaning of his loving words. Kirsta tried to stay calm, though her thoughts were spinning wildly out of control.

"I thought ... I mean, I was told you were ... dead," she stammered, still fighting with the slick leather belt behind her.

"I am," David laughed, holding up the black cane in triumph. "That is, David Belsen is dead. Let me introduce myself." He made a small bow. "David McLeod."

Kirsta froze, her blood chilled by his words. "David McLeod?"

"That's right. I've found myself." He moved closer, touching her shoulder with the silver ball on the top of his cane. "And now I've found you. I must teach you what it means to be an obedient wife."

A strong gust of wind nearly threw Kirsta off balance, but David steadied her with his free hand. She felt his fingers against her hip and shuddered. She nearly had one hand free of her bonds. Just another minute ...

"David," she said, trying to keep her voice from trembling, "please get me down from here."

He looked up into her eyes for a long moment as the rain beat down on them. Then, instead of helping her, he stepped away again.

"I can't do that, my love." He sounded almost sad, but Kirsta could see the corners of his mouth twitch.

"David!"

"You must be punished," he said, slapping at the palm of his hand with the head of the cane. "Surely you see that. You've deceived me and betrayed me. No decent woman would treat her husband like that. You deserve to die. But I'll bestow one last kiss before you follow your lover to hell."

He moved closer, and grasped the rope above her head, raising himself onto the stool, one booted foot on either side of her bare feet. Though the noose tightened, gagging her, Kirsta shrank away from his touch.

A desperate wrench of her hands and she was free. As he put his cold lips against hers, she brought her right hand around and drove the point of the brooch's pin into his cheek. David screamed and toppled backward. He lay sprawled across Sean's limp form, clawing at the silver brooch, still embedded in his face.

Kirsta drew her head from the rope and leaped down to the grass. Her feet slid beneath her, but she caught her footing, running across the lawn as quickly as she could. The rain had let up, but the wind still tore at the trees. Above the wind's howl, she heard David's shouts growing louder behind her.

He must be chasing her. With a sob of frustration, Kirsta tried to run faster, despite the stones and twigs cutting into the soft pads of her feet.

Suddenly, the topiary maze loomed before her. Kirsta slowed for only a split second, then plunged into the towering black fortress. Maybe David would get lost in one of the dead ends long enough for her to double back and escape. If she could get to the cabin for her car keys, she'd drive to the Pattons' and call the police.

Kirsta tried to concentrate, though David's voice and the pounding of his boots sounded very close. Obviously, he was not getting lost in the maze. Either he was close enough to follow her, or the David McLeod part of him remembered the pattern. Kirsta tried not to panic, but she realized she would be trapped in the center. Stray branches clawed and tore at her nightgown and the flesh of her bare arms as she ran madly on.

Then she was in the center, and the only direction she could go was up. Up into the sturdy waiting branches of the Marryin' Magnolia. She ran to the tree and began climbing, gripping the wet limbs with both fingers and toes, glad for the moment that her feet were bare. Shoes would only have made climbing the slick branches even more treacherous.

Below her, David shouted a name — she couldn't tell for sure whether he said "Kirsta" or "Indigo." Then he climbed after her. She heard his boots thumping against the slippery bark, and he cursed in pain several times when his feet slid.

Kirsta continued to climb, but she felt her energy flagging. She wondered how much higher she could go before he caught her. Or would she fall first, landing like a broken doll at the foot of the tree? Her lungs ached as she worked.

Then a hand gripped her ankle. Kirsta screamed in surprise and looked down. The clouds had released the moon, and silvery light distorted the maniacal leer on David's face.

"You're mine now," he muttered through clenched teeth.

"No!" Kirsta shouted, and yanked her foot as hard as possible, jerking it free. She nearly lost her balance, and clung to the wide tree trunk until she found her footing.

David was thrown backward against a large limb, and gripped a smaller one with his free hand. With the other, he lunged again toward Kirsta. But his booted feet chose that moment to slide on the surface of the branch below him. He fell forward, the small branch in his hand breaking beneath his weight. He plunged downward, limbs snapping loudly as he tried vainly to catch them.

Then there was silence. Kirsta dared to gradually turn away from her white-knuckled grip on the tree trunk. She looked down. She scanned the ground far below, but couldn't find David. Her heart froze. Maybe he still lurked down there somewhere, waiting for her to descend. Then he would grab her, and —

But then she saw him. He wasn't on the ground, but still in the tree, his neck caught in the fork of two branches. He dangled there unmoving, his head tilted at an impossible angle. This time, David Belsen was really dead. Kirsta felt a wave of nausea rise in her and closed her eyes until it passed. Moving to the other side of the tree, she climbed down and went to Sean.

EPILOGUE

Kirsta sat on the veranda two days later, balancing a cup of herbal tea on her knee. Sean shared the double-wide rocker with her, and the wicker creaked softly as they rocked. A tray of tuna sandwiches and potato salad lay on the table before them.

Kirsta sighed and leaned her head back against his arm, inhaling the fresh sweet scents around her. The air was clean and warm. The only signs of the storm were a few puddles in the driveway.

"I'm glad Daphne left with Etta and Henry," she sighed. "They certainly helped us straighten things out, but that was an exhausting conversation."

"You're not still tired, are you?" Sean asked, rolling his eyes in mock disgust. "I'd think nearly twenty hours of sleep would have been enough."

She grinned. "You should talk."

Kirsta had helped Sean into the house after her traumatic experience in the magnolia. The police had been called, and finally accepted an abbreviated version of David's "accident." Dawn was several hours past by the time Kirsta lay exhausted in Sean's bed. He'd tucked his comforter around her and held her hand, promising not to leave her side while she slept.

When she'd awakened at seven the next morning, Sean had been curled next to her on the bed, fully dressed. Daphne told them she'd called Etta and Henry the night before and asked them over for lunch, so they could all try to sort out what had happened.

"Well, we can all get back to our lives, now that it's all over," Kirsta said. Silently, she wondered what her life would be like now.

"It is over, I suppose?" Sean asked. Kirsta wondered what he meant. The question seemed twofold.

Hesitantly, she said, "I think so. Somehow I just feel … different. Like everything's going to be alright."

"I agree with that." He nodded. "I'm sure the evil, or haunting — or whatever you want to call it — is gone from Lost Oaks. Permanently."

Sean smiled. "I liked Henry and Etta's explanation for what went on. Though I have to admit, sitting out here in the sunshine around a plate of sandwiches, it does sound pretty strange — even unbelievable."

"But we both lived through it, remember," Kirsta said. "I think we're ready to believe anything. At least I am."

Sean nodded. "Me too. It's just so incredible to think Andrew Lucas's ghost has been trying to come back to Lost Oaks for generations. But, of course, that would explain all the ghostly sightings."

"But then, I show up," Kirsta said, "and suddenly there's a connection between events in the present and in the past. A lot of connections, actually."

"When you told us about your ex-fiance being named David, that made me even more certain we were on the right track. So, all of a sudden, the two time periods joined somehow, or became confused. And I guess I actually began to take on Andrew's personality."

"The worst parts of it," Kirsta said. "And as you and I became closer, you began confusing me with Indigo — at least when you were Andrew."

"Which only happened when we were here at Lost Oaks," Sean added for emphasis. Kirsta remembered the night in the cemetery, and felt her face warm.

"Right," she continued quickly. "But Andrew'd spent the last hundred or more years thinking of how Indigo had betrayed him — or he thought she did. And he decided to take his revenge. And Indigo kept trying to warn me; I see that now. But she wasn't quite strong enough to do anything about it until I got my blood on the brooch. I think that's what saved us."

Sean stroked her hair. "And then David showed up and joined the circus."

"Poor David," Kirsta said, her mood darkening a bit. She stood and walked to the railing. "I know he did some terrible things, unforgivable things. But I still feel a little sorry for him. Especially after the awful way he died." She shuddered. "If we hadn't all been dragged into this nightmare ..."

Sean moved to her and kissed her lightly. "Then we wouldn't have met, that's what. David was disturbed before any of this happened. You can't blame yourself."

Kirsta smiled up at him. "I don't, not really. It's just all these coincidences. It makes it hard to believe in random chance anymore."

Sean said, "Maybe none of it was chance. I've been doing some thinking, too, and it's hard to believe we weren't brought here together for a reason.

Other than to fulfill Andrew's revenge plan, I mean. There's got to be more to it than that."

Kirsta studied him. She marveled, for the hundredth time, it seemed, how different Sean was since the storm had passed. He'd completely lost the dark, haunted look she'd become all too familiar with recently. He laughed and smiled more. She felt her heart warm as their eyes met.

"What do you think, Ms. Linden?" he asked with exaggerated drama. "Coincidence — or something more?"

She smiled. "If it's a coincidence, it's a wonderful one. But maybe Andrew wasn't the only one with a plan; maybe Indigo had a plan, too."

"What do you mean?"

"I think it's possible that Indigo's tired of all the gloomy legends surrounding Lost Oaks, and wants to start some new ones. Someday, children in Allindea will tell each other about the night the ghost of Indigo McLeod saved the life of a yankee woman."

Just then, Sean pointed to a patch of sky beyond the tangled branches of the old live oak. "Look out there," he said. Above them, two white birds slowly circled the plantation. They silently glided three times around the house, then flew southward, side by side.

"Indigo and Andrew," Kirsta whispered, "together at last." Sean took her hand.

"There's another Lost Oaks legend that's about to come true," he said. "The legend of the Marryin' Magnolia. Since you looked down on me from its branches, we have to get married. It's destiny."

Kirsta's breathing stopped. She looked into his eyes. "Are you serious?"

"Deadly."

She put her arms around him, and they kissed for a long, long time.